THE FOOTPRINT
AND OTHER STORIES

Gouverneur Morris in his study

THE FOOTPRINT
AND OTHER STORIES

BY
GOUVERNEUR MORRIS

Short Story Index Reprint Series

BOOKS FOR LIBRARIES PRESS
FREEPORT, NEW YORK

First Published 1908
Reprinted 1970

INTERNATIONAL STANDARD BOOK NUMBER:
0-8369-3754-6

LIBRARY OF CONGRESS CATALOG CARD NUMBER:
70-142270 .

PRINTED IN THE UNITED STATES OF AMERICA

TO ELSIE

This ship of mine does not contain
    The precious stuffs that others do;
But bears into the raging main
    Assorted yarns, addressed to you.

Because, or course, fine, white or black,
    Or skeined or tangled to undo,
You always buy, and send not back,
    The yarns I always spin for you.

From day to day, from year to year,
    In easy times or in duresse,
You buy my yarns, and buy them dear,
    And pay for them in Loveliness.

A thousand times you've paid for all
    That I have ever spun. And, in
Outpoured advances, bought the call
    On all I ever hope to spin.

So men, of me, when I am not,
    Shall say, if anything —" Here lies
A merchant, whose unusual lot
    It was to trade in Paradise."

G. M.

AIKEN, S. C.

CONTENTS

CHAPTER   PAGE

I. *The Footprint* 3

II. *Paradise Ranch* 51

III. *Captain England* 85

IV. *The Execution* 123

V. *Simon L'Ouvrier* 147

VI. *A Carolina Night's Dream* 173

VII. *The Stowing Away of Mr. Bill Ballad* 193

VIII. *The Explorers* 219

IX. *The Little Heiress; or the Hunted Look* 237

X. *The Best Man* 271

XI. *The Crocodile* 305

I

THE FOOTPRINT

THE FOOTPRINT

I

BETWEEN TWO BAYS

We were waiting for the tide to ebb before resuming work on the schooner's bottom.   There was nothing the matter with her planks; but she had become so foul by months of cruising in the warm, fertile waters of the Gulf of California that she could not come about in anything less than a whole-sail breeze.   From the water-line down she had grown a yard-long beard of sea-greens that must have weighed several tons.   This growth, teeming with marine life—diminutive abalones, crabs, spiders, baby squids, and enormous barnacles that looked like extinct volcanoes filled with marrow—made the work of cleaning her difficult and repulsive.   With the least exposure to the tropic sun she stank like a rotten fish; the weeds clung to her planks as hair clings to the head, and we were forever slicing our hands and forearms on the barnacles.   We had warped her into

3

one of two small shallow bays, divided from each other by a high promontory of drifted sand; and as the tide receded, and left her drying and stinking, we worked against time and a slender larder to get her clean. When the unfinished work had been covered by the rising tide, and further barbering become impossible, we would retire to the sands that divided the two bays, to grumble and to smoke.

The sand of which the promontory was composed, though dry as dust, had a kind of inherent cohesiveness that caused it to maintain itself in hillocks and pinnacles and curious monumental forms, among which it was possible to find shade. Our favorite place to smoke and grumble was a hollow, round like a bird's nest, with one beetling elevation of sand to the west of it and another to the east. Except at high noon there was always shade in the hollow, and sometimes a kind of draught (less than the least breeze) was imagined to pass over it. Looking south or north from this nest the views were very much the same, except that in the foreground, or forewater of the south exposure, was the grounded schooner and the schooner's boat moored to the beach by a staked oar. To the eyes of instruments there may have been a calculable difference between the two bays of which we had the prospect, but to the human eye there was none; nor was there between the white desert shores, blotched with pale-blue shadows, that semicircled them. The two bays were like the upper-half of a vast pair of blue spectacles, of which the promontory dividing them was the nosepiece; the semi-circling beaches, the silver rims; the blue shadows, tarnishes. It was a prospect with which one soon sickened and soon grew angry. Of vegetation there was not so much as one dead stem.

During our periods of enforced idleness the prevailing atmosphere was one of pessimism. Our expedition had been a failure from the beginning. We were even ashamed to recall what we had once conceived to be its purpose. We said only: "Let us once get back to San Francisco and somebody will smart for his smartness." We had long since consigned the map, with its alluring directions in red ink, its infinity of plausible detail, and its general and particular verisimilitude, to the reddest devils of the deep sea. "Let Arundel get the rubies himself," we said. "Rubies—hell!"

There were five of us: four young fools, Crisp, Hawes, Meff and myself, and Morgridge, who was an old fool. We formed, together with Arundel, sick in a San Francisco hospital with tuberculosis of the bone (and lucky to be so well off, we thought), a stock company with a jointly paid-in capital of twenty-five hundred dollars. The company had paid Arundel two hundred dollars for his map, chartered the schooner (renamed her the *Ruby*), found her in water, provisions, and firearms, and, with Morgridge in command, set sail for the Gulf of California.

Arrived without mishap in those sharky, blistering waters, we cruised week after week, month after month, seeking the key to Arundel's map. "I can only tell you," he had said, "that there are two bays, very much alike, separated by high sand-dunes. The bay to the north is marked, where it bites deepest into the desert, by a kind of granite monolith that you can see for miles. It must be fifty feet high, and looks like an obelisk in the making. The trail starts a little to the north of this, and then you can apply the map, and it will tell you more than I can."

We happened to be seated, grumbling and smoking, between two such bays as Arundel had described. But they were not the first pair we had found, nor the second. The whole coast was pitted with semicircular bays, and it had been no great trick to discover pair after pair as like as the eyes in a man's head. The trick was to find one single, solitary needle of granite. And in that we had dismally failed. Indeed, in the course of a hundred landings at various points we had not found so much as one pebble bigger than a robin's egg. There was nothing but sand; there wasn't even sandstone. The only big, hard things were abalone shells that had been washed ashore. To have continued so long to hunt for a granite monolith in a region which emphatically denied the possibility of its containing one was a reflection upon the intelligence of all concerned.

Morgridge, who was near-sighted and never without his binoculars, lay on his belly and elbows, listlessly following the gambols of a porpoise-school in the waters of the northern bay. He remarked that the sight cooled him. Meff, with his eye on the tide, said that he was sorry to say we could get back to work in about twenty minutes; Hawes and Crisp were quarrelling desultorily over a game of piquet, in which was involved the filthiest, most dog's-eared pack of cards I ever saw. "I *said* you had point," said Crisp; "shut up and go on." "Tierce to the king, twice," said Hawes, not with any great hope. "You saw the discard," said Crisp, "I only took one card; you *must* know that I've got the knave quint in diamonds. It's awfully damn dull playing with you. I have to tell you everything." "Yes, you're the whole show," said Hawes. "Everybody knows that." The voices of the two, if sarcastic, were listless, and neither seemed capable of raising more than a shadow of resentment in the other. "Lead, fool," said Hawes quietly. "Twenty-one, Pinhead," retorted Crisp, and he led with the king of spades.

"Boys," said Morgridge suddenly, "there s a junk heading into the bay."

II

THE MAN WITH THE YELLOW UMBRELLA

The waters of the Gulf of California are rarely sailed; the shores more rarely tramped. Of the region's shadows no one is cast by the hand of the law. Diogenes would find there no honest face in which to shine his lantern. There men with itching palms, and pasts that clamor of unsuccess, voyage now and then in ill-formed craft, drawn by rumors. To some the inland mountains have yielded metals; now and then a lucky crew are enticed along a wake of ambrosial sweetness, to find in the waters a lump of ambergris that floats in the rainbow colors of its self-exuded oil, and is more precious than gold. From beneath the waters now and then are fished up bright and heavy pearls, orient, and abalone. But of the crews that go there is one that comes back with treasure, the mother of rumors, there are two that come back with nothing but scurvy, and there are seven that do not come back at all.

Only Chinamen, light of appetite and clean to the last nail, can long endure the climate, and only the Chinese expeditions strike an average of success. But in those unpoliced waters a junk of Chinamen is a thing for white men to avoid. It is a devil, sea-buffeting, and, before the wind, swift. It is filled with cheap lives, it

8

is full of greed, full of rifles, and formidable in patience and surprise.

That the crew of the junk now rounding the northern horn of the northern bay, perhaps a half-mile distant, would not soon discover us among the shadows and hollows of the dunes, was probable; and, of course, the schooner was completely screened from the most alert eye by the whole mass of the promontory which divided one bay from the other. But it was also probable that in the course of time the junk would round that screen and become unpreventably interested in our private affairs: interested surely, and perhaps involved. For if the junk's captain thought that we had anything that he wanted, he would try to take it. But not at once.

There would pass between the junk and the schooner very ceremonious and courteous greetings, and the junk would lumber away as if intent upon some far-off destiny. But she would not go very far; just out of sight around the next corner, and she would come back; not the same night, when all of us would be watching, nor the night after, when half of us would be still nervous enough to keep awake, but later by several nights, and at her own well-chosen and sudden time. She had a crew, probably of at least twenty-five, with a rifle, knife, and revolver apiece; she had a little machine-gun, probably. Surely she had no morals.

To the naked eye the junk presented little but a

color scheme, and it needed a turn at the binoculars to see faces and details. The color scheme, like that of all junks, was a sincere if misguided effort to achieve the beautiful. Her body was painted indigo blue; the square sail by which she was drawn slowly into the bay was pure vermilion. And aft some one had spread, to keep off the sun, a bright yellow umbrella.

From a brazier in the bow of the junk rose a tottering thread of bluish smoke, and beside the brazier (all this through the glass) stood a lofty Chinaman. He was nearly naked, and absolutely expressionless; a splendidly moulded, utterly lifeless statue of brownish-yellow clay. An enormous brass cymbal dangled by a thong from each of his wrists. The inanimate cymbals were the only things about him that moved. Amidships was a circle of half-naked men, squatting, gesticulating, and articulating, who seemed intent upon something in their midst. We hazarded that it was a game of fan-tan. In the stern, only a little less statuesque (because of more drapery) than the man in the bow, stood the helmsman, his hands clasped about the grip of a twelve-foot indigo oar, whose blade, half immersed, followed in the junk's wake like the dorsal fin of a shark. A little in front, and to one side of the helmsman, was spread the yellow umbrella. Under it was seated, cross-legged, a Chinaman, mountainous with robes and fat. He was more than a detail and, except for his umbrella, less than a complete tone of the junk's color scheme. His voluminous robes, mauvely and greenly brocaded with indistinguishable patterns, were of the richest and darkest blue imaginable. He exuded an atmosphere of ruches. You knew at once that he was many times a millionaire. You knew, too, that he had lived well, and revolved among pleasant episodes and people. There was an expression upon his face that I have never before seen upon the face of an Oriental—jollity. Through the glass we could see that from time to time he smiled, a broad appreciative smile, begotten doubtless of some sudden, transient thought. And whenever he smiled he twirled the handle of the yellow umbrella with his fat fingers. On his head was a little blue cap terminated by a large green button. Occasionally he fanned himself with a little round fan.

The junk's course was a long curve, parallel to that of the shore, and as close to it as the shelving nature of the beach would safely allow. As she was steered more and more to the starboard her big vermilion sail began to shut off our view of the stern and to cast its shadow over the fan-tan players. The helmsman and the man with the yellow umbrella disappeared, and as the junk veered more and more a funny fat little vermilion dinghy came into sight, trailed by a rope off her port quarter. The breeze had now sunk to a series of mild, unconnected puffs, and the junk's progress was very slow. She had covered half of the bay's curve, and was distant from us perhaps a quarter of a mile, when suddenly the man in the bow raised his cymbals and brought them together. As the cymbals separated for a second stroke, the clanging, brassy crash of the first concussion reached our ears; and with it a chorus of piercing minor falsetto notes from the fan-tan players, who had risen to their feet.

The junk swung more and more, and the yellow umbrella began to detach itself from the lower port corner of the vermilion sail. Two men ran forward to the anchor, and as the junk came into the wind and to the end of her momentum let it go with a fine splash. The junk's stern now faced the shore, and the man with the yellow umbrella rose and waddled to the rail. The little round fan disappeared up one of his voluminous sleeves, and from the same receptacle he drew what appeared to be a double-ended purse, well filled. This he flung into the water—a golden sacrifice, we learned later, to the gods who had given him leave to pass across their sea. Then he waddled forward, and, seating himself on the rail, swung his legs and the skirt of his robe outboard, dropped heavily into the dinghy, and precipitately seated himself. He was followed by the junk's helmsman, who, having cast loose, dipped with a long paddle, and directed the overladen craft toward the shore. The clashing of the cymbals and the chorus of

12

falsetto wails, which had never ceased, now redoubled in ardor and tempo, and as suddenly stopped when the dinghy bumped against the beach, and the man with the yellow umbrella clambered heavily over her bow and stood upon the shore.

He turned and watched the greatly lightened dinghy as she returned, powerfully driven, to the junk, and was swung aboard. He stood, a rotund, mauve, and blue glory under his yellow umbrella, and watched the lowering of the junk's sail. He did not move a muscle, only when the junk's anchor was raised and she, under the impulse of long sweeps that appeared mysteriously from her sides, began to crawl forward like a huge blue spider with legs, and turning to return upon her course, he produced his little round fan and fanned himself. But until the junk disappeared behind the northern horn of the bay he did not make any other motion, or take his eyes from her.

Then, however, he pivoted heavily and, waddling in a slow but determined manner, crossed the beach, his gorgeous brocades blazing and sparkling in the sun as their folds and surfaces shifted and rippled with his motion, and his right hand working the little round fan, and his left supporting the yellow umbrella, he began to mount, slow and determined, the tumbling desert dunes of sand that stood behind the beach. Up these and into them bobbed the yellow umbrella until, after one last bobbing, it disappeared from view.

"I'm going to find out where he's going," said Morgridge.

We fetched our rifles from the schooner and, reclimbing the promontory, in a body descended to the beach on the other side, and followed it to the point where its smooth surface was broken at right angles by the deeply marked footprints of the fat Chinaman.

III

RENEWED FAITH

We followed the track up into the dunes, with Morgridge leading by twenty feet and Hawes bringing up the rear. Meff and I, making jocular efforts to burrow aids to ascending locomotion from each other, "scrapped" along in the middle. I had hooked a surreptitious finger into Meff's belt, and thereby lightened myself during one entire step, when (it was just as Meff secured his release by planting an elbow in the pit of my stomach) suddenly Morgridge, who had reached to the higher levels of the dunes, ejaculated sharply and sprang out of sight. We scrambled briskly, all four of us, to be in the know, and found him, his thumbs in his armpits, a smile on his face (a jocosely assumed

14

attitude of low comedy), and his right foot planted high upon the curve of a gigantic weather-worn pillar of granite that lay in and out of the sand.

"Morgridge," said he, "that great leader in the act of discovering Arundel's landmark, and proving to a sceptical world that Arundel was not a liar. My God! boys," he cried, his expression shifting from one of low comedy to one of uncontainable greed and excitement. "My God! boys, we've as good as got 'em."

"The damn thing," said Crisp, "has fallen down, and that's why we couldn't see it. Kick it; somebody with stout shoes."

"Don't kick it," said Meff, "it's a good landmark to get itself found." He stooped and patted the monolith as one pats a good dog.

"Now this is where it stood," said Morgridge, "and Arundel's map says the course is due east from the pedestal.

"Direction due east," said Hawes, "and distance forty miles."

Attached to my watch-guard was a very accurate little compass set in striped tiger's eyes, a boyhood relic from Petoskey, Michigan. I looked from this to the tracks made by the fat Chinaman, and found that, having approached the fallen monolith from a little south of west, he had, on reaching its former base, veered a little and pointed his steps due east. Running my eyes along the line indicated, I had presently a glimpse, very far off, of the yellow umbrella bobbing deeper and deeper into the arid, scorching desert.

"Surely," I said, "our fat friend is going where we are going, but he won't do any forty miles in one clip. There must be stopping-places that Arundel missed."

"I believe you," said Morgridge. "We've only to follow the yellow umbrella."

"And when night comes?" objected Crisp.

"Stars," said Hawes, "stars enough to find *this* trail."

We laughed, because the very depth of the fat China-man's footprints recalled his humorous rotundity and the waddling, self-satisfied dignity of his gait.

"He will know where to find food and water," said Morgridge.

"Seriously, though," said Meff, "is it possible that he should really be entering upon a forty-mile walk in this heat—at his size?"

"Come along," said Morgridge.

"His food shall be my food," said Meff; "where he rests will I rest, his drink shall be my drink, and his rubies——"

"Shall be divided by lot," said Crisp.

We took up the trail, floundering heavily, and making slow way of it. We were unused to walking; the at-mosphere at the surface of the desert fumed and gyrated in the heat. The sun, now west of the zenith, lay upon the back like a garment of fire. Our sweat laved the unfertile sand. We had not, after the first quarter of a mile, a single joke or happy thought left among us.

At first we gained upon the yellow umbrella, and had the fat Chinaman looked over his shoulder there were times when he must have seen us; but he was intent upon his journey, and waddled eastward at a rate which was unpleasant to equal, and so difficult to exceed that we were soon content not to.

He preceded us by half a mile; in that atmosphere it had the effect of less; and he never swerved from his course, nor glanced to the right or the left. If my sweat-stung eyes had been keen for beauty, I should have admired inordinately the gorgeousness of color made against the silver desert by the blue robes and yellow umbrella of our celestial friend. But I was beneath admiring, and noticed only, and I do not know why, that, as the sun descended lower from the zenith, the umbrella was tilted further and further to interrupt its scorching rays, so that first the Chinaman's head disappeared behind its lower rim, then his shoulders, and then his trunk to the waist.

Thus passed a number of hours, but not the limits of that fat Chinaman's endurance and patience. Momentarily I expected to see the yellow umbrella turn to right or left and halt at some cache of water and

17

food. But we were destined to enjoy no such blessed nepenthe that day.

Serenely and indomitably bobbed the yellow umbrella, carrying its oval of shadow over innumerable desert miles. From a slender crescent it became a full orbit that flamed in the rays of the setting sun.

"We must get nearer before dark," said Morgridge, and he set up a herculean example of progress. But the fat Chinaman, whom we had laughed at for his labored waddling, began now to stand in our jaded minds for the very acme and poetry of motion. By dusk we respected him; but by dark, though we had gained a quarter of a mile and wished ourselves dead, we pronounced him, petticoats and fat considered, the most wonderful walker that the world had ever known.

At dark he lowered his umbrella, and for a time we lost sight of him. But as the stars brightened we could follow his deep steps, and had presently a sight of him, his robes silvery in the starlight, and perceived that he had faced about and was coming toward us.

Breathing quickly, but utterly fearless, he waddled into our midst.

"I come all the way back," he said, "to say I go altogether forty miles without no stop. I think it very fine courteous action to take all this trouble for strange gentlemen. You like to come all the way, I say nothing, none of my damn business. Only stop to tell you very

18

far away, all the way nasty sand. I very fine rich China merchant, and know how to give very fine courteous advices. You rest little while and go back. I go on now, and wish you very fine pleasant evening and return journey."

He turned and waddled away.

"Hold on," said Morgridge, "we're going with you."

The fat Chinaman paused and considered.

"Very well," he said, "we all travel together, more or less pleasant way to travel. Only I very clever, experienced fine traveller, and not put up with no complaints and damn swearing—— Like pleasant conversation and all good friends. We go along two miles in an hour, and by and by finish journey. You walk along by me"—he pointed to me with his fat finger. "You got very fine respectable face."

"My friends," I said with a bow, "have not had my advantages."

"Rascals?" asked the fat Chinaman. "Introduce their names."

I presented the four, and said my own name.

"My name Sang Ti—very fine, revered, damn name," said the merchant. "But like fine poet says of time, 'she flies.'"

I walked forward beside him, not knowing whether to laugh at the jovial absurdity of the gentleman who

19

had given me a character, or to cry because his indefatigable waddle was so hard to breast.

"You sweat much?" he asked in a friendly, interested tone.

IV

SANG TI

"Do you often go where you are going?" I asked.

"Go now for first time," said Sang Ti. "Chen Chan very fine old sacred holy place to end days in."

"You don't expect to end your days at Ch—Chen—Chan?" I asked. "Do you?"

"Oh, yes, before long. You see, I am dedicate from little boy to the High Gods. I am requested to have very fine high successful happy life, through intercession of parents and promises to the High Gods. All is accomplish. I go high up; lead a very fine benevolent life; accumulate very large fortune; do everything just right; and now must pay up promises made for me to the High Gods by parents."

The moon had risen, and the desert was as if flooded with quicksilver and ink. Sang Ti turned his fat, jolly face, beaded with sweat, and beamed at me. He thrust a hand under the silk cord that girdled him at the waist.

"On forty-fifth day of birth," he said, "I hand over this cord to priest of the High Gods; and he hand over to me to hold the ruby box and holy shark tooth; and I think a little while of the insignificance of life, and am soon strangled by priest. Then I have paid up."

"Do you mean to say," I exclaimed, "that you are taking all this trouble to get yourself strangled?"

"The promises of parents," said he, "now dead, is very fine holy sort of thing, not to be broken. I will arrange to have you and your friends see the strangling. It will be very interesting, dignified occurrence."

Though Sang Ti enjoyed, for a Chinaman, a very large command of the English language, I was concluding that he either could not possibly know what he was talking about, or that he was making an elaborate effort to "string" me, when, with the tail of my eye, I caught him in the act of feeling his throat, very tenderly, with a fat thumb and forefinger. His face for the moment wore an expression of wonder mixed with panic. But in a moment it passed, and with a sudden laugh he lowered his hand.

"You are considering me very practical joker," he said, "but I give you very honest man's word that being strangled at forty-five is very damn miserable joke. I am, however, a very fine philosopher."

"What's the holy shark tooth?" I asked.

"Him not too good to touch," said Sang Ti. "He take care of ruby box."

We labored on in silence, and the moon sailed higher

and higher in the heavens. A faint, hot breeze arose and blew in our faces.

"The night" said Sang Ti, "is a Nubian empress; her robes are sewed with diamonds; the moon is a gong of silver; the sand is the ashes of broken words."

"Are you making that up, or translating?" I asked.

"The wind, he said, "is some very fine high god sighing. I fancy Liang Tsang."

"Who is he?"

"Liang Tsang a yellow elephant by daylight, but by night-time a very potent, strong god that blows around the world. He a breeze when he sigh, and a wind when he groan."

"Isn't he happy?" I asked. "Why does he sigh and groan?"

"Because he an exile. He can blow everywhere but not over China. But when the end of the world approaches it is promised him that for one day in the spring of year he shall be a violet, with roots in fertile soil of Shan-tung. It a saying of us, 'Keep your promises, for the day approaches when Liang Tsang shall be a violet in the fields of Shan-tung, and the perverted shall be divided among a thousand thousand hells.'"

"Does your creed embrace so many hells?" I asked.

"Oh, yes," he said simply, "or what could be done with all Caucasian and European races? In Chinaman's creed there is very satisfactory place provided for everybody."

"The policy of the open door?" I suggested.

"Open to go in," he said, "and shut to go out."

I looked over my shoulder and saw that our company had begun to straggle badly. Only Meff and Morgridge were in easy speaking distance; Crisp was two hundred yards behind them, and another hundred yards separated Hawes and Crisp. As I looked, Morgridge called to me to stop.

He came up, followed by Meff, exhausted, angry, and completely blown.

"This not a proper time to stop," said Sang Ti. "I tell you before, too long a walk for you gentlemen. I see at once you not well bred for travelling. With me it very different matter. I come of very fine old stock; I am descended in straight recorded line from a camel and a shark. Must get a long way before morning; cooler now."

"We'll halt now," said Morgridge in an arrant, angry, bullying voice. "See?"

"I got no time," said Sang Ti. "You not able to come, I go alone, wishing you first very pleasant halt and subsequent journey."

"No you don't," said Morgridge, "you don't lose this crowd—not in this desert. You'll rest, yourself, till we're ready to go on."

23

Sang Ti stood his umbrella into the sand, and turned back the borders of his sleeves.

"You," he said to Morgridge, "are very uncivil, lazy, selfish damn rascal, and you, too."

He stood between Morgridge and Meff, looking quickly from one to the other.

"You interfere with Chinese gentleman, he teach you more respectable damn manners." So saying, and just as Crisp was coming up, he seized Morgridge and Meff by the backs of their necks and began to knock their heads together. He finished the lesson of courtesy by suddenly jerking in opposite directions and letting go. Meff fell in his tracks, but Morgridge, dropping his rifle, staggered for a long distance before he came to ground.

With a silvery laugh Sang Ti regained his umbrella and waddled away.

"I'll kill the dog," yelled Morgridge, springing with blazing eyes for the rifle which had been shaken from his hand.

"No," said Crisp. And as Morgridge sprang for the rifle he hooked his foot and threw him heavily. Then he sat on him.

Morgridge, with all the strength thrashed and pressed out of him, could only wriggle and swear obscurely in a whining voice. He was on the verge of tears.

I am far from suspecting Sang Ti of the fear of death,

but he reserved to himself the choice of its manner, and had dropped in conversation the hint that he was very earnest to be strangled. Anyway, though the desert was flooded with light from the setting moon, he disappeared from view in a wonderfully short time; and we (who were five fools) slept in our tracks while the night waned, and woke to see the dawn stream up behind the eastern rim of the desert like a conflagration.

I shall not soon forget the horrible march that then began, straight into the molten furnace eye of the sun. Whatever of moisture was in us was sucked out through the pores of our scorching hides and turned into dust. We felt ourselves grow light. All the constituents which had made human beings of us began to diminish except two: pain swelled in our brains, and in our mouths, our tongues. The heat that we had endured on the coast was temperate compared to the blasts of that inland desert.

We would have laid down and died, or some of us would (Meff was forever suggesting it) if very early in the morning we had not been led by the Chinaman's tracks to the top of a long rise, from which could be seen, far in the distance, what looked like purple feathers stuck into the sand on the further length of a piece of broken mirror, and which we knew to be trees growing by a lake. Indeed, specks of scarlet gleamed among the feathers, and we guessed that they were roofs upon the habitations of men.

Forward we went, and downward for an hour, and

then upward, until once more we could see the trees and the lake and the roofs. But they seemed no nearer than before. And all day it was so.

We began what was to be our last long ascent. During it the sun sank so low that our shadows reached the top an hour before our bodies. But the trees then and the lake had been drawn wonderfully nearer.

At our feet was spread the lake, shaped roughly like a vast human foot, and beyond it among the trees we could see pagoda-shaped buildings and, going and coming, long-robed Chinamen, and little children and dogs. We could hear the dogs. And as the dusk deepened, braziers began to twinkle palely here and there.

It was dark when we reached the lake, and, casting aside our weapons and watches, plunged into it, and felt the water rush in through our pores and begin to rebuild our wasted tissues and make rounded men of us once more. After a while, chin-deep immersed in deliciousness, with the rapture of hooked fish that have been returned to their element, we began to drink.

V

CHEN CHAN

We walked, dripping, around the end of the lake, and in close order, with weapons handy, for we did not know what reception to expect, passed down an avenue of ragged travellers' palms, and reached the first house of the single-streeted settlement. In the doorway of the house, smoking a long thick-stemmed pipe, sat Sang Ti. The water still running from our clothes, we drew up before him.

"Everybody gone to bed except me," was his greeting. "I of opinion that life too short now for sleep. Now suppose you look about a bit, and go back home. Priest say this very unhealthy place for white men. Only other white visitor name Arundel; some low damn thieving rascal. Priest say, if you come up, to say better go way again."

"How many people live here?" asked Morgridge in a voice which he strove to make civil.

"Maybe about thirty," said Sang Ti.

"Thirty men?" I asked.

"Oh, no," he said, "all kinds."

"You see," I said, "we couldn't go back right off. We couldn't walk a mile more to save our souls. We'll have to rest a bit."

"Priest not like that," said Sang Ti; "but never mind. Suppose all stay except that old rascal." He indicated Morgridge with his pipe stem.

"I guess we'll all stay," said Crisp firmly.

"All that contrary to rules," objected Sang Ti. "But all same contrary to rules to use force; so what can do? Why you come, anyhow? Maybe you come to steal very fine High God's ruby box?"

His eyes twinkled from one guilt-confessing face to the next, and he chuckled.

"Suppose, yes," he said, "and suppose you make off with ruby box, and suppose you go a little way and that uncivil rascal"—again he pointed to Morgridge—"feel sudden pain and die, and then that man——"

"My name is Crisp," said Crisp.

"Suppose then that man Crisp feel sudden pain and die, and so on. You think not very nice? Ruby box have live in Chen Chan for maybe two thousand years. Chen Chan oldest settlement in America. Very High God Liang Tsang cross desert one time, and have to put foot down once. That make very fine lake. All same time he drop ruby box and holy shark's tooth, and pretty soon he cross ocean, and see junk of China fishermen. And he blow into junk's sail, and she go ashore and break to pieces; and all the China fishermen and wives crosses desert, and stops at lake and builds temple for ruby box and shark's tooth, and then makes one man priest, and builds little holy village and call her Chen Chan. That mean in English 'The Footprint.'"

"Do many people come here?" I asked.

"Arundel," said he, "and he get away. That because he drop ruby box. Others have come never get away. First come Mexicans, five hundred years ago;

then some Spanish men, and then Arundel, and then you. And I tell you better go back, and leave very High Holy God's ruby box alone."

"Could we go to-morrow?" I asked. "We've got to have food and rest."

"Well, suppose you stop in house"—he pointed into the dark doorway—"and not disturb meditation any longer. Maybe you find some food," he went on. "And by and by, in the morning, you go away."

"Couldn't we wait till night?" I asked. "It's cooler going at night."

"I tell you," he said, "you wait till after strangulation, which takes place ten o'clock sharp. Then you go."

"If you are going to be strangled to-morrow," I said, "you are the calmest-minded man in this world."

"Between you and me," he said, "I think one very damn miserable business; but parents make promise, and what can do?"

He made himself as small as he could in the doorway, so that we could squeeze past him into the dark house. It had but one room; and by good luck and much feeling we found in one corner a vast bowl of cold-boiled rice. Crisp dragged it into the middle of the room, and, dipping with our hands, we gorged ourselves, and one by one toppled over and slept.

I was wakened by Crisp. It was broad daylight.

"What," said Crisp, "is all this talk about strangling?

Is he using a word that he thinks means something else? I've been having dreams about it all night."

"The whole thing's like a dream," I said; "but I believe, as I believe in—well, in hell—that Sang Ti expects to be put to death this morning. What time is it?"

"Nine o'clock," said Crisp. We waked the others, and among us finished the boiled rice. We had scarcely done so when, from outside, came suddenly the sound of persistent pounding on a brass gong.

We crowded out of the house to find the twenty-five or thirty inhabitants of the village—men, women, and children—in a group in the street, intent upon something that was approaching from its further end. We stood aloof from the little crowd, who, if they were aware of our presence, gave no sign, and craned our necks, to see what was coming.

It was Sang Ti, waddling along under his yellow umbrella and fanning himself. Behind him followed an emaciated Chinaman in flowing gray silk. It was the latter who was pounding on the gong.

As the procession passed the inhabitants of the village, all the inhabitants turned as if on one pivot to follow it. And a moment later our heads turned in the same way.

Sang Ti, with a jolly, contented expression, and looking neither to the right nor the left, having reached a point a little beyond where we were standing, turned and came back, always followed by the man in gray with the persistently pounded gong. This passage of the two up and down the village street was repeated many times without variation. But it was not till the third trip that we noticed anything further about the man in gray. Then we noticed, all of us at the same moment, that his little green cap suddenly loosened about his head, rose, perhaps half an inch, made a fraction of a revolution, and settled back.

Hitherto the procession had struck me as grotesque if not precisely humorous, believing, as I did, that Sang Ti's contented expression was muscular and not mental, but the sudden moving, without apparent agency, of the green cap, was horrible. It gave me the idea, I do not know why, that the cap concealed something that was alive and unclean.

The procession and the gong-beating was continued until nearly ten o'clock. Then, as Sang Ti made his usual turn just below where we were standing, the gong ceased and was followed by a silence peculiarly accented. Sang Ti passed up the street, followed by the man in gray, whose cap suddenly moved again, and by the whole population of the village, even the chow dogs.

And we, as unnoticed as if we had been invisible, made haste to follow in the wake.

The yellow umbrella halted in front of a dark-red pagoda of stained and carved wood. Sang Ti furled it and thrust it, point down, into the sand at one side of the steps that led into the pagoda. Then he passed through the door, and we could see, as the steps elevated him, that with his hands he was unfastening the silk cord which girdled his waist.

Inside the pagoda, or temple, there was not much light. We found ourselves in a high-ceilinged red room about forty by thirty. At the upper end, on a high granite pedestal, sat a hideous bronze god, blurred by smoke which rose from a blue-and-white bowl on his knees. Against the walls of the place were ranged long poles of polished teak, finished at their tops with enormous images, scroll-sawed out of shining brass; masks, roosters, turtles, scorpions, dragons, and strange fruits.

Immediately in front of the pedestalled god, and facing us, sat Sang Ti in a vast teakwood chair. He continued to wear his jolly, contented expression, but allowed his eyes to rest on no one.

The chair in which he sat had the central panel of its back prolonged, so that its top extended several inches above his head and projected on either side. This back piece was pierced to the top with two series of holes, each about an inch in diameter, parallel to each other and perhaps six inches apart. It looked like an enormous cribbage board.

Sang Ti handed his silk cord to the man in gray, and the latter, thrusting its ends through two convenient and opposite holes, and stepping behind the chair, drew them until the half loop of the cord lay loosely across Sang Ti's throat.

Then he knotted the loose ends, and, producing in some sleight-of-hand manner a golden casket incrusted with rubies of all qualities, from pigeon blood to pale pink, placed it in Sang Ti's hands. Sang Ti lowered his eyes and examined the casket. A very slight shiver passed through his fat frame, and he shifted his feet uneasily.

The priest now thrust under the knot at the back of the loop a long, heavy rod of stained ivory, and gave it a quick twist from left to right. The loose loop became tight across Sang Ti's throat, and at a second twist half disappeared in his flesh.

A horrid choking noise was forced from his half-open mouth, and he shot at me a sudden look of heart-breaking appeal that brought my rifle to my shoulder.

But I was not so quick as Morgridge. In that con-fined place the crack of his rifle was like the detonation of a small cannon. The place filled with smoke and the sound of scurrying feet.

We gathered about Sang Ti when the smoke envelop-ing him had lifted, and found that the bullet meant for the strangler had been aimed too low. The top of Sang Ti's skull was split down the middle, and only the loosened cords kept him from falling forward. But the bullet, nevertheless, had done its appointed work, for the priest lay behind the chair, shot through the diaphragm, and a great red stain was spreading over the front of his gray robes.

And now a very horrid thing happened. From under the priest's cap, loosened by the fall, crawled a little dust-colored snake with a venomous head, and ran at Morgridge. Morgridge struck at the reptile with the butt of his rifle, but not quickly enough. He screamed as its fang pierced his boot, and fell to the floor as if struck by a thunderbolt.

The snake, turning, darted for the pedestal on which the god sat, but not in time wholly to escape the butt of Crisp's rifle. Dragging a broken tail it disappeared into a crack between the pedestal and the floor.

We looked at Morgridge. He was purple, horrible. He might have been dead for a week. Then we ran—God, how we ran—through the village and out into the desert. We ran until Meff began to call from far in the rear that he could run no more. We waited till he came up, and hated him for delaying us. But when we found that even in the first burst of panic he had had the presence of mind to snatch the ruby box, we began to praise him and clap him on the back.

We passed it from hand to hand and wondered what the rubies would bring.

" I think Arundel overrated them," I said.

34

"Yes," said Meff. "But aren't some of them corkers? Look at that fellow."

"The light-pink ones," said Hawes, "aren't worth much more than glass."

"It ought to bring fifty thousand," I said. "See what's inside."

Hawes found the catch, and, as he raised the lid, suddenly screamed and flung the box high into the air. Over and over it turned, and there whirled free from it a little snake, and the two fell at a distance from each other. But the fate of that snake was sudden; turn and dart as he would, bullet after bullet grazed him and tossed him on spurts of sand. He was torn to pieces in five seconds, and we turned to Hawes. He had found the time to thrust his bitten finger into his mouth, and that was all. He was dead as a stone.

VI

CRISP AND MEFF

The first impulse of us three survivors was once more to bolt. But where, or to what purpose? About and about were the scorching undulations of desert. Behind the ill-omened visage of Chen Chan, where death lurked under men's caps and in the reliquaries of their gods. Ahead, but so far that it could not be reached by any sudden panic-born effort, lay the ocean and escape. **If** we were to get away at all it could only be by slow-sustained exertion, directed by the quiet mind. I think Meff was the first to realize this.

"I think," he said, "that we had better rest for a few minutes."

"We ought to bury poor Hawes," said Crisp. But one glance at the violet bloated corpse was enough. No man with a stomach could have handled it. There was left upon it no trace of a comrade through many vicissitudes. Personality, that so often lingers after death and so long resists the chemistry of the grave, was gone from it, and had left nothing of the friend. The eyes were repelled, and the muscles, that might have scraped a hollow in the sands, were turned to water.

The ruby casket lay at a distance. Meff caught it up (not before a cautious examination with the muzzle of his rifle), and we did not sit down to rest until we had placed a long undulation of the desert between us and the corpse of Hawes.

Our situation called for discussion. Whether to strike circuitously for the broad track which we had made in coming, or directly for the sea; whether to push through in one frantic march, so as to keep the start already made over possible pursuit; or to rest betimes, one to watch while two slept, and to trust to our rifles in case of attack by the looted villagers. We agreed, finally, to find our way to the schooner by compass rather than waste time by tedious indirections, and if we had the endurance, as we surely had the impulse, to make one march of it. We thought by so doing to have suffered less in the end. These matters being ordered, we got to our feet and set our faces to the west.

For the first hour Meff carried the ruby casket; but after that, for it was heavy and, having no handles, an akward package, we took turns. It was wonderful, and turn by turn we noticed it, what a handicap that small lump of treasure proved to the locomotion of the individual who carried it. Invariably he fell behind, with lagging legs, and at heart a petulance that undermined his resolution to go on. Had the carrier of it alone been to consult it would soon have been abandoned by the way. Its value was problematical. In the ultimate distribution of the gems incrusting it we were sure to be cheated, and meanwhile it was awkward to hold, heavy to carry, and a diminisher of speed.

Of our subsequent march that day there is nothing to record but weariness, until about an hour before sundown there was formed, by those agencies of nature which play tricks with the eyes of men, far to the north, a mirage. We beheld against the sky a range of the desert across which, his grass-green robes girded about his loins, there moved upon a course parallel with our own the wavering, yet distinct and gigantically magnified, image of a Chinaman. We had but a minute's view of him, vast and shadowy, like a storm cloud, or some vengeful and evil genius out of a dream, and then, presto, the desert refractions altered and the image vanished. For the first time in our desert wanderings, either going in or coming out, we felt cold—cold to the marrow. That the vast size of the Chinaman was an hallucination we knew, but we knew also that an actual man must have been the basis for the magnification, that his course was parallel to our own, and his sudden appearance in the heavens an illegible but disquieting portent. Had but one man of Chen Chan had the hatred to dog our steps? Or had a council decreed that to wrest the casket and perhaps our lives from us but one man was necessary? If the latter, and a certain fateful significance in the mirage impelled us to adopt it, what occult power could he possess to hold our vigilance and our rifle practice so cheap? And might we not with certainty look for him to strike in that hour of darkness which would precede the rising of the moon? In one presumption only was there any grain of comfort: that, forebodings notwithstanding, he might be, like Sang Ti, a solitary desert voyager intent upon a destiny in no way commingled with our own. But conscience told us that this was far-fetched presumption, and we moved uneasily forward, with roving and scared eyes.

To have been witness to, and part of, so many shocking deaths; to be bearing the fruits of an unjustifiable theft; and to have for accompaniment to our march a fateful and constant, although invisible, presence, was a torture to the mind and conscience. But it had, too, the effect of compelling a rate of progress that had otherwise been impossible, and casting a certain reticence into the demands made upon us by hunger and thirst.

Well, the dark hour before moonrise came and passed. Nothing happened. The moon rose, dripping light, and sailed toward the zenith. Nothing happened. And we began to believe in such slender promises of security; to go forward with less determination, and to suffer acutely from emptiness, parchedness, and fatigue. So that when Meff made the proposition to rest, and himself offered to keep the first watch, Crisp and I were only too willing. A man is seldom permitted to remember at just what advance of weariness his mind ceases to act, and he goes to sleep. But of the present occasion I seem to remember the exact point. I saw, with an eye of the mind, the unfortunate Sang Ti sitting in the temple to be strangled; I heard from Meff a kind of contented grunt; I shifted my right arm the better to sustain my head, and at that instant fell asleep.

I was awakened, I think, by the moonlight stealing under the brim of my hat and shining upon my closed eyes. I woke, I know, with a kind of dread catching at my heart. I sat up and saw that his promise of vigilance had been beyond Meff's strength to keep. He lay upon his back with his face completely covered by his hat. The fingers of his right hand were clasped tightly about one end of the ruby casket. There were no grounds for the feeling of dread with which I had waked. Yet the feeling abode. It was the feeling that a guilty man has who believes rather than knows that he is being watched. I looked beyond Meff, across the desert, and my heart froze. I had seen—I could swear it—for one fleeting instant, a yellow face that ducked away behind a near-by ridge of sand.

I seized my rifle and rushed to the point at which it had vanished. From there I obtained an expansive view of the desert. But there was no form to show that a man had been lying in the sand, nor any tracks of feet. I was mentally staggered, and, after rushing a few purposeless steps this way and that, returned, thoroughly dazed, to my companions. The noise of my sudden upspringing had not disturbed them. They continued heavily asleep, and had not moved a muscle. Only it seemed to me that Meff's hat had slipped a little from his face; and as I looked it actually shifted a little more, and then—to my horror—it rose a little and settled back. It was preposterous to think that Meff's quiet breathing could so move the heavy felt. Then, as if to settle once for all the agency of the motion, Meff's hand, that had been clasped about the ruby casket, went up to his hat in a kind of petulant way, and removed it.

Whether it was Meff's scream or mine that broke the silence I shall never know. I only know that I was on my feet, wildly firing at a streak of gray that hissed as it ran and dodged the spurts of sand tossed by the bullets.

Crisp was on his feet, rifle in hand, staring wildly about him.

"What is it?" he cried.

"It was under Meff's hat all the time," I shouted back. "It's the one with the broken tail—that hid under the altar. That Chinaman is hunting us down with it," I shouted on; "I tell you he is. Damn him! We're goners—goners. Look at Meff!"

But it was not good to look at Meff.

"Which way did it go?" said Crisp in a sombre voice.

"That way," I said. "You can see the track; see how the broken tail had to drag."

"You missed it—of course."

"Yes," I said, "of course. I nearly got it once. But I didn't, and that's all there is to it. Except it will come back. It's following us. It and that Chinaman. We must hurry now. We must hurry. We mustn't stop again, and we must look back all the time."

Crisp stopped and picked up the ruby casket.

"We must leave that," I said, "it isn't ours, you know, Crisp. You'll leave it, won't you, Crisp?"

"No," said he. "By God!"

VII

CRISP

But the sun, rising hot upon our backs, found me in a saner condition than Crisp. For hours he had been cursing and swearing because he was thirsty; but now he began to talk with a kind of crazy boastfulness, saying that he was not the man to go without water when there was plenty of it to be had for the mere seeking. He knew the signs, he said, and as soon as he saw them would lead me to a spring hole. I needn't be afraid; he would see to it that I had a good drink. He even warned me against drinking too fast. "When we strike water," he said, "you'll be for rushing in and swigging a bucket, but mind what your uncle says, and don't. First you want to moisten a rag and suck it, and when you get used to that you can swallow a few drops, and then after you begin to swell a bit you can negotiate your bucket." And so on all the long hours. His eyes, wide and glassy, roamed the horizon in search of signs, and toward noon he began to mistake hillocks of sand for vegetation, and I was obliged to join with him in long zigzags that ended in disillusion and wasted precious time. To have gone against him in his craziness might have ended murderously. There was no good in his eye. After a while he began to visit his disappointments upon me; to curse me because the green bushes were sand, and to say that I ought to have told him so in the first place. Several times, too, for he would not suffer me to carry it, he dropped (impelled, I think, by a kind of insane mischievousness) the ruby casket, and we had to go back for it. It was beyond patience. But I was not man enough to cross him, or to say what I thought.

Suddenly he stopped and pointed to the right.

"Well, my boy," he began, "what did I tell you? Are those green bushes or not?"

I could see none, but before I could say so he broke out violently:

"Don't lie to me. Say 'yes' or 'no,' but don't lie. If you lie," he went on with a very horrid expression, "I will kill you. Now, then, which is it, bushes or not?"

It entered my mind to shoot him down, and perhaps I made a threatening motion. Anyway he sprang at me, wrenched the rifle from my hands and retreated warily.

"You're gone crazy," he said, and, rather kindly, "a drop of water'll fix you up. Now you watch out for that"—here he flung the ruby casket at my feet—"and I'll go fetch you a drop of water. Sorry you're crazy."

He turned and, like Robinson Crusoe, a gun under each arm, started away toward his imaginary patch of green. But was it imaginary—this last patch? Or was my mind, too, going? It seemed to me at one moment that there was a patch of green, at the next that there was not. I stood irresolute, and rubbed my swollen eyes, blinked, and then made a step or two after Crisp. But he had developed a wonderful acuteness of ear, and heard me.

"You stay there," he shouted, "or I'll fix you."

I stood and watched his slow course toward—yes, it was a patch of green. Of the color I was now as sure as Crisp had been, but of the substance, no. If it was vegetation—a sudden fear gagged me for a moment, and then I shouted to Crisp.

"Look out!" I yelled. "It's silk!"

I saw his head turn and he called to me.

"Water," he called, "it's water."

But it was not water, and Crisp, blinded by his infatuation, walked straight up to the Chinaman of the mirage, who, in a girt-up green robe, had risen in his path. It seemed to me that the Chinaman made a gesture with his hand, as of a man casting something quietly on the ground, and then I saw that Crisp had flung the rifles from him, and was running toward me with frantic leaps and bounds. He was sane enough now, poor fellow, and no less aware than I of the gray death that struck at his heels. I had one moment of clear vision. The Chinaman had vanished. With a scream, that still rings in my ears, and in a shower of sand, poor Crisp went down, and then there was darkness in my eyes, and I was running, running desperately, and clasping something heavy to my breast.

In my frenzied panic I must have snatched up the ruby casket, for when I came to my senses, how much later I do not know, but soon, for I was still desperately running, I had it clutched with one aching hand to my breast. I had been running up a long incline of the desert, but the impulse of terror came to an end, and I stopped short. There was no sweat in me to run out; but I glowed and burned like a furnace, and for a long time my only vision was a kaleidoscope of crazily swirling white dots. I looked behind me when my vision had cleared, but there was nothing to be seen but sand, blazing in the sun.

I climbed then very slowly a few inches to the step, to the top of the rise, and saw before me, very far, between hills of sand, segments of the blue and tranquil sea.

VIII

THE CHINAMAN IN GREEN

Had I been alone in the desert I would have had eyes for nothing but those placid and refreshing stretches of blue; but it was peopled for me and haunted: by the

45

ghosts of comrades, and by the Chinaman in green who hunted me, and by the broken-tailed snake that he could loose against me when he conceived that the hour of his opportunity had struck. I must have cut a grotesque and horrible figure of fear and caution; halting to look behind with wild eyes; starting, stopping; sucking at the hot desert air, now breaking for a few yards into a lumbering run; and now dragging my feet as if to each there had been riveted a ball and chain. So a guilty man, and one hounded by fear, might act in the night-time or the dusk, in a city street, convinced that in each dark doorway, or behind each corner, the fearful lurked to spring upon him. But here was I so acting in broad sunlight, in a region that for miles in every direction was open to the eye like a book; levelish and free of cover toward every point of the compass, and still I advanced, starting, cowering, running, halting like an actor of melodrama rehearsing a rôle of terror.

The direction that I followed thus stageily intersected at last the broad trail that our little company had made on its march to Chen Chan. Here were the deep footprints of Sang Ti; the shuffled marks of Morgridge's big feet; Crisp's firm and even tread; Meff's small and neat impress; the long stride of Hawes; and here I had gone on well-arched, buoyant feet. Of all that company I only could now write my progress in the sands; I only lived on for a time.

At another time that broad and tragic spoor nad turned me aside to break a fresh and unsuggestive path; but now I had a sense of companionship with it, and followed it feeling no longer so utterly lonely, afraid, and alone.

I passed the fallen monolith, and saw in the bay, half full of tide, the schooner, riding in safety, and the schooner's boat moored to the beach of the promontory by a staked oar. On board that schooner was water—food—home. I had an exhilaration of escaped danger that lent me wings. I ran along the hard beach toward the boat and my feet splashed in the advancing rim of the tide. There was a breeze in my face, and my fears were blown from me and fell behind. I shouted as I ran

It was but half a dozen strong strokes to the schooner. I snatched up the ruby casket from the seat where I had lain it, and sprang aboard, and found myself face to face with the Chinaman in green. His robes were dripping sea water, and there was a kind of smile on his lips. In one hand, held tenderly as a girl holds a pet bird, was the little gray snake. White lids covered its eyes, and its broken tail hung from between his fingers and dangled listlessly like a bit of string. The smile on the Chinaman's face wavered and broadened. There was a kind of friendliness in it. I smiled back at him. And when he held out his other hand, open, I placed in it the ruby casket. And he, gently and quietly as a girl might slide a necklace into a jewel-box, slid into it the little gray snake, dead now, for what reason I know not, and closed the cover with a faint snap.

I ferried him to the shore, and stood watching him until he had disappeared over the brow of the desert with his face toward Chen Chan.

II

PARADISE RANCH

PARADISE RANCH

I

During the five years that it had served him as home, work, and recreation, the Paradise Ranch had seemed a real paradise to Emmanuel Mason and Jim Stanley, his partner during those years, a kind of better angel. The ranch was a masculine paradise; two thousand acres of rich meadows and black forest looking boldly forth between two barren hills upon the open sea, planned, toiled for, worked, cultivated, inhabited, and owned by men. The trade-winds blowing up the little valley had never given occasion to a member of the gentler sex to snatch with one hand at her petticoats and with the other at her hat. The lamps of the long white ranch-house had never looked upon the festive dance, nor had the moon ever discovered a pair of lovers seated hand in hand upon the long veranda. The lamps had never looked upon anything gayer than a poker game, nor the moon upon anything more exciting than men who smoked and talked. Seasons came

51

and went. But as yet no woman had found her way into the Paradise Ranch, and if one had she would have been politely shown the way out.

But a change was coming; a fact which the telegram that Emmanuel Mason held open in his hand betrayed —a telegram that had been brought fifteen miles over the hills from the railroad at the gallop.

Stanley had been East anent a will in which he had figured to no great profit, and the telegram was from him:

My wife and I will be in San Mateo Monday. Send over a team to meet us.

That was the whole matter, a sudden violent blow between the eyes for which the recipient had been in no way prepared. The marriage must have been very sudden—as all marriages are—but the courtship must have been like chain lightning; shorter, perhaps, as Mason thought with the flicker of a smile, than the ceremony. The circumstances, however, did not matter to him in the least; it was the fact. Paradise was to be invaded, as of old, by a woman, and the next comer, of course, would be a serpent—a serpent of old habits laid aside, old times discontinued, furniture moved to new positions, tobacco frowned on (perhaps); liquor relegated to the nearest saloon, fifteen miles away; wholesome meals turned into finical courses, and last,

52

and worst, the lazy Sunday shave changed into a matutinal or vespertine regularity.

Emmanuel Mason mourned for lost friends. He must share "Jim," the sweet-tempered, the big-boned, the guileless, the gentle, with another. When he had worked all day and become tired and dirty and lazy— he would have to wash and dress. When the "heap pain," as they called, it, should pierce him from temple to temple, he could no longer stamp the veranda till dawn, Jim's hand on his shoulder, and swear. When the "heap pain" waked him in the night he could no longer thrust open Jim's door and call upon the comforter to come with him out under the stars, and talk to him lest he should go mad. That door must not be opened at random any more, it must be knocked upon. And the spacious, plastered, airy room beyond looking south-westward upon the sea, would that receive a coat of paper and come to be referred to as the "blue" room or the "pink"?

With the exception of the "heap pain" all had been paradise till now; it would become purgatory, and the pain remaining would make the latter hell. The "heap pain," hitherto the only cloud on the horizon, had never occurred with sufficient frequency to cause Mason any real alarm. It came two or three times a year, usually during the rains, remained a day or two, hurt fearfully, and went. The pain was similar, only much more

violent, to that which is known as a "stitch in the side."
Mason had it in the head, from temple to temple, and
though he had consulted doctors its cause and nature
remained unexplained.

With so many grounds of foreboding it was not un-
like the man to make the best of the situation, and,
grumbling deeply, to set the house to rights from end
to end. He decked it with great boughs of pungent
bay and fragrant yellow acacia; he filled it with roses
and calla lilies; he straightened the chairs over and over
again. He had a dozen nervous interviews with Jue
Fong, the cook; he saw to the team, the trap, and the
harness which were to go and fetch the bride and groom.
He shaved and donned costly raiment and intended to
drive over the hills for them himself, and then came
the "heap pain," and sent him writhing to his bed. He
lay until he could lie it no longer. He rose and walked
till he could stand it no longer. He groaned and blas-
phemed. And about four of the afternoon the pain
became worse.

Emmanuel Mason clapped a hand to each temple and
literally ran for the low-built clump of huts where his
Chinese laborers dwelt. He smote with his foot upon
the door of Sam Ah and strode in.

"Sam," he said in a thick voice, "have you got any
opium?"

"I no smoke," said the righteous Sam Ah.

"Who has some?"

"All boys allee samee," said Sam Ah. "Him no smoke."

This was, of course, a righteous lie. Mason groaned.

"You don't understand, Sam," he said. "If I don't get smoke I'll die."

"Allite," said Sam Ah, "me go city?"

"You get me smoke," said Mason, "then you go to the city and raise hell."

The wily one smiled pleasantly.

"Allite," he said.

And from a room which contained absolutely nothing but a pallet bed, a mattress, and the bare insides of four walls, he produced a pipe, a rectangular can half full of opium, matches, a tiny spirit lamp with a glass shade to keep the flame steady, and a sort of thin metal skewer to roll the pill on.

"I don't know how, Sam."

Sam Ah indicated his bed with a hospitable gesture.

"You sabe lie still," he said. "I make pill."

Presently he had lighted the lamp, gathered on the end of his skewer what appeared to be a lump of soft tar, and fell to rolling it in the flame. Instantly an indescribable, penetrating odor (that seems as if it ought to choke one, but doesn't) filled the room. The opium sputtered and spat, and the lump seemed to shrink into itself and become a shape. Every now and then Sam

Ah took it from the flame and gave it a quick telling mould with his slim fingers. When he was satisfied with its shape and consistency he slipped it into the tiny bowl of the pipe, let it cool for a few seconds and withdrew the skewer. Mason put the pipe in his mouth and inhaled the smoke, while Sam Ah kept the pill burning by a constant application of the lamp.

"More fast," he commanded, "more in."

Mason puffed as rapidly and deeply as he could. The burning pill guttered, sputtered, and roared like a miniature volcano.

"More fast," commanded Sam Ah, and in half a minute the smoke was finished, and Mason, gagged and gasping, was conscious of no wonderful dream or any pleasant effect whatever. His head was shot with pains as before. Meanwhile Sam Ah was rolling another pill. But scarcely had Mason drawn a breath of the second smoke into his big lungs than the tormenting pain left him. He pushed aside the pipe, rose and shook himself.

"You're a good man, Sam," he said.

"Good men heap scarce," said Sam Ah, and prepared to finish the relinquished smoke himself.

When Emmanuel Mason came into the outer air he felt like a happy child. He wanted to laugh and turn hand-springs. A hedge of artichokes seemed to him more beautiful than a hedge of roses. An hour later he was conscious of a slight rawness in his throat and a slight headache, but not the old torture, nor in the old place. A little later still he felt perfectly normal.

Then came the sounds of wheels on gravel, a halting of horses, and steps on the veranda. Emmanuel Mason flung open the door and advanced with a broad smile of welcome and outstretched hands.

Jim Stanley's wife was tall and girlish-looking. She had a big sweet mouth which Emmanuel Mason had once considered beautiful. He started at sight of her: then took both her hands in his and made her welcome in Jim's name and his own.

"You've not changed much," she said.

"But I never expected it would be *you*."

There was all the unnecessary clipped talk of question and answer which the occasion warranted, and the two friends and the woman went into the house.

"My dear," said the woman to her husband, "now do go and put something on your hands. . . . He *would* drive," she explained to Mason. "He wouldn't wear gloves, they were *already* chapped, and now look what the sun has done to them."

Indeed, Stanley's hands were a study in raw, cracked red. It was nothing new to Mason, however, for he had often seen them as bad or worse.

"I tell him to put cold cream on them," said the bride. "There's nothing like it for chapped hands."

"Vaseline is better," said the groom in an eager, gentle voice. "But that doesn't do mine any good."

II

The men, of course, altered radically in their habits of life; shaving daily, disposing of yesterday's mud, and dressing for dinner. But these alterations came from a natural desire to please rather than from the hounding of a woman's tongue, for if the Ranch had been at one time a man's paradise, at least the Eve who had entered it was a man's woman, so that nothing of what Emmanuel Mason had feared came to pass. Instead, he was by way of being more comfortable than he had ever been; and it was long before he realized that to live in the new condition was no less dangerous than to live in a house built over a sleeping volcano. To this ignorance, perhaps, the rains which, for so many weary weeks, had been appeasing the thirst of the land, and clothing it with green grass and flowers, contributed by suddenly coming to an end. There commenced the long dry season for which California is famous, and during which every moment spent out of doors is a complete blessing. All day the sun blazed and the strong salt trade-winds blew in from the ocean. Each evening, as the sun set, and the winds thus shorn of heat smote the hot earth, fog arose along the whole line of the coast and rushed inland. But, later, the fog diminished until the stars showed through, and presently all the glittering heavens appeared. Day after day, night after night, month after month, it was thus. Every drop of surface water was sucked from the earth; the green of the hills yielded to golden brown; the soft muddy roads became bands of white, hard as iron. Growing things rested from the labor of growing. The world was at peace with itself.

It was not too hot by day, nor too cold by night; much that made for human calm and happiness was an atmospheric condition. There was no excuse for morbid depression; the cattle became fat on the dry stubble. In irrigated districts fruit swelled and ripened. There was great prosperity throughout the State, merrymaking, and out-of-door life. During this period matters progressed peacefully and with pleasantness at Paradise Ranch. The woman was firm in the saddle, strong in the surf, and subtle of tongue; to be with her was to be gay. And Emmanuel Mason found himself thinking that if he had his life to lead over, he would like to marry her himself. As a mere boy in the old days he had enjoyed the chance. He had been her first fancy and she his. They had construed fancy to mean love (and Heaven only knows whether it does or not) and they had plighted their troth. Lack of money had stood in the way of immediate marriage, and Emmanuel Mason had gone the way of the sun to carve his fortune. He toiled in mining camps and in lumber camps, drove fence posts, was partner in a livery stable, clerk in a bank, was by turn prosperous, on the verge of riches, poor, dead broke, and again prosperous. At this stage he fell in with Jim Stanley, and together they bought Paradise Ranch and other adjacent properties, which they managed to work with much pleasure and considerable profit. Entering upon such vicissitudes as a boy, he was soon developed by them into a man, and during the transition became heart-whole and fancy-free. It was the same with the girl. Long separation, as usual, killed their mutual fancy. They stopped writing peacefully enough—but felt as if they had quarrelled. If Emmanuel Mason had made a visit to the East he would not have called upon her.

With all that he had gone through and with all that he had accomplished, it is not to be supposed that Mason was altogether a strong man. Free from restraint and at an early age his own master, full of red blood and high spirits, there had been periods in his career which are still spoken of with awe on the "Barbary Coast" and similar districts. He had raised many kinds of Cain, painted many towns red, had killed a man, been co-respondent in a divorce suit, and achieved a notoriety which had been very difficult to live down. Good sense, coupled with the first intimations that the "heap pain" was to be an irregular permanency, strong words from a physician, and perhaps mature years, had all contributed to shape his present healthful and respectable form of existence. He drank sparingly, smoked rather too much, and worked long vigilant shifts in the open air. He looked like a man who had inherited tell-tale lines of face, rather than a man who had made them. He was as brown as his adopted hills in the dry weather; short, broad, erect, gray-eyed, and powerful. There was something of the tiger in his long, quiet stride, something of the hawk in his glance, and something of the holiday school-boy in his smile.

The summer at Paradise Ranch brought three types of happiness to three people. Jim Stanley was happy, because in possessing the woman he loved he was not renounced by the friend he loved. Emmanuel Mason was happy because he liked his partner's wife, and because the year was a prosperous one. But the woman was happy in a very different way. It was not the peaceful in life that she most enjoyed. She knew that Emmanuel Mason, who had once fancied her and now admired her, would end by fancying her again. It seemed inevitable—a kind of poetic retribution for his former neglect. To rouse the dormant fancy intrigued her mind, amused her, and made her happy. Unfortunately she did not realize that playing with matches is

often the cause of a conflagration which may not only
destroy one's neighbor's house but one's own. To
make matters worse, she had a real affection for her
husband—and did not love him in the least. Therefore
she was as tow, and in striving to set fire to Emmanuel
Mason's heart was in a fair way to consume her own.

At first Emmanuel Mason thought that Alice Stanley
was "nice," "sensible," and "amusing." Then that
her face was "pretty"; then, as of old, that her big,
sweet mouth was "beautiful"; then that her face was
beautiful. And after that he began to carry her image
in his mind's eye, and to shorten his hours of work that
he might be with her the more. His first regret was
that he had not married her himself, and his second
was like unto the first. He regretted that she was not
still free. "If she were still free," he thought, "I
believe I would fall in love with her." That under the
circumstances he might as readily fall in love with her
was a supposition which he did not for a moment entertain. And it was not until the unexpected ending of a
vacation which he had decreed unto himself that he
began to perceive danger in the supposition. The
ending of that vacation was in this wise.

Emmanuel Mason was an ardent and jealous lover
of fly-fishing. Once a year, sometimes twice, he jour-
neyed to a section of river which he controlled in the far
Sierras, and fished to his heart's content. Being a

jealous lover, and of an adventurous disposition, he always went alone, built his own camp, and did his own catching and cooking. It befell, therefore, that a strong desire to fish came upon him, and his good-bys were as brief as those of a thirsty drunkard departing for his club. It also befell that he came to the far river, cast his fly, and struck three pounds of shifty muscle, speed, and endurance. This had often happened before, but that there should be no joy in the struggle was an entirely new sensation. All that day, however, he fished conscientiously. The luck ran with him, the fish were big and strong, but the old ecstasy was gone. Emmanuel Mason had left his powers of enjoyment in Paradise Ranch.

The next day he did not fish at all. He sat in the shade and watched the strong, bright rush of the river until he was dizzy. He lay on his back and regarded the intricate patterns drawn by the lofty tree-tops upon the sky. He thought upon the days of his youth, neglected opportunities, opportunities seized, moneys made, moneys lost, manly truths, subtle lies, success, failure, times of comparative virtue and times of rank vice. He thought upon his gains and his losses. He thought of how he had gained in experience of men, in capital, in sense of living, but he thought also of how, in the gaining, he had lost the most precious of gifts— innocence. He became melancholy and restless in the shade by the river. A week before he had smoked and planned with Jim and Alice for the future. Now he smoked and wondered about the end. For the first time in his life he felt old; for the first time he felt that most harrowing and unmanly of feelings, self-pity. A glorious night of stars came, but brought with her no gift of sleep. Emmanuel Mason thrashed in his blankets like a newly landed fish. He thought almost with agony of what was and of what might have been. For hours he tormented himself, and then fatigue began to exert itself, and from logical thoughts and facts he passed to Spanish castles, and thence at length to dreams. In what *is* there is seldom peace, in what *was* there is less, but man is saved from madness by the thought of what still may be.

Emmanuel Mason arose with the sun and bathed in the river. His face, far from being harrowed by the unquiet night, looked younger than it had in years. He was exalted and stimulated by the unwise dreams. He burned his fingers at the cooking and laughed. He packed his blankets and his rods, and sang aloud. In an hour he was riding down the mountains with his face toward the sea. And as he rode he laughed and sang.

Love is a wonderful and beautiful affair, but it is most beautiful when it is unalloyed with passion. When he who loves is first aware of his love, and is abashed in the presence of his beloved, when for a moment the hardened sinner recovers his lost innocence, and the world seems as it should be from pole to pole, there is no sense of danger, nothing exists but the beautiful. And so it was with Emmanuel Mason. He was wildly happy at finding himself in love, but more wildly happy in the delusion that he was content to possess his love alone. He did not feel the slightest temptation to declare it. Jim and Alice were man and wife. He was their friend. He loved them both. He could not be happy away from them. Therefore he would go where they were and stay there, and be, if he could, their good angel. If ever a man rode innocently into an ambush, that man was Emmanuel Mason. If ever a man believed that love, pure, good, and proof against the poison of desire, had come into his life, that man was Emmanuel Mason. If ever a man deluded himself, that man was Emmanuel Mason.

He reached Paradise Ranch on the evening of the second day, and, crossing the broad piazza with his long, quiet, tiger-like strides, pushed open the door of the living-room and went in.

Stanley and his wife were seated on opposite sides of a small table, reading. They looked as if they had not spoken to each other for hours. As a matter of fact, Stanley had made several offers in the way of conversation which had been rejected without too much civility by Mrs. Stanley. At Mason's entrance both rose and hurried to greet him. In both faces were looks of real pleasure. But the look in Stanley's face was mingled with wonder; while, if a heightened color and sparkling eyes are to be trusted, that in Mrs. Stanley's was alloyed with a feminine feeling of triumph.

"But for Heaven's sake what has brought you back so soon?" cried Stanley, grasping his friend's hand.

"Why, he couldn't stay away from us, Goose," said his wife.

"But the fishing must have been bad?" said Stanley.

"Awful," said Mason, "not a strike the second day. What do you think of that?"

This statement was perfectly true, but Mason blushed in delivering it.

"How disappointing," said Mrs. Stanley. But she had noted the blush and could not conceal a smile.

"But you must be famished," said Stanley eagerly. "I'll go to the pantry myself and see what there is."

"Wouldn't you rather I went?" said the wife.

"No, you stay right here, and hear all about it. . . . I'll be right back."

There was a pathetic awkwardness about Stanley which belied his manly qualities. When he moved he seemed to be all knees and elbows. They watched him out of the room, and it is just possible that Mrs. Stanley raised her fair shoulders the least fraction of an inch.

"Why did you smile just now," said Mason suddenly, "when I said that I didn't get a bite the second day?"

She looked boldly in his eyes and read as in a primer what was written there.

"The difference," she said slowly, "between a man and a woman is that a man lies with his tongue and tells the truth with his eyes. But a woman lies with both."

And she turned her own eyes down, and half covered them with their soft lashes. Color rose in her cheeks, and Emmanuel Mason realized that his love was not to be a solace and a delight to his secret heart, but a menace and a tragedy. He made a step toward her.

"Good-night," she said. "No, I'm not going to stay and watch you eat your horrible old dinner. I'm tired out. Don't let Jim sit up too late. Good-night."

At the door she turned. Her eyes met his and mocked them.

"I'm glad you're back," she said softly. . . . And vanished.

III

It was November, but as yet no rain had fallen. The country was beginning to feel distressed. Farmers looked anxiously and often upward for signs of clouds;

their brows became puckered from too much gazing
upon the blank, blazing sky. In the reservoirs water
was so low that it was impossible to draw a clean bath.
Along the roads, dust, like dirty snow, enveloped the
trees. Even the dwellers in cities were tired of the
bright weather. Alone the Chinese smoked their
opium and went with calm faces and patient eyes
indefatigably about their business.

Emmanuel Mason and Alice Stanley rode at a walk,
northward, along the ocean beach. On the right hand
the naked brown hills, baked to the hardness of brick,
gleamed like metal in the sun. Upon the left hand the
long blue combers came unbroken from afar—like regi-
ments in line of battle—and were broken among the
shallows. Ahead, the beach extended like a broad tortuous white road between the tumbling ocean and the
steadfast hills. The wind blew greatly from the
southwest.

"I know that, in the world's eyes, what I have proposed to you is wrong. I have been brought up to
believe so. I do believe so. I have no defence to
make. Do I care? Care? I want you to come away
with me, that is all. I want it with all my strength.
The more wrong it is the less I care and the more I
want it. If I had not gone away—'way back at the
beginning of the world—you would have belonged
to me, wouldn't you? The situation that we are in is

only an accident. We were meant for each other.
You know it."

"But you went away, and we forgot each other,
didn't we?"

"Yes, like the pair of young fools we were. If I
went away now, would I forget? Would you? You
are wretched with this—with Jim. For God's sake
give yourself a chance to be happy. Say the word.
. . . You're afraid of conventions, dear, aren't you?
Is that it? Tell me."

"May be. How should I know? I don't know
what to think."

"Let me think for you. Convention is a base and
false fabric that has been erected by the vast majority—
the vast pitiful majority which has ever been unable
to occupy itself with real issues. Convention——"

"I believe that at this moment you love me, let us say,
with all your strength. But how can I know that it will
last? How dare I think that it will? We were lovers
once who met in after years as strangers. We——"

He snatched the word from her as it were.

"We are lovers now. That is all that counts. At
this moment we love each other. What is the use of
supposing things that are not very probable? If a
shadow *should* come between us, is it worth antici-
pating? And, furthermore, I tell you that it can't
come. I won't let it. . . . We are lovers *now*."

"Yes, but I am a woman, and I am afraid of the shadow."

And of a sudden their faces were both in shadow, for a dark cloud blown up unperceived from the ocean had come between them and the sun. The woman laughed nervously for a second.

"*I* told you," she said. "Do you think it will rain?"

"How do I know?" said the man almost roughly.

"Ah!" she said, "you would speak to me like that after a while. . . . No, thank you."

"Alice, dear," his voice was all tenderness, "if I spoke rough, I wasn't thinking rough. I wasn't thinking about rain, I was thinking how I love you and want you." He looked upward with great humility. "Yes, dear, I think it *will* rain."

"Then we'd better go back."

As they turned the first drop fell. The rain was slow in getting under way. It seemed as if it were out of practice, and not exactly sure what to do. And just as an army sends out scouts and then skirmishers to prepare the way for the main attack, so the cloud sent down experimental drops and little showers before commencing to pour.

"It's going to be a good one," said Mason; "shall we canter?"

Both Mason and Mrs. Stanley were conscious of a suppressed feeling of excitement. The wind seemed to

70

blow stronger and the surf to run higher. Even the ponies were excited by the coming of the rain. They began, as they cantered, to fear the waves to which they were perfectly accustomed; to prick their ears forward and back, to snort, to shy at dark stones and lumps of seaweed. The canter became a gallop, the gallop a run, the run all but a runaway. And in the midst the cloud let fall its contents, and the earth and sea rose in smoke to meet them.

Mile after mile and side by side the ponies raced through the deluge. Water, sweat, and foam poured from them. They began to gasp and labor in the sand. The rain and the surf combined in one deafening roar.

Mason shouted something to his companion. She shouted an answer. It looked rather than sounded like the query, "What?"

"This won't do,." Mason bellowed. It is not known whether she heard or not; it is enough that she understood. They reined in the ponies till they walked.

Presently the heavens grew lighter, and the rain slackened. It continued to fall for some time, but mingled with it were bright rays from the sun, and presently it ceased. The brown parched hills were streaming with little brooks, that sought ways across the beach and so into the sea. There was no longer any dust. The air was cool and greatly fresh. It was as if nature had suddenly been cured of a fever.

"Wasn't it glorious! Oh, but I loved it!"

He looked at her. Her habit hung shapelessly upon her. He only thought her figure the better. Her face was wet and her eyes were still brimful of rain. He thought her face the more beautiful.

He reined to the left until his knees touched her pony's ribs. He slipped his left arm about her.

"Alice," he said, "I have not kissed you since I was a boy."

If the madness had left the scene it had not yet left the actors.

She shivered slightly and drew a deep breath. Then she turned her face toward his; the big sweet mouth was trembling. As their lips came slowly close it seemed to each as if the face of the other was half hidden in a wonderful mist. One moment and the eager lips would have met.

Emmanuel Mason's head was suddenly jerked back on his shoulders. He relinquished his bridle. His riding crop fell to the ground. He drew his arm from about the woman he loved and pressed his hands to his temples. His eyes rolled and his mouth writhed. His face had become a frightful mask upon which was depicted agony incredible.

"For God's sake, what is it? What is it? Can't you speak to me?"

A groan was wrung from him. It is possible that

the woman had not really loved the man until she saw him enduring his torture.

He took his hands from his head and gathered up the reins.

"Never mind the crop," he said. . . . "I have these things once in a while." He spoke between clinched teeth, his face the color of dust. "They strike like hot iron. It's the suddenness that . . . that hurts . . . after that I can stand 'em."

She was trembling with alarm and concern.

"We must hurry home," she said.

Emmanuel Mason strove without success to look natural and to smile.

"First I want my kiss," he said.

"Not now," she said, "we must hurry. . . . Oh, man, man, I love you . . . I love you!"

Again they put the ponies to the proof.

But as they tore along the beach the pain in his head was so frightful that Emmanuel Mason had no thought of the beloved at his side, who loved him and would endure all things for his sake.

Instead, he thought, with the intensity of a monomaniac, of the low-built clump of huts where his Chinese laborers dwelt, and of the instant relief to be found in the quarters of Sam Ah.

And an hour later, as he lay sucking the heavy, hot, white smoke into the innermost recesses of his great

73

lungs, it seemed to him as if the guttering, sputtering of the fusing opium was the sound of the rain roaring about his ears.

IV

It was late in February before the lovers were able to think of putting into effect the plan which they had matured for the elopement. The rains, long in coming and prayed for in all the churches, made up in profusion what they had lacked in punctuality. The world became green, and all night the tree frogs sang loud and sweet.

December was a wet month, January a wetter. In the first half of February there was only one bright day. It seemed as if the prayers addressed to God must have been heard by the devil and answered in a spirit of malice. In particular the winter was a hard one for Emmanuel Mason. He received and recovered from attack after attack of his trouble. But on each occasion it took more of the subtle art of Sam Ah to repulse the enemy. A Chinaman can begin young, smoke opium hard, do his work, and live to be sixty-five. The toughest white man will go to pieces in a fifth of that time. Emmanuel Mason was a strong man, but the pain told on him some, and its cure told on him much. He became almost a shadow of himself, haggard, petulant, and without repose. The whites of his eyes

74

took on a yellowish tinge, and it was noticed that he no longer loved his tobacco. But the more sick and more tragic he became the more the woman loved him.

It is to the credit of both that during that trying winter they kept apart as much as possible and were indefatigable in their attempts to be nice to Stanley. Nor was this a studied hypocrisy of demeanor. They were truly sorry for him, and, incredible as it may seem, truly fond of him. They were like a pair of children preparing to run away from home. Nothing should prevent them, but they were sorry to go.

Mason's health was so much improved during February that he implored Mrs. Stanley to fix the hour for their departure. And in the end she named the first day of March, on which date the big new steamer of the Maru Line was to sail for the Orient. Mason made one trip to town to engage the best suite of rooms on the hurricane deck, and a second when the ship had reached port to look the rooms over and to make note of anything lacking to promote Alice's comfort during the voyage.

By a miracle the day was sunny and bright even in town. Mason felt better and happier than he had all winter. And so used had he become to the idea of an elopement that he no longer regarded it as either wrong or unusual. He made an early start, so that he might return to the ranch the same day and report to

Alice. This was the next to the last day in February. They were to come to town together on the 1st of March, and the ship with them aboard was to sail early in the afternoon. There was to be no commotion. No bother about trunks. Alice had made several trips to town to buy a new outfit and new trunks to pack it in. For this purpose she kept a room in the Palace Hotel. Mason had made his preparations in a similar manner. There would be little scandal. Paradise Ranch was little visited, and its inhabitants were less known. Mason was glad for himself and very sorry for Stanley, that was all.

He boarded the steamer, and was shown to the suite which he had engaged. It was capacious and comfortable. Two bedrooms, a big bathroom, and a pleasant lounging room containing a writing-desk and various easy-chairs. Mason spent some time in the little apartment, fixing its geography and possibilities in his mind so as to describe them correctly to Alice. He made up his mind which of the bedrooms should be hers and which his. Then he tried the easy-chairs in the lounging room, one after another. He had a thousand pleasant dreams to the minute. He was very happy. At length having completed his list of things needed, fruit, wine, books, writing materials (to whom could they write, pray?), etc., he rose to go. Before doing so he permitted himself a last look into the room

which Alice was to occupy. He pulled aside the curtain
(the door was hooked back) and thought for a moment
that he had mistaken her doorway for the one opening
on the deck. It was a momentary hallucination, to be
sure, for there was the fold-up basin, the rack with
bottles for drinking water and glasses to drink from,
or to hold tooth-brushes; there was the brown carpet
whose pattern had struck his fancy, the swinging lamp,
the hooks upon which to hang clothes, and there was
the brass bedstead with its expanse of immaculate sheets
folded back over a rose-colored counterpane, embroidered with the company's crest and monogram.

Emmanuel Mason stepped suddenly into the room
and looked upward at the ceiling. No, the ceiling was
perfectly solid, and not, as he had fancied, pierced by a
skylight. He had even fancied that the skylight had
been left open and that— But how utterly ridiculous.
. . . And yet. . . . He stopped and felt of the carpet.
It was perfectly dry, of course. . . . And yet. . . . But
he laughed nervously and went ashore.

About this time it began to rain. And it kept on
raining. During the month of March it rained thirty
days out of the possible thirty-one. The curious thing
was that day after day the rain never varied in appearance and effect. It was not the roaring, black rain that
comes out of low-hanging, swiftly driven black clouds,
but the long, gray rain that falls from thin gray clouds,

drifting slowly through the upper strata of the atmosphere. It had the effect of making things intensely damp rather than actually wet, but for turning brown into green and producing frogs and tree frogs it was incomparable. For instance, Emmanuel Mason had seen a brown carpet whose pattern had struck his fancy become a new grass-green almost the moment the rain struck it. He remembered that the carpet was in a kind of bedroom, which he had left because the newly born tree frogs had suddenly burst into a loud sweet singing which was intolerable to his ears. Another peculiar property of the rain was its power to penetrate opaque substances. It fell upon the floors in houses, as if there had been no ceiling to protect them, and turned them green. On leaving the ship he had made his way to the Palace Hotel and taken refuge in the bar-room. The court-yard of the Palace Hotel is covered by a glass dome, and it was natural enough for that to prove no obstacle to the rain, but that it should penetrate a roof and all the floors of a seven-story structure so as to reach the bar-room in undiminished volume was astonishing. Emmanuel Mason felt a delicacy in asking the bartender why this should be. Instead, he contented himself with saying tentatively: "Doesn't it seem very damp to you in here?"

"Not to me," said the bartender.

"I must be mistaken then," said Emmanuel Mason,

and he shivered slightly. For all that, he was convinced
that the bartender had lied.

Almost from the first the rain got on his nerves. He
felt that it would be absurd to return to the country in
such weather. He would wait until the sky was clear.
Meanwhile he was damp to the bone, and really troubled
about the singularly penetrating quality of the rain.
He was afraid of his old trouble. He remembered that
in Nevada it was nearly always dry. He stepped into
a rainy ticket office and inquired the price of a ticket to
Reno. He had not enough money to pay for it and
crossed the street to his bank to draw a check. Although the ink ran badly, he managed to fill in the blanks
all but the one for the signature. He could not fill
that, however, for the very annoying reason that he had
forgotten his name. It took him two days and a whole
night of hard thought, during which he walked the
streets in the rain, to remember it. When he had done
so he hastened toward the bank.

On the way he encountered a tall, slim woman, who
made an involuntary gesture toward him with both
hands. Although she smiled and had a big sweet mouth
which seemed oddly familiar to him, he was perfectly
sure he was not acquainted with her. So he smiled,
shrugged his shoulders, looked upward, and was for
passing on. The woman endeavored to block the way
and tried to catch him by the sleeve. But that was a

familiarity which Emmanuel Mason did not propose permitting to any woman. He ducked under her outstretched arms and ran up the street like a big cat. When he felt that he was safe from pursuit he laughed loud and long.

That same day he went to Nevada and was disgusted to find that rain was falling in every part of the desert State. He left at once for Colorado, but there it was also raining, and he felt obliged to give it up after an hour's trial. One thing struck him as odd; the fact, namely, that he met nobody who carried an umbrella. He longed to tell them to go in out of the rain, but remembered just in time that it was a kind of rain which it was impossible to avoid. It really began to worry him. And why in the devil was there such a mighty chorusing of tree frogs in regions where there was not a tree to be seen? It was clear to him after a while that if the frogs didn't stop singing, and if the rain didn't stop falling, he would be obliged to go mad.

It was a clever thought to go to Quebec and try a little snow for a change. But high over the Plains of Abraham slowly drifted gray clouds, and from them perpendicularly fell the long gray rain. It was true that the rain fell upon heavy deposits of winter snow. But even as Emmanuel Mason looked the snow turned green, and from the umbrageous gully by which Wolfe had made his immortal ascent there arose suddenly a great, sweet, intolerable singing of tree frogs.

As he thought of Wolfe's immortal ascent the lines of Emmanuel Mason's face smoothed themselves and he smiled. He must ascend. If there is rain under the clouds there is surely blue sky above. A moment before he would have offered his soul to the devil for a sight of blue sky, in spite of the fact that although the devil has been trying for years to make a corner in souls, a sight of blue sky is never the price which he pays. But now there was no need of that. He would ascend above the clouds and owe the devil nothing.

From the Plains of Abraham to the top of Madison Square Tower is but a step for an active man, whose stride used to be compared to that of a tiger. But at that elevation he was still beneath the pitiless clouds, and the beautiful naked Diana from whom the wet dripped was not potent to retain him. He hastened to Paris (cursing the delay, for it took him nearly an hour to get there) and ran nimbly up the steps of the Eiffel Tower until he reached the topmost platform. But still the clouds were above, and from them descended the long gray rains, always at the same pace, always perpendicular to the earth. "God!" he thought, "if it would only fall parallel for a moment—just a moment!"

He turned and began wearily to descend the steps. Suddenly he stopped and began to roar with laughter.

81

"You fool! You fool!" he cried, and he resumed the descent at the run. Reaching the foot of the tower, doubts began again to assail him, and for the second time he paused. "Of course," he said, "to get high enough, I must go up in a balloon, but it takes the devil of a while to make one—and I can't wait. Poor Emmanuel Mason—can't wait. Because, if he waits—if he waits another minute—this rain will drive him mad."

He took out his watch and contemplated the second hand during one revolution.

"Well, I'm not mad *yet*," he said, and put back the watch in his pocket. "Perhaps I can hold out until the balloon is made."

He started to run, stopped, leaned against a railing, and for the second time roared with laughter. When he had done laughing he assumed the attitude of an orator, and with one hand pointing heavenward he cried to an imaginary audience in a great voice: "And if the balloon is out of the question, there yet remains harnessed for the service of man the eternal principle of the balloon. . . . *Why does the balloon rise?*"

It was night. Three gas jets flickered through the rain and illuminated the room. Emmanuel Mason locked the door and the windows. One after another he blew out the three lights.

And then he lay down in the darkness to wait for the time when he should ascend.

82

III

CAPTAIN ENGLAND

GUTTA PERCHA

CAPTAIN ENGLAND

You gentlemen of England,
That live at home at ease,
How little do you think upon
The danger of the seas!

When the stretch of waves between the white coast of Britain and the oaken sides of the *Hynd Horn* had widened to an impassability for the most enduring swimmer, the two mariners with pistols in their sashes quitted the presence of Mr. England, to which they had clung with pertinacity ever since the elegantly buckled shoe of that gentleman had first touched the deck. Mr. England smiled with sweetness after the last disappearing hall-marks of his various misdemeanors, and seated himself on the rail, where he balanced with niceness and behaved so alluringly that the ship's cat leaped to his knee, purring. Thence the cat climbed to his shoulder and rubbed against his cheek.

"O cat," said Mr. England, "in the course of your nine lives, have you ever been hanged?"

The cat yawned, from the sea-freshness, and elevated his ample tail.

"And was it painful?" said Mr. England. "And were you, despairing, made to leave the most beautiful of all tabbies to the machinations of other toms?"

Mr. England's delicate hand passed in caress the whole length of the cat from his nose to the tip of his tail.

"In the midst of life, O cat," said he, "we are in need of the poets, and

> If she be not fair for me,
> What care I how fair she be?

But to be hanged, puss!—a dolorous priest—a knot under the left ear—a drop—kingdom come, and be damned to you!"

The cat purred loudly.

"What is life?" said Mr. England. "A shoe too tight to wear. What is death? An ineptness of nature. Let us die cheerfully, puss, the stem of a rose between our teeth, and our feet clad in easy stockings."

Mr. England sighed and looked back on that fast-sinking shore where he and his crimes and the law had all met in the same ale-house.

"Feline," said Mr. England, "I am to be judged where I was born, hanged where I was bred, and buried where four roads cross, with a stake through my susceptible heart, and a devil to make me dream. But you, lamented sir, will die of an indigestion,—cat, 'ware rat!

—and be hurled by the tail into some corner; and our respected talents will die with us. Do you draw a lesson from that? Then down with you, sir, for an ignoramus!"

Mr. England shifted his shoulder so suddenly as to send the cat scrambling to the deck. There he gradually lapsed from an attitude of surprised indignation into the first position of washing.

Mr. England mused with half-shut eyes.

"Ah, Mr. England," said the captain, "you are comfortable, I trust, in body and mind?"

"The sea does not make me sick in body," said Mr. England, "neither do my thoughts make me sick in mind. But I *am* sick at heart, for I have not yet been presented to Lady Pelham, and on that straight, short road which is between me and the gallows there is no other petticoat in view."

"Mr. England," said the captain, "when I agreed not to put you in irons during good behavior, but to give you the run of the ship, I made it clear that you were not to seek the society of the other passenger, and you promised a ready obedience to my wish."

"But I thought the other passenger would be a male," said Mr. England.

"I had not made the proviso," said the captain, "if it were to have been a man."

"But, captain," said Mr. England, "think of the

lady! How may we find it in our hearts to oblige a lady—a beautiful, an accomplished, a fashionable, a *young* lady—to endure a voyage of inestimable length and dullness, which might be rendered a shadow less disagreeable by the society of one who, though not to the manner born. has been to court, mastered the graces, the languages, the poets, the game of piquet, and other arts which, while not to be mentioned before honest men, have in no wit detracted from his knowledge of the world or his powers of conversation?"

"To the point," said the captain. "But how can I present to this lady, whose guardian and protector I am for the time being, a man who, however accomplished, is for all that a——"

"Spare me!" said Mr. England, with a shudder.

"You see," said the captain.

"But she is so beautiful!" said Mr. England.

"I deplore," said the captain, "that duty which causes me to disoblige a gentleman whom I frankly like and to deprive a lady, whose loneliness I myself can do little to alleviate, of his charming society."

"But surely," said Mr. England, "there would be no harm done. Has crime pock-marked me? Am I loathsome? Is not the great sweetness of this lady proof against contamination? I ask only to be allowed to render her those delicate attentions which are her due, and to bend such small talents as I may have to

88

the shape of her amusement. And can you not, sir, consider me at all? A few weeks—a short trial—a speedy hangman—a dead England! How gayly could those weeks be passed in the nearness of a beautiful lady! How one could disregard the savage judge in the memory of those weeks! How featly one could tread the scaffold imagining it a well-pitched deck beneath an August moon! Would you send me onward, my captain, with no gentle memories? Must I grave it to the recollection alone of murder and of sudden death? Oh, for a gentle memory at the last—perchance a tender word to cling to, perchance a kerchief given in jest, the memory of a sweet profile against the moon, the memory of eyes that gave back stars to heaven! Such memories are fresh garlands hung upon the dying tree, to which, in the very clutch of death, I could whisper with the poet 'Hang there like fruit, my soul, till the tree die.'"

Mr. England turned half away with some show of bitterness.

"Mr. England," said the captain, moved, "my duty is as plain as the north star on a clear night; but in utmost sincerity your sentiments are tearing my mind."

"Let me appeal to *her* great graciousness," said Mr. England. "Let me tell her who and what I am, and then, if she stand for me——"

"You *will* tell her who and what you are?" said the captain, weakening.

"My word!" said Mr. England. "At the worst, she can but spurn and despise me and I shall have played the story-telling Moor."

"You shall have your chance," said the captain. "And now, see, she comes hither."

"Her eyes are like the morning," said Mr. England. And he added: "Captain, in the constant and diverting repetitions of history, it often occurs that when Mohammed cannot go to the mountain—you know the anecdote? I will lay my best gilt buckles against a half-dozen of your Burgundy that the lady takes the part of the pirate."

"Mr. England," said Lady Pelham, jestingly, "the time is come when you did promise to confess your manifold sins and wickedness before all men."

The time was night. The full moon like a round of mottled marble, hung in the heavens. Her sweet light radiated across the dancing sea, and the white sails of the *Hynd Horn* were lighted by it.

Mr. England held up his head proudly, and Lady Pelham clasped her pretty little hands attentively.

"Lady Pelham," said Mr. England, "it is a poor thing that boasts of its own gallantry, but I have been no stranger to the giving and taking of blows, nor to encounters with wild beasts, of which some were lions and serpents, and some men. I ask you to believe that, whatever the fear that has tugged at my heart I have never run away. But now I would fain run from *you*, for what I have to tell will lower me unspeakably in your gracious sight."

"Mr. England," said Lady Pelham gently, "your voice sounds tired and melancholy, like that of *Prince Hamlet* in the play when he becomes sickened of his part in life. If what you are about to say can in any way sever an acquaintance so prettily begun, I pray that you will leave it unsaid. We are two young people in a wide ocean, cut off from each shore with weeks of weary sailing before us. Let us leave behind those things which have been, and be content with what is. If you are truly gallant, you will not leave the queen of this ship without a solitary courtier."

"Such a mantle were a cloak to any sin," said Mr. England. "But such shreds of honor as I may lay claim to require that I speak. Our queen must know her courtier for what he is."

"I will pardon my courtier in advance," said Lady Pelham, "for I need his service."

She looked up at him with a wonderful girlish sweetness.

"I am beyond pardon," said Mr. England, "and forgiveness. I dare not hope that those gentle elements of which I am at this moment composed can secure me toleration after the monstrous composition that I have been. Will you listen, lady, from the bitter beginning to the bitter end? It may be that no woman will ever listen to me again."

"I will listen," said Lady Pelham.

"We are to understand," said Mr. England, "that all those littlenesses, such as tears and laughter, and crime and goodness, which go to make up the Almighty's universe were established by some primal cause. In this way it is possible to conceive of a man who is not answerable for what he is. But I am answerable for what I am. I think I had no primal cause. I adhered to my will when it was good; I clung to it when it was wicked. I cannot say in my defense, 'Had my parents not beaten me, I had not done thus and so.' Therefore, Lady Pelham, you are to judge of a life which was not made for a man, but which a man made for himself.

"Down to the southward," continued Mr. England, "there was an island of the sea. Seen from above, it was like an outstretched hand upon the waters: long, safe harbors were between its fingers, and the five knuckles were redoubtable mountains, susceptible to rare defenses—to the overwhelming of narrow gorges— to the rolling down of irresistible rocks. But from the ocean that island was more sweet; for frothy blue waves lapped the white sands on the one side, and to the other came troops of trees and greenery that knelt and bowed like worshippers. In the harbors of that island was a great safety and hiding-place for a certain ship, and on the shores were deep-thatched homes for men. Plantains and many manners of trees gave fruit; other trees, deep shade; swift brooks, cold water; the mountains, game. There were storehouses full of silks and satins and brocades, and spices, and all manner of good things. Many a chest of gold and silver was in the secret keeping of the strong sands. Dusky women of the island made welcome with soft voices, and the captain of the ship, who was a leader of men, gave good rule to that calm place."

With a little sigh of approval Lady Pelham settled deeper to the mystery of listening.

"There was a ship," said Mr. England, "so shapely above and below the water, and served with such cunning sails, that not one other ship in all the world was so swift upon the seas. This ship was manned by a crew of a hundred men, and captained by a devil."

Lady Pelham shifted uneasily.

"The men," said Mr. England, "were men of Devon in England and of Portugal and Holland and Spain and of the Americas. In only two things was there similarity among the men: each had the heart of a lion and the cruelty of a snake. But the captain!—oh, the captain! He was a rare bird—a pretty gentleman to look

93

upon, if you like; a man of letters and breeding; a man of easy language, who could pin a compliment to a heart and slap his Maker's face in the same breath; a sweet swordsman, a sure shot, and"—Mr. England's voice rose almost to a note of command—"a leader of men."

A look of aversion began to creep into Lady Pelham's eyes.

"Now, what manner of kingdom was that, Lady Pelham?" said Mr. England. His voice was almost fierce. "Whence came those satins and brocades, those chests of gold? What manner of men lived in those deep-thatched homes and sailed that ship? What manner of man was their captain? I will tell you, Lady Pelham. We were bloody pirates, and *I* was our captain. We robbed and murdered on the high seas. Those who despised us we shot; those who were for us we hanged; those who besought us we hauled down the barnacled keel. We made coffins of ships——"

He paused, sweating from the energy of his discourse. Lady Pelham shivered.

"Right," she said; "right; you have said enough." She rose and swayed slightly.

"To the bitter end—to the bitter end!" cried Mr. England. The sweat was on his forehead and upper lip. "I have your Ladyship's promise."

And, as it was in the beginning, the woman listened to the serpent. He spoke in a lower, less shocking voice.

"A wave of us," said he, "went up and over the side of a rich ship. When all was finished, and while the sea, sucking at the shattered bows, was dragging her down, two brother sstood in the cabin. One was honorably, one basely, born. One was Henry, Lord Clearwater; one was Thomas England, pirate. One was a kingly boy with golden hair, and the pride of honor and innocence set like a crown upon his brow. The other was a hard man, whose heart was set upon grimness.

"'Sir,' says my Lord Clearwater, 'if you are truly my brother, I shall be obliged to take my life, which has become unendurable to me, now that I am connected with such vileness. I beg, in view of this, that you will retract your statement, in which case I can consent to live.'

"The boy was white, and he shook, for it was in his mind to take his own life, because I was his brother, and he loathed me, yet he feared to die.

"'Henry,' says England, 'you *are* my brother, and I will save you in spite of yourself.' Oh, the horror of it, Lady Pelham! The words were not free of my mouth when he shot himself—here in the forehead he shot himself, through the very crown of his pride and his innocence. I knelt and kissed the blood from him, for he was my brother, and a kingly boy."

Though Mr. England's voice broke at the tragedy of its own conjuration, he sighed with relief when he saw the look of aversion go from Lady Pelham. He went on falteringly.

"I cut a lock of his yellow hair, and we committed him with honor to the deep. Then I bade haul for England, and I laid the lock upon his mother's knee, and I said, 'Do not weep, lady, for he was a brave and kingly boy.'" Mr. England controlled his voice with effort. "I turned at the door and, looking back, saw the gray head bent over the yellow hair."

Lady Pelham was crying. Mr. England watched her furtively.

"Lady—lady," he said, almost piteously, "does the bitterness of that atone a little? As I rode down the long avenue from the castle, I repented of my shudder-able life, and said over and over again, 'God help me! God help me!'"

Mr. England's hand lay upon the rail, white in the moonlight and frail like an appeal. Lady Pelham touched it with her fingers.

"God help you!" said she.

Mr. England turned from her so that she might not see his face.

"There is more," said he, presently. "It is the bitterest part, for it is the death-blow to the new life then begun. In London is an ale-house where, it is said, if you sit for a year and a day you shall see all the people in the world. There are famous meetings in that ale-house. And who do you think met together there one day? Why, Tom England and his crimes and the law they met there, and, so help him God! he is being taken to the place where he was born, to be tried for all of his crimes, and for any one of them to be hanged by the neck until he is dead."

He leaned toward Lady Pelham.

"It was to lay a lock of hair upon a mother's knee that I went to England," he said. "Gracious, merciful, and beautiful lady, have I spoken my last word to a woman this side of the grave?"

"No," said she, and hot tears coursed down her sweet cheeks, and she ran below without another word.

Mr. England was joined by the captain, who had been prowling about in the night.

"Well?" said the captain.

"Captain," said Mr. England, with the utmost cheerfulness, "I am your creditor for six bottles of Burgundy. With your agreeable and esteemed acquiescence we will open one of them."

And he added to himself:

"That was a saving invention about the brother."

Infinite compassion of woman; infinite forgiveness; infinite desire to mould and make new; infinite power to leave her great, tender, true, beautiful, silly heart in the most brambly places.

97

Those eyes of Lady Pelham's, which Mr. England himself had said were like the morning, looked into the eyes of Mr. England, and saw nothing there of all that horribleness which she had forgiven. She saw there only the purity and nobility of purpose with which he had promised her to live until he died; and in the bottom of her silly, golden heart, she said: "He has repented. He loves me—he must be saved."

Behind them were three weeks of fair and foul weather, a thousand pages of the poets, a hundred games at piquet; conversations wherein were laid down the laws of life, the meetings and partings of true lovers. Sometimes they had spoken of death, but more often of the beginnings of happy lives; sometimes of the delicate perfections of verse, sometimes of predestination, sometimes of the champ of war, but mostly of love.

A bright sun was in the heaven, a following wind was on the sea, and between the *Hynd Horn* and her port was an ever-narrowing distance. But between Priscilla, Lady Pelham, and Mr. Thomas England was no distance at all, for her elbow touched his arm, and a wisp of her hair brushed his cheek.

"Beautiful princess," said Mr. England, "I see now, when it is too late, that the gods have loved me all along, for, through circumstances too horrid for another to contemplate, your favor has caused me to be happier than the heir of a kingdom about to mount the royal throne. I make it my hourly duty to thank God for the wealth of peace which he has given me. The end, which had presented itself to my view amid surroundings of such boundless dishonor, seems now like the gentle coming of night. I shall bid you 'good night,' and fall asleep to dream of you. But there will be no morning, my princess, after that last good night."

"There must be morning somewhere," said Lady Pelham.

"Do you wish it?" said Mr. England.

"I wish it," said she.

"Ah, lady," said Mr. England, "there is such bitterness in brief days! How can you, looking back upon the glory of this time at sea,—when I am gone,—believe, in your heart of hearts, that I was a true penitent? How easy it were to play any part for so little a space! There is scarce a difference between my case and that of your sinner who, feeling the tides of life run agonizingly out, the sweat on his brow, the rattle in his throat, turns with an ecstatic valedictory from his sins (which he can commit no more), and writhes to be forgiven. There is such doubt. Tell me, lady, that you believe—that you believe me other than that."

"I have given you my trust," said Lady Pelham.

"Golden heart!" said Mr. England, and a real tear ran down his cheek. "Oh," he cried, "for a full fragment of life wherein to step from the slough that was into the broad thoroughfare of a true knight! To march prospering, with her kerchief on one's sleeve, with her eyes looking upon one from the high tower, with her trust in one's keep, with her love to return to! I tell you, if I had a year to live I would prove before all men and such a lady that chivalry is not yet gone from earth, and that dragons are still to be found in the enchanted forest."

There was such a deep ring, as of gold, in England's voice, and such an undercurrent of pain and missed opportunity, like the tolling of a dirge, that Lady Pelham's heart was torn, and became bursting with a desire to help that same rebirth of chivalry and knightly deeds upon earth. She laid her hand on his arm.

"If I were Tom England," she said, "I would not yet give over. Rather a plank in the ocean, a gallant struggle, one last fight for that same year of life. If I were a leader of men, I would not suffer myself to be led meekly like an ox to the slaughter by men."

"A plank?" said Mr. England, looking at the great waves. "Ah, lady, not a plank!"

"The plank was a figure," said Lady Pelham. "Can you not think out some stratagem—some desperate chance?"

"And leave you?" exclaimed Mr. England. "Ah, beautiful princess!"

"At the end of such a year as you spoke of," said Lady Pelham, "you could seek me out, and come before me, haling the dragon after you."

"And the reward?" said Mr. England.

"The year were its own reward," said Lady Pelham.

"True," said Mr. England, dolefully. "Then you wish me to escape?"

"Oh, I do!" said Lady Pelham, vehemently.

"I bless you for that," said Mr. England. Then he looked into her eyes for some moments.

"Thank God!" he said at length. "My lot is happier than that of kings and emperors, for in my life I have found one person I can trust."

Lady Pelham's eyes filled with tears.

"And you will try," she said, "for my sake?"

"Listen, dearest lady," said Mr. England. "It has come to my mind that when I am cut off from the sight of your bright eyes I must have leisure wherein to turn back my heart and recollect them. Therefore, being a man of some resource,—the result of experience, not boasting,—I did decide to essay one desperate chance."

"Ah!" said Lady Pelham. "And that——"

"I have some power over nature," said Mr. England, mysteriously, "and I have altered the course thereof."

"Altered the course of nature!" said Lady Pelham.

Mr. England took from a pouch a piece of heavy stone, the color of lead, and the size of a thumb-nail.

"I had two of these," said he. "You have heard how the coffin of Mohammed was raised from the floor of his tomb by the power of the roof, which was lodestone. This is part of the roof of Mohammed's tomb, and so was the other piece. The other piece is now playing ducks and drakes with the mariner's compass by which our good captain confidently thinks he is steering the *Hynd Horn* direct for the port where I am to be hanged. As a matter of fact, she has been running in a somewhat southerly direction. Strange ports offer strange chances to those who are willing to chance it."

Mr. England laughed softly out of pure satisfaction.

"And now," said he, "observe our astute captain and his able officers. It is twelve o' the clock, and they are about to take the sun with the sextant, and locate our exact whereabouts upon the face of the waters. But they will not do this, because our prying skipper shall find within a minute that his instrument—by the way, the only one now on board—has been irreparably deranged."

Mr. England smiled blissfully at Lady Pelham, and hummed from the ancient ballad of Sir Patrick Spens the lines:

> O whare will I get a skeely skipper
> To sail this new ship of mine?

"And, thank God," said Mr. England, "there is one person in the world to whom I can tell this thing."

102

"You trust me like that?" said Lady Pelham, a tender light in her eyes.

"I trust you," said Mr. England, "more than I trust myself."

The captain and his officers stood for a long time scratching their heads.

"At any rate," the captain had said to his officers, "we can trust to our compass, which is an excellent instrument of the latest pattern. At night we must watch out with redoubled vigilance, lest we fall a prey to some uncharted body of land. But it's God's own pity that so pretty a sextant should have met with so untimely an end."

Though the nights were cloudy, the weather held to the satisfaction of all on board, especially to that of the captain and Mr. England, for each was holding himself responsible for the navigation of the ship. Each spent several hours a day in reassuring Lady Pelham. The captain told her that the piny shores of Massachusetts were dead ahead. Mr. England spoke of palms and guavas.

"It is so warm," said the captain, sententiously, to Lady Pelham, "because we are approaching the New World, where it is warmer than with us."

"It is so warm," said Mr. England, "because we are approaching the equator, where it is hotter than in the infernal regions."

"O Lord," said Lady Pelham, on her knees, "make it right for me not to betray his secret, for he is thine own true penitent, and I am thy daughter that adores thee.'

One morning the fan of a palm was seen by Mr. England to pass to leeward in the boil of waters. A little later he showed Lady Pelham a school of flying-fishes, and about noon the lookout cried to those on deck that he beheld land under the port bow. The two faces which Mr. England wore as the *Hynd Horn* bore down on that island—for island it now showed itself to be—were of an exact oppositeness. To the captain he showed a drawn lip,—a beginning-of-the-end face, as it were,—to Lady Pelham the most dancing of eyes, the most radiant of smiles. But if the expression of his face was joyous when he turned it on Lady Pelham, what must have been the feeling in his breast when the dim bluish cloud on the horizon began to assume a familiar shape?

"By the splendor!" cried Mr. England's heart, "I have hit the nail on the very head."

The *Hynd Horn* ran nearer and nearer to the island, and the captain, who was forward, glass at eye, suddenly lurched like a drunken man. He made a new focus and looked again.

"My God!" he cried—"palms!"

Mr. England was at his elbow.

"The tropics!" said he, sweetly.

"This is the devil, Mr. England," said the captain.

"I begin to think it is," said Mr. England. "Sir, the loan of your glass."

Mr. England looked long and eagerly, and his heart leaped and bounded, but he kept countenance.

"Sir," said he, "these waters are familiar to me, and we are in imminent danger of our lives; we are in the midst of shoals and reefs——"

"Condemn that sextant!" cried the captain.

"Sir," said Mr. England, "I beg you to let me take the wheel before all is lost."

"We will turn back," said the captain. He was dazed at finding his ship so far to the southward.

"It were foolhardy to turn back," said Mr. England. "We have no sextant, and the compass has proved as fickle as woman. I beg you, sir, let me take the wheel. There is not a moment to lose. We can talk as—as we save our lives."

The two gentlemen hurried aft, and Mr. England snatched the wheel from the helmsman's hand.

"Ah!" he sighed, as if relieved of a great burden.

"And now, sir, what do you intend?" asked the captain.

"That island," said Mr. England, "is a great putting-in place for ships short of water and supplies. It is inhabited by a gentle race of—of islanders, who will treat us with courtesy. I propose to conduct the *Hynd Horn* to a safe anchorage, and there we must lie until some other ship touches and we can beg a sextant. Sir, I pray that you will send a safe man forward to take the soundings."

"I will do it myself," said the captain. "Sir, you are proving yourself a man of spirit and resource."

"I think I am," said Mr. England to himself when the captain had gone forward. He patted the wheel and added: "Oh, the simplicity of steering through imaginary shoals and reefs!"

Presently the captain cast the lead.

"Mr. England," he cried, "there is no bottom."

"Thank God!" Mr. England called back. "Then we are in the channel."

The *Hynd Horn* was now skirting the shore of the island within three cable lengths. Mr. England still steered, and the captain still cast the lead and found no bottom. Lady Pelham was standing close to Mr. England.

"It is a sweet place," said she.

"Sweeter than you know, lady," said he. "Do you notice anything particular about the scene?"

"Only that it is fresh and green and beautiful—a blessed island!" said Lady Pelham.

"Mark," said Mr. England, "how the frothy blue

waves lap the white sands on the one side, and to the other come troops of trees and greenery that kneel and bow like worshippers."

"Mr. England," cried the lady, in excitement, "it is not—it cannot be *your* island?"

"In the midst of doubt," said Mr. England, "we must turn to the poets."

He raised his shapely head proudly, and turned his eyes on the lady.

"Princess," he said,

> "I am monarch of all I survey,
>   My right there is none to dispute.
> From the center all round to the sea
>   I am lord of the fowl and the brute."

"You terrify me," said Lady Pelham, "when you look like that."

"Oh, my lady," cried Mr. England, "my good, my blessed angel, how can *I* terrify *you?*"

"I have given you my trust," said Lady Pelham, "and I will not fear you any more."

"My people shall be your lambs," said Mr. England.

The shores kept unfolding great beauties, so that it was a sheer delight to look upon them—on the surpassing freshness of the green, the wonderful whiteness of the sands, the slender perfections of the palms, the bright-colored flashes from the flowers. The extreme coquetry of nature ornamented those shores.

Now and again the captain's voice arose from the main chains, where he was using the lead:

"There is no bottom."

Now and again Mr. England spoke reassuringly to Lady Pelham.

Nature had done much to conceal the narrow mouth of the tortuous harbor into which Mr. England steered the *Hynd Horn*. Conceive a bottle from which a fragmentary and rotten cork has been three parts drawn. The cork, a dozen little islands, as round as coins, and densely wooded, was in, and projected from, the neck of the bottle. These islands were so placed and related that the channel, in any direction, was blocked by some one of them; and so close were they to one another and the main island that to even a near glance they gave the appearance of being one unbroken shore. Their inanimate deceits and contrivances so tricked the eye that it was as if that Providence which watches over the evil-doer had taken a handful of everlasting dust and thrown it in the face of Justice.

The channel itself was like a narrow tidal river: the trees on each bank were exceedingly well grown, and formed, with the various flowery and thorny creepers which bound them together, an unbreached and impenetrable wall; for, whereas the top of the wood waved energetically in the wind off the sea, the waters of the harbor were as still as death, and the *Hynd Horn* seemed to be advanced less by the impulse of moving air than by a kind of delectable wafting.

A quiet came over the *Hynd Horn*, and only those men who were preparing the anchor spoke at all. Mr. England, his lips pressed tightly together to keep back any show of that eagerness and triumph which was almost bursting his sides, turned the wheel to right or left with delicate and precise movements of his white hands. Lady Pelham stood close beside him. She was very pale.

For a long time that ribbon of still water continued between its twin vegetable hedges, and then came a turn, beyond which everything spread. The channel opened into a great placid fan, dotted thickly with wild fowl. The matted trees stepped back from one another, and halted at stately distances, as in an English park. The shore ahead rose to the dignity of a hill, and discovered among its waving plantains and traveller's-palms a well-ordered village of deeply thatched cottages. But no atom of humanity was stirring, and that land-locked, fan-shaped basin, with its park-like shores, had been as peaceful as paradise, save for the intrusion on its shining surface of the shape of an ominously powerful ship, painted as black as the pit.

As when, at a game of pure chance, it is suspected that a certain player is causing the intrusion of skill, the other players begin to look at him askance, so the officers and crew of the *Hynd Horn* began to eye Mr. England. There was as yet no handle to seize upon; but the inhuman silence of that place, and the sardonic power and blackness of the vessel at anchor, worked upon the imaginings of men like unexplainable sounds in the night season. All faces became long and grave, save only that of Mr. England. Alert and flushed, his eyes glittered coldly over the captain, the officers, and the crew; even over Lady Pelham, from her head to her feet, for he knew that the others began to divine that they had been betrayed.

Lady Pelham, poor dove, stood close to the snake and trembled.

"Mr. England," said the captain, in a deep voice, "what place is this?"

"A harbor," said Mr. England, sweetly.

"Sir," said the captain, "I would feel safer on the high seas without rudder or compass than in such a harbor."

"The tone of your statement," said Mr. England, "makes the issue personal rather than geographical. I brought you here. Am I to understand that——"

"You are to understand," said the captain, "that I have trusted the lives in my care to dangerous hands."

"Ah," said Mr. England, contemptuously, "and your final judgment?"

"I reserve that," said the captain. "And in the meanwhile I will run no risks. We will turn about and make for open sea."

Mr. England stepped back from the wheel, releasing the spokes.

"You are too late, captain," he said jauntily. "The channel up which we have come is now divided by an indivisible chain of iron, retreat is cut off, and, further-more—furthermore, we—are—aground."

It was true. The *Hynd Horn*, either from being left to her own guidance, or from some last subtle impulse which Mr. England had given to the wheel, ran, with a scrunch, upon a submerged bank of soft, clinging sand.

Instantly all was bustle and menace, but before the latter had taken the shape of an attempt to arrest the person of Mr. England, that gentleman had found time to kneel at Lady Pelham's feet, kiss both her hands, say in his most tender voice, "Farewell, charmingest," to mount lightly on the rail, leap gracefully overboard, and swim leisurely ashore. Not a gun or pistol could be fired, for none was loaded; not a marline-spike was thrown, for the thought came to no one.

Mr. England stood dripping on the beach, in easy view from both vessels. He stood so for a moment, and then, turning, disappeared among the trees.

Instantly a port opened on the pirate ship, a gun

was run out, there was a thunderous discharge, generating thunderous reverberations, and a ball screamed between the masts of the merchantman. The water-fowl rose from the surface of the harbor with a terrific roaring of wings, and swung over the trees with terrified cries.

The captain of the *Hynd Horn* hauled down the flag.

And Lady Pelham sank sobbing to the deck.

The afternoon passed without a sign from the pirate ship or the land. Long and short strings of water-fowl returned to the harbor, and all was as before. That island world stood still, waiting until Mr. England should give it command to move.

He might have been seen pacing moodily in a glade of the forest. For the first time in his adventurous life he did not know what he was going to do next. He was possessed of a magnificent devil which was tempting him to act like a gentleman.

About ten in the morning a small boat was rowed to the *Hynd Horn*, and Mr. England came over the side. He was white and drawn, and there were blue circles under his eyes, but he had been at some pains to dress himself according to the latest mandates of fashion. To the captain, who greeted him, he bowed shortly, and said:

112

"I have come to speak with Lady Pelham. Where is she?"

"If you have come to insult her, which I doubt not," said the captain, stoutly, "you shall have the pleasure of doing so across a number of dead bodies. I may have hauled down my flag of commission, but you shall find my flag of honor nailed to the mast."

The men of the *Hynd Horn* began to close in.

"For God's sake," said Mr. England, "don't make me angry! Where is she?"

"I demand your intentions," said the captain.

Mr. England pursed his lips and looked the captain over.

"My good man," said he, "I spent last night in hanging you for safety's sake and sparing you for courtesy's sake. I did each about nine hundred and eighty times. I have barely reached a decision comfortable for all concerned, when you begin to annoy me and make me wish to retract. Now I want to speak with Lady Pelham. Where is she?"

"Sir," said the captain, "whatever decision you may have reached as to hanging me or not hanging me, I stand in the place of a father to that young lady, and I ask why——"

"Why in——," said Mr. England, fiercely, "don't you act as if you were grown up?"

"I'm condemned if you shall stand there insulting me!" cried the captain.

"I'm condemned if I sha'n't!" cried Mr. England. "I tell you—" began the captain, hotly.

But just here came an interruption in the lovable form of Lady Pelham herself. The very exquisiteness of her sudden apparition upon the deck—for she was all in white, and her eyes were like the morning—cooled the glowing tempers of the two men, as sweetly as rain cools parched ground.

"Speak to her if she wishes," said the captain, with a bow.

"Captain," said Mr. England, with a flourish, "I am under many obligations to you already. I should like to place myself under one more. I desire to speak with Lady Pelham alone."

The captain and crew of the *Hynd Horn* went forward in a body. Mr. England removed his hat and advanced slowly to Lady Pelham.

"What are you to-day?" said Lady Pelham, not coldly, but with deep sadness.

"Do you mean am I penitent or pirate?" asked Mr. England.

Lady Pelham's head drooped in acquiescence.

"I think that for to-day and for many days," said Mr. England, "I shall be neither pirate nor penitent, but only a common man—with a broken heart."

"How well I know you now!" said Lady Pelham, with even more sadness.

"Lady," said Mr. England, "I did not think you had found me out. But since it is so——"

"It was yesterday," said Lady Pelham, "when your eyes glittered so, and you looked me over as if—oh, the shame of it!" A great blush rose on her cheeks.

"Oh, lady," said Mr. England, "I want you to listen to me *so* much!"

"Yes," said Lady Pelham; "and for what reason?"

"For these," said Mr. England—"for the sake of the moon, and the freshness of the sea."

"I think that you are only going to make me one of your speeches," said Lady Pelham. "But I will listen to you for the last time."

"You are right," said Mr. England—"for the last time."

"And for afterward," said Lady Pelham, almost piteously, "I have a pistol, which I have been shown how to use."

"You have the right," said Mr. England, "to hurt me more than you are hurting me now—if that is possible. But there will be no afterward, for I shall never see your face again."

"What!" cried Lady Pelham.

"Will you listen to me, most gracious lady?" said Mr. England.

"I am listening," said she.

"I am all that you think," began Mr. England, "and

worse. I have done nothing but lie to you. But until we sighted this island I had no evil design. Then it came to me like a flash that I could have my escape and you, too. That was why my eyes insulted you. But, lady, just before I went ashore, when I stole those kisses from your dear, innocent hands, do you know what happened? I fell in love with you. And I walked out the night in mortal combat with my worst enemy—myself. And in the morning the cur laid down his arms and my heart broke. And that is why, gentlest, sweetest, dearest lady, I am going to send the *Hynd Horn* on her way rejoicing, with all that I ever cared for on board."

Mr. England's voice was very tired, and he stood wearily.

"Are you going to say anything to me?" he said.

"I am going to tell you," said Lady Pelham, "that I know you have been speaking the truth, and that you are an honorable man."

"For your dear sake," said Mr. England, "I would leave the old life if I could, but it is too strong upon me. I am a little king upon this island, and my people are mine, heart and hand. It is not all murder and robbery. There are fair nights and white moons, and sometimes you can find, deep in the woods, places where innocence lurks, and you can go back to it for a little. Heaven can do no better than that, lady. Indeed, I

think heaven is a place where we recover our lost innocence. If there is any good in me, lady, it is the love I
bear my kingdom. And I cannot begin again, even for
you. I was born by chance, and chance used to be my
only goddess. I know that I must go back to her, and
to her sister, the spirit of desperate adventure. At their
feet I shall one day die, and be damned, as I deserve."

"I shall never think of you as—as a pirate," said
Lady Pelham.

"For your dear sake I will try and be less hate-
ful," said Mr. England. "But sometimes we are just
like anybody else. Will you try to think of me like
that? Why, lady, there have been true lovers on
this island."

"I shall think of you often," said Lady Pelham.

"To-night," said Mr. England, "as the *Hynd Horn*
passes the mouth of the harbor, will you wave your
scarf to me? I shall be on the point."

"I will," said Lady Pelham.

"Thank you," said Mr. England. "It will be sweet
to remember your having done that. And now I am
going to say good-by to you, dearest lady, but first you
will let me look at you a little, for I shall never see your
face again."

Lady Pelham's eyelids drooped, and her graceful
head drooped.

Mr. England looked on her for a long time.

"I have never seen anything so beautiful and pure," he said.

A tear stole down Lady Pelham's cheek.

"Good-by, dear," said Mr. England. He stooped quickly and kissed her hand softly where it hung at her side.

Lady Pelham burst into tears.

All that day she lay in her berth and cried, and made great moan, saying:

"Oh, how terrible—how terrible—for I love him!"

There was a wonderful moon that night. She came brimming out of the sea, dripping with light, and swept up the heavens, and the fire of all the stars in her path went out. Only the very youngest stars that had strayed to the most remote places remained to look at their mother; and even they became dim.

At the mouth of the harbor, leaning against the stem of a palm, stood Mr. England. He was back from the beach in a kind of recess among the trees. Every line of him expressed fatigue, and his face was very sad.

Presently out of the stillness came the creaking of rigging and the vowel sounds of commands.

"The end," said Mr. England. He stood more erect.

The *Hynd Horn* slipped by like a ghost.

Mr. England followed her with his eyes, at first

eagerly, then surprisedly, then dejectedly, then bitterly. No scarf was waved to him from the deck of the outward-bound. She slid behind one of the little islands, and he saw her no more.

"The end," said Mr. England. He put his hands over his eyes, and pressed tightly. After a little he took them down and said:

"She didn't mean to hurt me so."

Then he looked up at the moon.

"Now I will go back to my kingdom," he said.

But a new sound broke the stillness—the splash of oars unhandily plied. The sound drew nearer, but the strokes occurred with less and less frequency, as if the boatman were tiring. Mr. England stepped briskly to the shore.

A few yards off, and to the left, a boat was headed for the beach. The boat contained a lady.

Mr. England sprang forward.

"Glorious, golden, gracious, wonderful, beloved, beautiful!" he cried. It was as if his voice caught fire and blazed up.

The boat grated on the sand.

"Will you help me out, please?" said Lady Pelham.

IV

THE EXECUTION

THE EXECUTION

I

The room was dark as the pit and its midnight
silence was accentuated rather than disturbed by the
soft, steady, grating sound of a rat gnawing in the
wall, and by the loud metallic ticking of a clock.

Suddenly upon one of the walls appeared a perpendicular thread of pale gray. This widened by grada-
tions that were almost imperceptible, and which were
accompanied by faint creaking noises like those made
by iron hinges that have not been oiled. The thread
widened to a rope, to a broad ribbon, after a while to
the width of a broad window. Through the rectangles
of the sash appeared a swirling gray vista of falling
snow, half shrouded by the dark figure of a man, his
cap and shoulders thatched with snow. A pane of
glass fell to the floor with a sharp *pang*. The rat in
the wall ceased his gnawing; and only the clock continued to break the silence. Presently the lower half
of the sash began to move upward, until there was a
sufficient opening for the man to pass through. Before

entering he shook the snow from his cap and shoulders, and, seated on the window-sill, his body in and his legs out, brushed the snow from his feet. Then he swung his legs into the room, one after the other, and, turning, reached out his arms and drew to the shutters. The room was again dark as the pit. A faint sound, between a crunch and a squeak, told that the man had closed the sash.

Presently the man struck a match. The spurt of blue and yellow flame showed a thin, white, shaking hand and a thin, white face—a young face aged by care, by premature cleverness, by suffering and by sin. It had a hunted look. The match went out. The man lighted another and moved about the room as if looking for something. He lighted match after match, moving about the room as he did so, so that its disposition and its effects were gradually disclosed: a great fireplace with big logs laid upon split shingles and newspapers, the dark hollow of an old, high-shouldered leather chair, a grandfather's clock, doors leading to other parts of the house, four windows, a table covered with an oil-cloth, a big mirror in a cheap veneered frame.

From time to time during his stealthy peregrinations the man felt of his throat with his left hand. The gesture had the effect of a something characteristic and habitual; it was as if the man had once been afraid

124

for his throat and had got into the habit of feeling to see if all was still well with it. When he came before the mirror with a lighted match in one hand, the other, which went again to his throat, instead of being quickly withdrawn, remained, and its thin nervous fingers clasped and pressed here and there, as one clasps and presses one's throat when it is sore to locate the exact area of inflammation. With the last flicker of the match (still feeling of his throat) the man leered at his reflected image, and nodded to it. And his lips seemed to form and give out, without any actual utterance, the words, "you'll do."

His next move, which was to the deep leather chair in which he seated himself, proved that, whatever his ultimate motive in entering the house might be, he had no immediate intentions to the burglarious or murderous. Indeed, his loud, steady breathing betokened that he was on the point of falling asleep. But at the very moment when his senses were passing heavily into oblivion the grandfather's clock, after a kind of mechanical throat clearing, struck twice. The man roused himself, drew off his heavy boots, lighted a match, and, yawning again and again, walked quietly to one of the doors leading out of the room, opened it, struck another match, stepped over the threshold, and closed the door behind him.

The whole house creaked and groaned in a sudden

gust of wind; a dribble of soot and old mortar fell rattling into the fireplace. The ticking of the clock sounded louder after the extraneous noises had ceased. The rat began once more to gnaw in the wall; guardedly at first, but soon with a rasping steadiness that made it seem as if his whole heart were in the act. The rat might have been likened to a prisoner who was trying to work his way out of jail.

Presently the man could be heard moving about in the room immediately above that which he had just quitted. But not for long. The sound of his steps soon ceased.

II

Hours later, in the same doorway by which the young man had left the room, there appeared, palely illumined by the candle which she carried, the emaciated figure of an old woman. Her thin, bony face, with its deep sunken eyes and high-bridged nose, suggested the face of a hawk; the thin, harsh lips and the harsh, protruding jaw gave her a look of strong will and inflexibility, but the snow-white hair, drawn tightly to a knot at the back of her head, suggested, it is hard to say why, a gentleness and motherliness which the hawk face belied. She was shabbily dressed in black; her skirt did not reach below her ankles, and disclosed a pair of bony feet encased in coarse white stockings and broken-down slippers. Her movements, though brisk and sure, were those of a person who does not see clearly; and she seemed to be laboring under an almost irrepressible agitation. Her first action on entering the room was to hold the candle very close to the face of the clock, and to advance her eyes equally close to it, so as to ascertain beyond doubt the exact position of the hands. The hands indicated that the hour was exactly a quarter to six. The old woman pressed her hand nervously against her lean breast, and groaned. Then she set the candle on the table, and kneeling on the cold board floor, her face in her hands, began to mumble and mutter as if in prayer, prayer in which there were a thousand things to pray and only seconds in which to pray them. Tears came through her fingers and trickled down her bony wrists.

In the doorway there now appeared a young woman, also illumined by a candle which she carried. Her face, thin and white, had a kind of gentle prettiness about it and was crowned by glories of dark hair. The young woman was also dressed in black, but her gown, though of an old fashion, hung gracefully and was of a decent fit. The young woman had evidently been crying, but had composed herself. With a pitying glance at the old woman who knelt, and prayed and wept, she crossed to the fireplace and thrust her candle among the papers and kindlings laid to start the big logs. Having assured herself that the fire had caught, she set the candle on the table, slipped her hands under the old woman's shoulders, and raised her to her feet.

"Mother!" she said, "I hoped you'd sleep through it."

"No, dear—no, dear," said the old woman. She wiped at her eyes with the backs of her hands.

"Come by the fire, mother, the cold is terrible."

The old woman suffered herself to be led to the fire, where she spread her lean hands to the blaze that was beginning to leap among the logs. She had managed to stop her tears (it is easy for the old both to begin tears and to stop them) and to regain a certain composure.

"Yes, it is terribly cold," she said. "I don't remember such another storm as we've had. On the north side of the house the snow is almost up to the second story windows."

Her eyes sought the face of the clock, but at that distance she could not see the hands.

"What time is it?" she asked.

"It is just five minutes to six, mother."

"Are you sure the clock is right?"

"Yes, mother."

The old woman began to nod her head repeatedly, as old people are prone to do when their minds are far away.

"Sunrise," she said, "is just at six o'clock to-day."

"Yes, mother."

"But we shan't see the sun to-day, even if the clouds pass. We must keep the shutters closed all to-day."

"Yes, mother."

"They always say 'at sunrise,'" said the old woman querulously, "but they mean the time when it rises, not the sight of it. In the eyes of the law sunrise means a certain time."

"Yes, mother."

"What time is it now?"

"It is nearly four minutes to six, mother."

"You'll keep an eye on the clock, won't you, dear?" said the old woman. She rocked before the fire, her hands still spread to the warmth. "Just at sunrise we must go on our knees and pray to God."

"Yes, mother. You are trembling with cold; let me get your shawl for you."

"I don't want my shawl," said the old woman. "I would have put it on if I'd wanted it."

The young woman knelt by the fire, and readjusted the logs with quick, dexterous movements. Combustion answered to the bettered draught and began to roar up the chimney.

"Beyond the grave," said the old woman, as if answering a question, "there are no clouds." She went on, still as if questions were being put to her: "Beyond the grave there is mercy; the Governor of Heaven will have mercy on those who have sinned."

"Yes, mother."

"I tell you," cried the old woman in a kind of prophetic ecstacy, "we shall all meet beyond the grave."

If further questions arose in her soul she answered them by mutterings that were not words. The young woman crossed to the door by which she had entered, closed it and returned to the fire.

"What time is it now?" asked the old woman.

"It is three and a half minutes to six."

"He has finished his breakfast now," said the old woman, "and they are leading him out."

"There came faintly from some inner and upper portion of the house a sound as of a floor creaking.

"Do you hear anything?" said the old woman, a kind of awful expectancy in her face. "I thought I heard the creaking of boards. I thought I heard the scaffold creaking."

The sound was repeated.

"It's in the house," said the young woman, "upstairs somewhere. Some one is moving about. Listen."

There came now a distinct sound of slow, heavy steps.

"There is no one in the house but ourselves that *can* move," said the old woman.

"Could it be father?"

"He hasn't moved for three months; you know he can't move; he's crippled with his rheumatism. He'll die of it."

The young woman's eyes widened with terror.

"It's coming down the stairs," she said.

The old woman, erect, courageous, full of fight, stepped briskly between her daughter and the door. It opened, and in the frame appeared the bent figure of a gigantic old man. He was clad in a rough heavy overcoat, the collar turned up; below the skirt of the coat showed a foot of coarse white nightgown. His hairy shanks were bare, and his feet were thrust into a pair of enormous carpet slippers. A Jove-like head and face, streaming with white hair and beard, crowned the motley figure. But the face had, instead of eyes, sockets, and, held to its left ear by an immense, sinewy, hairy hand, was a long, old-fashioned ear-trumpet of japanned tin.

"What is wrong?" said the old man, in a voice that sounded like a heavy wagon crossing a wooden bridge.

The old woman seized him by the shoulders and began to shake him.

"You will kill yourself!" she said. "There is nothing wrong."

"Stop shaking me," said the old man fiercely.

The old woman's hands dropped from his shoulders, but she continued to scold him.

"You had no business to get up," she said. "You must go right back to bed. Do you want to kill yourself?"

"Something is wrong," persisted the old man. He pushed his wife aside as if she had been a feather, and groped toward the fireplace, talking as he went.

"Do you think I could have got up and walked if there hadn't been something wrong," he said. "Why are you all up?"

The old woman hovered, so to speak, on the flank of his advance, anxious, frightened, between scolding and tears.

"There is nothing wrong," she said.

"You lie," said the old man. "Is it about my son?"

He turned his head heavily from his wife to his daughter, as if he could see them with his empty sockets and read in their faces the truth.

His daughter advanced and took him by the arm.

"Nothing has happened, father." She spoke briskly and cheerfully. "Come to the fire. How good it is to see you walking about, just as natural as life. Isn't it good to see him walking about, mother?"

"Yes, yes," said the old woman, but without conviction, "it is wonderful." She turned her near-sighted eyes to the clock and tried to read the time.

The old man was conducted by his daughter to the

large leather chair. He sank into it heavily, as if he had been a load of stones.

"Your poor feet," she said, "are blue with cold."

After an anxious look at the clock she bent and commenced to chafe them briskly between her hands.

"You are both keeping something from me," said the old man. "When mother got up she thought I was asleep, but I wasn't. I knew when she left her bed. And I knew then that something was wrong. Is it about my boy?"

"No, father."

The old man removed the trumpet from his ear and laid it across his knees. By that action he cut himself off from the world of sounds and, blind and deaf, frowned terribly and worked his bushy eyebrows up and down. It was at this moment that the clock began to go through its usual throat clearing preamble to voicing the hour.

The women, white as death and trembling violently, sank to their knees and, as if by prearrangement, the same prayer came brokenly from their lips:

"Almighty and most merciful Father: We have erred, and strayed from Thy ways like lost sheep——"

The old man's terrible rumbling voice broke in upon them, and while he spoke, though they continued the prayer, it was in silence.

"As long as we are all up," the old man boomed and rumbled, "why doesn't somebody get breakfast ready?"

The clock had finished striking.

"A full stomach is the thing to keep the cold out," he said, and, seizing his ear-trumpet, thrust the small end of it into his left ear.

"What are you saying to mother?" he said.

"Nothing, father."

The old woman kept on praying.

"Why don't you tell me what is wrong? I'm not a log. I could tear this house down with my hands if I got angry. I'm not a child. Maybe you heard a noise and thought somebody had broken into the house. Was that it? Answer me."

He staggered heavily to his feet, and turned his empty sockets this way and that.

The two women rose from their knees and glanced at each other. Without speaking a word the daughter managed in that brief glance to ask a question and the mother to answer it. The daughter turned to her father. The mother sank once more to her knees. The fire roared in the chimney.

"Father," said the young woman, speaking into the mouth of the ear-trumpet, "it *was* a noise. Mother heard it and woke me. She thought she heard some one open a window and then close it. But she must have dreamed it, mustn't she? We . . . we've been all through the house."

"I ought to have been called at once," said the old man. "Just because I'm deaf and blind you think I can't look after what belongs to me. Another time . . . are you sure you've looked everywhere?"

"Mother must have been dreaming."

"You thought you heard steps, mother?" asked the old man.

"Yes, father." The old woman rose, tears pouring down her cheeks.

"Just think," said the old man, "it might have been somebody after my money."

"But it *wasn't*, father."

"And she thought she heard a window being opened?"

"I thought I heard it open and then close," said the old woman. "But I must have been dreaming."

The old man rose heavily and groped his way to the door, and fumbled till he had the knob in his hand.

"I'll just go about and make sure," he said. He passed out into the darkness and closed the door behind him. The two women heard the key turn in the lock.

"Father has locked us in," said the young woman.

"He doesn't like to be interfered with. Let him go. He'll soon find that there's nobody."

"Mother," said the young woman, "have we done right not to tell father?"

"Done right not to tell father about—about—— "

"Yes, mother—*have* we?"

"Father's days are numbered in the land. His heart's threatened. That's what the doctor said. Any sudden shock would kill him. I think you'd best make a cup of hot coffee to give him when he comes back."

"It's terrible to think of him groping in those dark rooms."

"He couldn't see any better if there were lights in them. Besides, there's nothing to hurt him."

"How quietly he moves, mother; I can't hear a sound."

"Most likely he's standing still trying to listen with his old trumpet."

A curious change had come over the old woman. She seemed to take a kind of martial pride in the fact that her blind, half deaf, half crippled old husband had gone forth so boldly to hunt for a thief. She stood more erect; she had stopped trembling.

"Mother," said the young woman suddenly, "what are all these burnt matches doing on the floor?"

"Why, so there are," said the old woman. She picked one up and examined it. "It's not our kind," she said. The two women looked at each other in bewilderment; bewilderment that changed gradually to horror.

The old woman ran noiselessly to the door by which her husband had gone out, and tried to open it.

"There *is* somebody," she said. "We must get to father."

The young woman dragged her away from the door.

"If you make a noise," she said, "you will put them on their guard. Father must take his chances. We can't get to him without making a noise. We can't anyway; *we* can't break that door open. Maybe they've gone."

The two women leaned against the locked door listening with strained ears.

Suddenly, loudly and distinctly, footsteps sounded in the room above their heads, light, crisp, firm footsteps.

"They're in my boy's room," said the old woman.

"Mother—mother," said the young woman, her eyes blazing with excitement. "Don't you know that step—don't you know it?"

The old woman listened carefully. Her heart began to rise and fall rapidly. Her deep-set eyes seemed almost to protrude, so great was her wonder and fear.

"It *is*—it *is*." Her voice dropped and broke in her throat.

"He has got away, mother—he must have got away."

"I wonder," said the old woman excitedly, "if your father hears him and knows who it is. Why *did* he lock this door. We've got to get it open. Your old—father—so deaf—blind—might get hold of him, and not

137

realize who it was, and, and—God in heaven, girl—quick, get that poker."

The young woman flashed to the fireplace and back, bringing the long, solid, old-fashioned wrought-iron poker.

"Let *me*, mother." She tried to find a purchase between the door and the doorstep, but could not at first.

"Try higher up," said the old woman. "Stop—do you hear anything?"

They listened intently.

"Not a sound, mother. We must get it open."

They worked at the door frantically, but without success.

"Stop," said the old woman. "Why don't we warn him?" She began to beat a tattoo with the poker against the ceiling. "Boy!—boy!" she cried in a thin, piercing voice. "Answer me—it's mother."

There was no answer. The silence was leaden, horrible. "Boy!—boy!" screamed the old woman.

She listened. There was a sound of heavy steps descending the stair.

"It's all right—father's coming back," said the young woman. "Nothing can have happened."

"Then why didn't he answer me?"

There was a kind of fumbling sound upon the door, then the rasp of the key being turned. The old man stepped heavily into the room. His face had a high color, and he was breathing quickly, as an athlete flushes and breathes after putting out his full strength. He had removed the key of the door, and now, after much fumbling, reinserted it, gave it two rasping turns, and dropped it into his overcoat pocket. Then he turned to the women, rolling his sockets from one to the other. He put his ear-trumpet to his ear.

"Daughter," he said, "when it gets to be really daylight you must go for the sheriff. In the meanwhile keep out of the room that is above this one—your brother's room. The man was coming out," he went on, "and he ran right into me."

Slowly and heavily the old man extended his right hand; the enormous thumb and fingers clawed into a trifle more than a semi-circumference—the circumference of a medium-sized man's neck. The thumb and fingers moved sharply inwards, became rigid, knotted, and began to tremble violently.

"A hangman," said the old man, "couldn't have done it better with a rope."

The hand fell nerveless, the tin ear-trumpet clattered hollowly on the floor. The color faded from the old man's face; his cheeks and chin took on a bluish tinge in the candle light. A kind of shuddering spasm passed through him from head to foot.

"Take me back to the fire," he said. "I am cold all

over." He had never before spoken in such a quiet dependent voice.

The old woman, her face working with fear and horror, led him to his big chair. The young woman stood as if rooted, her face the color of salt; only her fingers moved. They kept picking at her skirt.

The old man fell, like a sack of stones, into his chair.

"I want to hear what you're saying," he said presently. His voice whined. "Give me back my eartrumpet. I dropped it by the door."

The young woman, apathetic and numb, moved to where the trumpet had fallen and picked it up. It fell twice from her jerking fingers.

The old woman, a black and white flash, crossed the room and seized her daughter's arm.

"Don't give him that," she cried. "Father mustn't know what he's done . . ."

The old man's voice once more, heavy and sonorous, broke over the old woman's words like a wave and drowned them.

"I can't hear what you say," he rumbled. "Give me my ear-trumpet."

"Not yet," said the old woman quickly; "father must never know what he's done."

The young woman's mouth opened and shut several times without uttering a sound. Her swallowing muscles worked violently and she kept licking her lower lip.

140

Suddenly her half-palsied speaking machinery emitted a voice that was between a wail and a scream.

"He got out of prison"—the voice soared to its highest register—"and he came home."

"Quiet," said the old woman. Her voice was sharp and sudden, like a steel spring breaking. "Your father must not know of this." She seized the young woman by the shoulders and shook her.

"Can you be calm now?" she said. "Can you collect yourself? Can you speak in your natural voice?" The young woman could only gasp and mumble.

"Let me do the talking, then," said the old woman, with a sharp note of impatience. She snatched the ear-trumpet from her daughter and, flashing back to her husband, thrust it into his hands. They were lying open on his lap. The fingers did not close on the trumpet. His head had fallen forward as if in rumination.

The old woman, brisk and graceful—a young girl had not been more so—knelt and laid her ear to the old man's breast. Then she thrust her hand inside his overcoat and laid it on his heart. She felt rapidly of his hands, his feet, his legs. They were cold as ice.

She rose heavily, and began to stroke the dead man's streaming white hair.

"He knows all about it, my dear," she said. It was difficult to tell if she was addressing the dead man or his daughter. "He can hear and see now."

141

The young woman approached with halting, leaden steps.

"We must get him to his bed, somehow," said the old woman, "even if it breaks our backs. Nobody must know that he ever left it. Nobody must ever know what father has done."

There was not a trace of emotion now in the old woman's voice. It was the voice of a calm and zealous housekeeper, giving orders during a spring house-cleaning.

"We must hide all the traces of what has happened," she said. "It wouldn't do to have people know what father has done. The snow will have covered all the tracks leading to the house. People must never know——"

"Mother—mother, if you talk so heartlessly I shall go mad."

"Help me now, we must get your father back to his bed, and then——"

The two women, the one calm, self-reliant and unmoved, the other hysterical, gasping and useless, were unable to stir the gigantic body of the old man.

The old woman stood for a long time in thought. Then she took the door-key from the dead man's overcoat pocket and thrust it into her daughter's hand.

"Get our bonnets and shawls," she said, "and the money."

"What—for—mother?"

"Do as I tell you."

The old woman occupied the moments of her daughter's absence by dragging the fire piecemeal from the fireplace and reconstructing it against the ancient tinder-dry wainscoting of the room.

The young woman returned to a room full of smoke, in which the candles made dim yellow halos.

"Mother—mother, what have you done?" she cried.

"My dear," said the old woman, "we couldn't have gone on living in this house. By the time we can fetch help there will be nothing left of it but ashes. Come."

V

SIMON L'OUVRIER

SIMON L'OUVRIER

I

The other day Simon L'Ouvrier died. A good half of the New York dailies, supposed to be devoted to the promulgation of news, made no mention of the fact. A number misspelt his name, and at least one had it that he was a painter. Thus a remarkable man and a remarkable talent made their exit from this busy stage, receiving, from the jaded audience, adieus the most hasty and undignified; scant thanks for past entertainment, and, presently, oblivion.

These days a great man makes as much stir as a stone thrown into a pond—a splash, ripples, nothing. The bigger the man, the bigger the splash. Yet for all the smooth and placid air of forgetfulness assumed with unseemly haste by the stirred water, the pond is forever affected by the sinking of the stone. Its general level is raised. And if the stone was big enough, it shows eternally above the surface like an island. Such a stone flung into Europe was Napoleon. Such were Shakespeare, Cromwell, and the other prodigies that man is willing enough to forget, but unable. A man could as easily forget his own sins as Shakespeare.

Simon L'Ouvrier was a small stone, but perfectly round, and in his time was flung into the pond with such violence as to make a very great splash. And then, forgotten, sunk to the bottom, covered with mud, he was fished up and flung in again. It is given to few men to make more than one splash. Twice L'Ouvrier set the pond agog, twice sank to the bottom, and was twice forgotten. And the other day, by the grace of God, came death to put him out of his misery.

Simon L'Ouvrier was born in Tours, in sight of the statue of De Balzac. His father was a cake-maker of much talent and address—a man who put as much genius into a new frosting as Bernard Palissy gave to his enamels. To the child it matters little if the transmitted influences toward thoroughness and application come from a cake-maker or a maker of ballads, if only they come. L'Ouvrier himself believed firmly in heredity and often spoke in proof of it. "This is how I came to have a talent," was the beginning of his favorite anecdote, which went on: "My father, the day ended, left some cakes to bake in a slow oven. His heart was set on them, for the ingredients were mixed in entirely new and promising proportions. His heart was equally set on the return of my mother, who had been spending

148

the week at Blois with her parents. My mother returned, and after the usual embraces proper to such an occasion, and the rapid, mutual accounts of the days passed in separation, the worthy couple ascended to their chamber and prepared for bed. It was November and bitterly cold, the kind of night when leaving one's bed is worse than going into battle. 'Now I call this comfort,' said my mother; 'kiss me good-night.' My father kissed her, but she felt that his heart was not wholly in the tenderness. 'What are you thinking of?' said she, slightly piqued. 'I was thinking, my dear,' said my father, 'that it would have been better to have put the pistache cakes on the warmer side of the oven; the apricot paste will bake with less heat.' 'Never mind that,' said my mother, 'do not invite a cold by descending to the kitchen.' 'Very well,' said my father, 'I can try again to-morrow. Ah! but it is good to have you back.' 'Don't talk to me in that tone,' said my mother, 'you are still thinking of the cakes.' 'That is true,' said my father, 'and I would like to take just one little look to see how things are going.' 'In the name of God,' said my mother, 'go. But you are inviting an inflammation of the chest.' So my father got out of bed, put on his slippers, and pattered down to his famous cakes. When he returned he said: 'I have shifted the cakes and raised the heat one degree, and now, my treasure, I have thoughts of you only,'

'You are shivering,' said my mother. 'That is for you to think about,' said my father."

"It is to these circumstances," L'Ouvrier would conclude, "that I owe the qualities which have brought me a measure of success: passion and the capacity for taking pains. But for a thorn to modify my pleasure in these roses, I am diabolically subject to colds."

On one occasion, having concluded this anecdote, a friend asked him this question: "And what do you owe your mother?"

"Everything," said L'Ouvrier; "she was a Jew."

II

At an age when most boys are flying kites or dreaming of the approaching holidays Simon L'Ouvrier was plotting the steps by which he should ascend to eminence.

He was slight, dark, large-featured, big-eared, bright-eyed. and singularly phlegmatic. He worked long shifts in the bakery, lending an amazing address to the work, and thought long thoughts. This is curious: that in those days he had never been inside of a theatre, but had already determined to be an actor. We have his own word for it. To quote from his journal, a bulky volume, long out of print: "I have but one dream—to be an actor. To this end I am determined to devote whatever is in me of inclination, capacity for suffering and power. I will not allow myself to fail." Any other boy of fifteen, possessed by such a dream, would have let it out in some manner to the family circle. But Simon had the great gift of reticence, the greater gift of consideration. "Why talk," said the journal, "when I have as yet formulated no plan of procedure? Why trouble my father, who wishes me to devote my life to frosting and pistache? Why trouble my mother, whose dream it is that I should one day marry a lady? . . . By working diligently at a trade which does not interest me I am gaining character. . . . I have bought a mirror to make faces in. It is five inches in diameter, weighs but little, and goes easily in the pocket."

There is nothing, to my mind, more characteristic of L'Ouvrier than that mirror. Can you not picture him, in his blue blouse and baker's cap, waiting till the ovens can take care of themselves (he never neglected his work—if we can trust the journal; and I think we can), whipping out the mirror and making faces in it?

"The time," he wrote, "is inevitable when I shall be caught with my mirror and pronounced an imbecile." Later he wrote: "I have learned to prick up my ears like a dog, to move my scalp up and down, to frown horribly, and to stare my own self out·of countenance." Again he wrote: "My practice is to imagine myself in

151

a situation: to brood over it until, according to its nature, I am either (and in real fact) happy, unhappy, terrified, jocose, pathetic, heroic. Arrived at such a state of mind, I glance in my mirror, and try to catch, and store away for future use, the expression written there for the moment in lights and shadows. By a diligent pursuit of this method it must arrive that in the end I shall be able to look jocose without feeling so; heroic, though afraid. . . . I have discovered something: the emotions of a quiet nature—tenderness, gentleness, archness (if that be an emotion), courtesy, whimsicalness, are expressed by the soul; that is to say, a man, more easily a woman, can look these things without moving a muscle. The passions—jealousy, hate, fear, indeed all except greed—are expressed by the muscles. Greed may be expressed by either method. . . . I make an analysis of a given character; then try to put myself in the mental attitude of that character, and then study the reflection of it in my mirror. Thus I have arrived at the ability to look like any one in the establishment—my father, my mother, the apprentices, the maids, etc. This morning I tried to look like the archbishop. I thought for a long time of good deeds, quiet cloisters, the crucified Jesus, and charity. Then I looked into the mirror, and saw there a face not in the least like the archbishop's. I then imagined myself an archbishop; I

developed the ambition to become a cardinal, then
Pope. I plotted ways and means, I played at politics—
I looked in the mirror, and, in the name of a thousand
saints, I was the archbishop's self! . . . I have tried
another experiment. I became, with all the intensity
possible, myself—my whole self—self-centred, ambi-
tious, single-minded, sure of success, full of courage to
endure the means to my self-announced end. I looked
in the mirror, and saw the face of a conqueror. . . . I
looked at myself so long that, for the first time in my
life, I allowed the cakes with which I had been entrusted
to burn."

III

Simon did not swerve from any of his purposes.
He kept his own counsel. His parents died in peace
and left him the bakery, ten' thousand francs which
they had saved, and five locked volumes of culinary
secrets. Simon sold the bakery and his good-will for
the sum of forty thousand francs, tucked the culinary
secrets in a corner of his trunk, the mirror in his pocket,
nodded in a friendly manner to the statue of De Balzac,
and took the train for Paris.

Up to this time—he was now seventeen—he had never
been inside of a theatre nor read a play. Neither
played a part in his scheme of education. Still, the
theatres and the book-stalls of the capital tempted

him, but not beyond his strength. "In ten years," says the journal, "I promise myself a performance each night and a whole library of plays. Meanwhile, I must devote myself to life, to joy and to sorrow, to nature and the development of all that is best in me, to the knowledge, if not the exercise, of all that is worst." The journal tells us further that Simon quitted Paris for Marseilles, and played all the way, much to the alarm and annoyance of other travellers occupying the same compartment with him, the part of a young fellow who has contracted consumption, been taken out of college by his doting parents, and sent South. "I tell one old fellow, much to his horror, that I have had three hemorrhages and am likely at any moment to have another—*alors vous verrez du sang—va!*" He went to Algiers, to a hotel frequented by consumptives, and continued for many months to play his part, acquiring, he tells us, from observation and practice, a sufficient perfection to deceive a doctor.

"There is one woman here who will not recover. I am watching her closely, and causing my own malady to progress symptom by symptom with hers. But one of these days she will die, and I will take a turn for the better. In the cough I am past perfect. I eat little for two reasons: to appear pale and to husband my resources. Sometimes I cut my arm so that I may show blood on my handkerchief. . . . A young girl came by to-day's boat. She is very beautiful, but far gone with the malady. A part suggests itself: A man dying of consumption is in love with a woman dying of consumption."

The journal does not tell the girl's whole name; only the Christian part of it—Cloise. Simon made love to her, so he tells us. They were the talk of the hotel. "The situation is pathetic in the extreme," he writes. "Without meaning to, I have made her love me. I will never let her know that I am deceiving her. . . . To-day she said: 'Simon, dear, if you would only take a turn for the better, I think I would.' This is very curious. I wonder if there is any truth in it. To-morrow I will cough less. . . . It is very wonderful; as I improve, she improves. She is happy—oh, so happy. Suppose she should recover? I do not wish to marry her, for I do not love her in the least; but would it be honorable to do otherwise? . . . This morning I pretended to be worse. But I must not do so again. She had a hemorrhage, poor child. . . . If I can save her by recovering, I will recover; if I must marry her, I must. . . . This morning I appeared at breakfast with a beaming face. 'Cloise,' I said, 'I only coughed once during the night.' Ah, such joy—such joy! I imitate her joy faithfully. We are like two happy birds. . . . Cloise continues to improve. I shall have to marry her. This is not at all in my scheme of life. . . . It is six weeks since Cloise had her hemorrhage.

I have asked her hand in marriage from her parents.
. . . It is very cold to-day; we shall not go out . . .
a note from Cloise to say that she can not leave her
bed, she has taken cold; will I pass her door sometimes
during the day? It will comfort her, she says. . . .
Have just come from passing her door. She is coughing again. Poor child! I love her a little; that much
is certain. . . . To-day it is still very cold; no note
from Cloise. I must make inquiries of her parents.
I reach their door. Within is a low moaning. . . . For
a moment, I confess it with shame, I am tempted to
rush in and play the heartbroken lover; but only for a
moment. I, even, have better feelings. I will say
nothing. I will go away. Maybe she died happier for
thinking that she was loved. . . . I can not make up
my mind what to play next. I am sick of disease. I
think I will be a man of iron—one of these boisterous
fellows that has no ailments, no fatigues, nothing but a
vast energy, a vast appetite, a loud mouth. I shall be
disagreeable enough, I dare say, but pouf! Suppose
that beneath a gruff exterior I ill conceal a heart of
gold?"

IV

That, then, was the way Simon L'Ouvrier went about
learning his art. He lived out hundreds of parts;
sparing no pains to be perfect in the whole and its

components. In the privacy of his own room, in complete solitude, sometimes for whole days of solitude, he never swerved, he tells us, from the character he had assumed for the time being. Now he would be a military man, disappointed in his aspirations; now a successful man of affairs; now an explorer; now a priest, author, photographer, lawyer. To the playing of each character he gave an infinity of thought, research, and temperament. It is said that there are few professions in which he could not have practised with aptitude, and perhaps distinction. The journal tells us of many failures—parts which at first he was unable to play. To these he returned again and again until, for so he would have us believe, he succeeded even in deceiving himself. At one period, toward the end of his self-appointed term of practice, it became his ambition to visit Lhasa, the forbidden city, in the guise of a pilgrim. He gave two whole years of the most searching preparation for this feat, living close to the danger line, studying inflections and Buddhism; accustoming his body to bear the desert sun. "I am now," he writes, "so seasoned that I can lie naked in the sun a whole day and be none the worse. It will not be long before I am the right color from head to foot. I pass readily for a native, and shall burn my bridges and join the next pilgrimage."

It seems that on this journey he penetrated to within

five miles of the forbidden city successfully, and was then exposed by a holy man who had come out to inspect the pilgrimage. "It was terrible," he wrote afterward; "there was something in his eye which I could not meet. He questioned me; I lost my presence of mind, and stammered. I suffered, I think, from what is called stage-fright. I was an impostor, patently, self-confessed. They stripped my clothes from me," the narrative continues, "and suspended me to the wall of a house by means of two nails driven through the palms of my hands. . . . I remained there hanging a day and a night in mortal agony. . . . I said: 'Simon, you have elected to be a player of parts. Act now the stoic.' But as God is forgiving I could not. To strangle my screams ere they were fairly born was the utmost that I could do. Nor, indeed, is any philosophy potent in the presence of such pain as I endured at that time."

He was taken down after hanging for twenty-four hours, and escorted out of the country by men who struck him terribly with whips. He writes: "When the illness following this barbaric usage had passed, I found myself still firm in the intention to visit the forbidden city. It may be that it will be my last part. Let me leave no stone unturned to be perfect in it."

The second attempt succeeded. He penetrated the forbidden city and came out alive; unharmed and undetected. The two attempts, with the preparation for them, cost him five years. He had devoted already, from the time of purchasing the mirror, twenty years to the study of his art.

"I am thirty-seven," he writes. "What does that matter? I can look eighteen. I have done my best. I shall now take the world by storm."

I cannot, in justice to my subject, refrain from quoting another passage from the journal, written on the journey from the Far East to Paris: "In every part that I have undertaken to play I have touched perfection, except in one. It is impossible for me to be a gentleman. Nor can any self-love convince me that I shall ever succeed with that illusive and exquisite rôle. The many will not know, but the few, those who are *born*, will never be satisfied with my interpretation. I have drunk this bitter cup to the dregs, and no longer care."

V

It would be interesting to know if at this period, slightly anterior to his intended *debut*, Simon L'Ouvrier had any doubts as to how the public would receive him. The journal voices none; L'Ouvrier never admitted to having had any. Acquaintances (friends the man never had) affirm that doubting had no rooting-place in his character. De Maupassant is said to have said:

SIMON L'OUVRIER

"L'Ouvrier? He would play God if they would let him. Except for purposes of mimicry, he does not know what modesty is, or conceit for that matter. Give him so much as a cotton thread and he will hang himself beautifully; give him a dish of crumpled paper and you will behold a connoisseur eating ortolan. Give him nothing and he will be everything."

Madame Bernhardt was present at L'Ouvrier's third or fourth performance (as, indeed, was all Paris). During the first entr'acte she said: "It is horrible to feel clumsy all at once." During the second entr'acte she said, with tears in her golden voice: "I am willing to admit that I am not an actor, but a buffoon; nevertheless this public demonstration of the fact is hard to bear." The curtain rose on the third act; L'Ouvrier appeared; Madame Bernhardt burst out laughing; so did the whole house. Ten minutes later the divine Sarah was in tears. The curtain fell. The house was sobbing. Coquelin Ainé left his seat and approached Madame Bernhardt. Tears were streaming from his comical eyes. "I am going," said he; "farewell." "Where are you going?" she asked. "To Père La Chaise," said he, "to bury myself." "I will go with you," said she. "But in the name of God let us wait till the performance is over. If I know anything of stage-craft there will be another occasion to make us laugh. I would not miss it for assured salvation."

"Admit," said Coquelin, "that I am a lumpish amateur." "Never! But admit, you, that my voice is full of cracks!" "Never," said Coquelin, and he hastened back to his seat, for the signal had been given for the curtain to go up. During the act Coquelin was heard to say: "Those feet—oh, those feet, how eloquent!" And when the performance was over he sought out Madame Bernhardt, and said: "I thank God that at least this man is a Frenchman." "And I," said Madame, "thank God that he is a Jew."

But all this is advancing matters too much. How did L'Ouvrier get his chance to play before Paris? In a manner thoroughly characteristic. Says the journal: "Having ascertained that Monsieur Didot was alone in his office, and, indeed, in the whole theatre, except for a boy to answer the bells, I took the latter, an intelligent gamin, into my confidence. 'I am an actor,' I said, 'and I have a grudge against Monsieur Didot. I am going to frighten him, but I shall not hurt him. If he calls for help, do not hear. I am only going to play a trick on him.' Then I gave the gamin a couple of francs and ascended to Monsieur Didot's office. I assumed the face of a madman, entered without knocking, locked the door behind me, and put the key in my pocket. 'They say I am mad,' I said; 'what do you think?' Monsieur Didot is a large, courageous man, who has fought a number of duels. He rose and placed himself so that his large desk was between us. 'I am not really mad,' I said, 'but sometimes I feel in my muscles a superhuman force, and I have to exercise it. That,' I said, in a confidential tone, 'is how I escaped. There were bars in the window. I took them in my hands; they came to pieces. It is good to be strong. Sometimes I feel as if I could tear a man's head from his body with my hands.' Here I advanced a few steps, looking more and more insane. 'I must try it some time,' I said. Monsieur Didot was trembling violently, like a man in a malarial chill. 'But I'm not mad,' I said, 'and the proof is that at times I imagine myself to be a dog.' Here I began to yelp, bark, and snarl. Monsieur Didot's hand closed on a heavy ruler. 'See,' I said, and I held up my hands so that he could see the scars in the palms, 'I have been crucified. Do you wonder that I am a little queer at times? And the queerest thing is this, that I have never been in a theatre and yet at times I imagine myself to be an actor. Nothing soothes me like reciting. See, at the thought of it, the mad look leaves my eyes. Would you like to hear me recite?' He nodded. He was too frightened to speak. I let the madness go out of my face, and in a heart-broken voice counted from one to twenty in Arabic. When I had finished tears were rolling down the manager's face. 'That was how I lost her,' I said. Then I began again at one and counted

162

to twenty in a comic manner. And though he was
shaking in his shoes, laughter burst from Monsieur
Didot's mouth before I had finished saying the number
five. 'See,' I said, 'how rational I can be if I am
humored.' Then, suddenly kneeling, I began to make
love to a chair with the most soul-moving passion.
Again Monsieur Didot wept. Then I scolded the chair,
pretending that it was my little boy and that he had
fallen down in the mud in his Sunday clothes. Then I
made it my confessor, and confessed to the most idiotic
crimes and sins. Monsieur Didot roared with laughter. Then I became, in a moment, perfectly rational.
'Confess,' I said, 'that you have been entertained. I
am not in the least mad. I want you to stage me in a
play which I shall select. That is all. Perhaps you
have not seen enough of my art to judge. Give me
five minutes, and I will die of consumption, waste away
before your eyes, and spit blood. It is not pretty, but
I can do it, though it is disagreeable to bite the inside
of one's mouth. Or, if you prefer, I will have an
epileptic fit, or strangle myself. Or, if you like, I will
go mad again and frighten you to death.'

"Monsieur Didot vented a long sigh. 'Whatever you
do,' he said, 'don't go mad. It was horrible. But I
will stage you in whatever play you select. You are
wonderful. But what was that first piece you recited?
I could not understand a word of it, yet it made me

163

cry.' 'That,' I said, ' was the Arabic for the cardinal numbers one to twenty inclusive. And so was the second piece, which, if I am not mistaken, made you laugh.'"

That was how L'Ouvrier induced a manager to give him a start. The rest, the first night—Œdipus—belongs to dramatic history. On the one side the audience and critics, experienced playgoers hostile to new blood; on the other side to do battle against them, a little Jew, who had never faced an audience till that moment—a little Jew with big ears, clad in the classic robes of a Grecian king. The result was never in doubt. The little Jew appeared—enormous and dominant. His voice sounded like a great bell tolling. The rigid tragedy throbbed with passion and life. Horror appeared like something tangible on the most cynical faces. At the point when Œdipus appears, after putting out his eyes, to say farewell to his children, many persons in the audience screamed and fainted. For days all Paris talked of a Greek king dead these thousands of years.

A critic is said to have asked L'Ouvrier at this time how, being a smallish man, he managed to make himself look large.

"By thinking large," said L'Ouvrier.

"And with whom did you study eloquence?"

"With silence."

Pressed to explain himself, he said: "I went into the

desert, at a season when no winds blow, and day and night there is complete silence. I stood it as long at I could. Then I began to talk. At first I had no effect on the silence, but gradually I forced it out of my vicinity. I pretended that I was a little village. I learned to produce all the sounds of one—the women scolding, the children howling, the hens clucking, the dogs barking. I peopled the solitude and amused myself vastly."

VI

Simon L'Ouvrier became the talk of the town. People rushed to see him, and scrambled to know him. His journal was published. He was proclaimed a conqueror, not over nations, but over matter and mind. The French, with their strong leaning to fanatical worship, set him upon a solitary pinnacle, in the clouds above other pinnacles, and saw in him the true apostle of art. Nor was L'Ouvrier backward in propounding his gospel. He had worked, suffered, sacrificed, sowed—now he would play, rejoice, smell the grateful incense, and reap.

"In the beginning," he said on one occasion to a reporter, "there were three ambitions in my family: my father's, to have me bake cakes well; my mother's, to have me marry a lady; my own, to become a great actor. The other day a Royal Personage took luncheon at my house, incognito. I offered him a little cake which I had compounded and baked with my own hands. He pronounced it delicious. Thus my father's ambition for me may be said to have borne fruit. I have received two offers of marriage from women who, to judge by name and position, if not conduct, are ladies. Thus my mother may rest in peace, for, while I shall not marry either of them, I could if I would. As for my own ambition, I need only say that I have been received with ovations by the people of Paris, with whom rests the last word in things appertaining to art. If I am a great actor it is because I have worked hard. If I am not, it is because I have not worked hard enough."

By what kind of a moral code did this curious man live? What was he like? The first question is the more easily answered. He gave money in charity, lived frugally and free from all breath of scandal. The second question is difficult, but, from combining the accounts of those who knew him best, I have concluded that he was polite, self-assured, without offense, a little stiff and distant, a better talker than listener. He dressed quietly, was scrupulously clean, and quite without the vagaries of lesser stage favorites. He played steadily night after night and was open and consistent in his business obligations—in short, a man of his word, who took no liberties with the existing school of manners. He deserved the success for which he had given so much mind and so much courage. There could be no better proof than the fact that his brother and sister artists admired him with all fervor and no jealousy. He must then have been a very happy man at this time: financially and socially secure, enjoying excellent health, and the promise of many years during which he should give infinite pleasure to multitudes of people—gloom them with tragedy, burst them with laughter. But fate had an awful blow for him in her bludgeon.

When he first met Aimée de Longueville is not known. It was not even known for months that they were anything but acquaintances. Then came the announcement of their engagement and approaching marriage. All Paris rose to applaud. Then came the Charity Bazar fire, and Aimée de Longueville, in her youth, beauty, and innocence, was burned to death—horribly, beyond recognition.

Simon L'Ouvrier did not receive this blow in a manner worthy of his manhood and his genius. He left the stage and plunged into every excess which his genius could devise. Houses were no longer open to him, society cut him, the press forgot him. So fast a pace did he go that in less than a year he presented a barely recognizable shadow of himself, a malevolent, evil shadow, forever dogging the footsteps of vice. He was dubbed by vicious associates "the Wandering Jew."

All this is very unpleasant to think about. Let us hasten to the end.

It came out that Aimée de Longueville's mother was starving. The directors of the Français organized a benefit, sought out Simon L'Ouvrier, and begged him to take part. Besodden as he was with drink, it took him some time to understand what was wanted. When he did, he said: "Very well, I will play the farewell scene from 'Œdipus.'"

The fact that L'Ouvrier was once more to exercise his genius set Paris by the ears to obtain seats at the benefit. And those who were lucky enough to bid themselves into the theatre were treated to a performance which, though great, was not in the least what they had expected. L'Ouvrier appeared with his crown on the side of his head, two enormous glass eyes hanging around his neck by strings, his ears wiggling, and his toes turned in. He spoke, indeed, the heartrending words of Œdipus, but he lent to their utterance the most comical inflections and by-play. For half an hour the theatre crashed with laughter; people howled and held their sides. When the curtain fell the applause and cries for L'Ouvrier lasted five minutes. The manager stepped before the curtain.

"Monsieur L'Ouvrier," said he, "wishes me to thank you for your kind attention, and to say further that he has gone home for ever, and bids you farewell. He wishes me to thank you further on behalf of your kindness to the memory of Aimée de Longueville."

Simon L'Ouvrier on his deathbed with consumption played one more part.

"How long have I to live?" said he to the doctor.

"It is a question of minutes, my poor friend," said the doctor.

"How little you know," said L'Ouvrier. "Look, I am improving—I am getting well."

The doctor affirms that color came into L'Ouvrier's cheeks, that his temperature and pulse became normal, that he gave orders for a hearty meal, laughed and joked like one who has suddenly and successfully passed a serious climax, and then, exclaiming hilariously: "I can still do it," collapsed and died.

VI

A CAROLINA NIGHT'S DREAM

A CAROLINA NIGHT'S DREAM

While I was dressing for dinner the moon rose, and I could see, beyond the firm island studded with live oaks, miles of shaky rice swamps from which protruded the mouths of straight, narrow canals, looking in the moonlight like garden paths of silver. Far to the left a winding screen of trees hinted of a river at its feet, while here and there among the swamps groups of live oaks, bushy, low-headed and immense, like Cyclopean orchard trees, signified that the region was either in process of yielding to the ocean or of establishing more consistently the hoop of a continent. Through my open window came the loud, consumptive coughing and chugging of an old-fashioned stern-wheeler, which presently ceased and yielded to the shouts and yells of negroes. And I knew that the bi-weekly steamer trom Georgetown was being made fast to my host's wharf and that the servants were welcoming a guest. But it all sounded like an act of piracy.

My host knocked and asked if I had what I wanted.

"Yes," I said, "come in, will you?"

He entered—a long, thin, gracious young host, in

spotless white linen dinner clothes which contrasted delightfully with his crimson bow tie and shining brown face.

"Who's being murdered," I asked.

"It's my grandfather Creighton," said Creighton. "He knew that you were to be here to-night, and many nights, and he proposes to be among the first to express satisfaction."

"How far has he come," I asked.

"Forty miles by buggy and steamer."

"How old is he?"

"Eighty."

"I wish," I said, "that I could do something to deserve so much honor."

"You can," said Creighton.

"How," said I.

"By taking a drink whenever he does," said Creighton. "I can't, because I'm married. You'll be down in a minute? If not, the old gentleman will visit you with a cocktail. The mixer and ingredients are on the hall table waiting for him—" Creighton opened the door and listened. "Come here," he said. Then we both began to laugh. "He has arrived," said Creighton.

We could hear the unmistakable and delectable sound of ice and liquid being shaken in a cocktail mixer. By this time I was dressed and we started downstairs. On the landing we met Grandfather Creighton coming up.

He had not had time to remove his hat or long cloak, which were streaked with salt-water stains, for, as he afterward said, it had been rough crossing Georgetown bay. He was a charming little old gentleman to look at, smooth-shaven and delicately fashioned like a porcelain. His slender hands were almost as white as the silver tray which he carried and upon which were three straw-colored cocktails in heavy cut glasses. The old gentleman held the tray steadily with one hand and employed the other in an easy and graceful removal of his hat.

"I attribute this meeting," said he, "to the good fortune which has followed me for eighty years. *Help* yourselves."

Creighton took his grandfather's hat so that the old gentleman could have a drinking hand, and we put down our cocktails with one gesture, as it were, and one swallowing noise, as if three soldiers trained to an act of discipline.

"I feel that we are better acquainted already," said the old gentleman. "I shall be forgiven if I do not put on my evening clothes? My granddaughter by marriage waits for no man. At my age a man should think twice before letting his soup grow cold."

He then led us downstairs to the hall table where he found the cocktail things just as he had left them. Attributing this to the good fortune which had followed him for eighty years he mixed three more, and we joined our hostess in the drawing-room.

"Why, Grandfather Creighton!" she cried. "Could nothing but a miserable stranger bring you to see us? What have you been doing with yourself all this time?"

"I have been suffering from thirst," said the old gentleman. "That I have occasionally found relief I attribute to the good fortune which has followed me for eighty years."

During dinner champagne was served before I had swallowed my oysters. The old gentleman was silent and uncommunicative. But as he prefaced this attitude by stating that he could not do more than two things at once, on account of his great age, we allowed him to eat and drink in peace. But when Mrs. Creighton left us and coffee was brought with gigantic cigars and fiery brandy, the old gentleman said that he never smoked until he had drunk as much as he could, and began to carry the bulk of the conversation. This at length fell on ways of getting rich, legitimate and other ways. Grandfather Creighton at something I said about so and so being no better than a pirate chuckled immoderately.

"Why," said he, "we Creightons are rich and all our money comes from piracy, entering vessels on the high seas, and murder. We didn't do it ourselves; it was done for us. We reaped the benefit. Those pearls which Rob Creighton there wears in his shirt bosom came from a pair of Spanish earrings that had black hairs tangled in them and their clasps broken as if they had been torn from a lady's ears. My father had them broken up—the earrings—because my mother thought the design unlovely, and because, to tell the truth, which is not an elegant one, the settings were greasy. All this Santee region," the old gentleman went on, "its rivers, tideways, swamps, seaward ponds, lagoons, harbors and turtle-backs of dry land, was infested by pirates. When I was a big boy my father took me to Charleston on a visit, and while I was there I escaped from him and went to see one hanged. It was not a spirited scene. The poor wretch had begged a bottle of laudanum from his jailor and was in no condition to seize the opportunity which fortune had given of making his exit in a gallant and sympathetic manner. But when I was a little boy pirates were not so sodden. It was then that the golden harvest of their nefarious doings was gathered by us Creightons and put once more to Christian employment; that is, to drawing interest. One-eyed Limb, an escaped slave, was the particular devil of this vicinity—a great pirate, sir, as black-hearted as skinned, astute, cunning, of a skill with weapons that bordered on the divine, malicious, humorous, and of an audacity and sheer courage that compelled a kind of admiration, even from white men.

A CAROLINA NIGHT'S DREAM

"I was the last person, sir, to see one-eyed Limb alive. He met his God or his devil, sir, over yonder on the sea beaches where Gunpowder creek flows into ocean.

"The fresh sea-gull eggs, mackerel and flood-gull, and the certainty to hook a drum, frequently drew me thither when I was a little boy. My nurse's stories of the horrible deeds upon bad little boys of one-eyed Limb and other notable pirates of our Carolina coast as frequently inspired me to stay away. Even the grown folk did not feel entirely secure. For, from time to time, we could see from these very dining-room windows the glow of fires far off reflected upon the sky, and hear the sounds of wild men in liquor. There were more pregnant alarms than these sometimes, and once, sir, my father and a number of gentlemen who were his guests, firing from the upper chambers, stood off a deliberate attempt of one-eyed Limb to raze the plantation. On that occasion there was enough carnage among the pirates to reduce their ambition. My nurse carried me in her arms to the carriage-house where the corpses had been ranged. There were eleven of them, with eleven types of bad faces—black, white and yellow. My mother was for having them decently buried, but my father gave orders to have stones attached to their necks and to sink them in the river.

"Among Limb's crew were a number of escaped slaves—two from this very plantation—and it was not, therefore, unnatural that rumors of what the pirates were about doing or intending reached us from time to time through the quarters. We heard, for instance, that Limb would take a terrible revenge for the loss of his eleven companions, and for nearly two years my father maintained an elaborate system of outposts and signals; but with the exception of a few shots fired upon the house from afar and quite at random, and the mysterious disappearance from the quarters of three plump wenches, nothing of a permanently alarming nature occurred. . . . You are neglecting the brandy.

"The pirates had their village by the fresh-water pond on Long Bear, where we will take you wild fowling when you are less tired than you will be to-morrow morning, and, always through the quarters, we heard of their government and civic life. These consisted in allowing matters to run from bad to worse, until one-eyed Limb himself could not endure the disorder. He would then rouse himself, go forth armed from his cabin, do a murder or two, put the quiet of death upon the village and return to his wives. Once we heard that the yellow fever had broken out among the pirates, and that they were in a fair way to be exterminated. That alarmed us far more than any rumor of attack. As a fact, however, the village was agreeably and healthily situated, and autumn breezes off ocean put an end to the plague.

A CAROLINA NIGHT'S DREAM

"It was the spring following that a longing came upon me to know if the gulls had commenced to lay. I attribute this to the good fortune which has followed me for eighty years and to which I will empty this diminutive glass of liquor.

"I gave orders to have my canoe provisioned and in readiness for a start two hours before sunrise. I threatened my body servants—I had two, big hardy young bucks, Yap and Yaff—with a hundred lashes apiece if they overslept, and sent them early to bed.

"At about the appointed time we started, Yap in the bow, Yaff in the stern, and myself amidships, with my little fowling-piece and a number of soft rugs. The night fog was still upon the water, cold and opaque. I ordered the paddlers not to loiter, and, drawing the rugs about me, lay flat and slept. I was twelve years old then, and now I am eighty. In all the intervening years I have never lost the power to sleep. When we retired in order after Gettysburg, sir, I slept in the saddle for six hours. I have thus ever been able to give myself relief from mental anguish, which is the secret of longevity.

"I awoke at the commencement of sunrise, in time to admire the dissipation of the fog and the looming into view of our wild amphibious landscape. We were descending Gunpowder Creek at the leaping pace of a strongly paddled tide-borne canoe. I could hear already the cries of the gulls and the reverberations of ocean beating upon the hard beaches. A wholesome salt wind had arisen and was blowing strongly in our faces. We had entered that part of Gunpowder Creek where its swampy shores yield for a while to firm banks dense with bushes and salt-stunted trees, when Yap, who had the bow paddle, relieved a hand and held it up for silence. Yaff let his paddle, too, trail in the water and we listened. The wind bore us the sound of oars grinding against tholl pins and the murmur of a voice humming in a minor key.

"'Black man's voice,' said Yap, and under his own ebony hide appeared a sudden visitation of leprosy-white blotches. It was a credited story among the negroes that one-eyed Limb went about the more devilish of his deeds sweetly singing.

"'Land!' said I.

"In a few seconds we were back in the bushes, canoe and all. But had it not been for the strength of the wind and its direction we must have been heard and, as events bore out, run to our cover and murdered. Mindful of what was expected of me as white and a master, I left the negroes, enjoining them to lie flat and make not a sound until I returned, and proceeded to work my way through the bushes to the open marsh behind them, a matter of not more than thirty yards, then down stream, perhaps a hundred yards; and then diagonally, once more through the bushes, to gain a view of the creek beyond the bend which I had thus eliminated.

"Toward the sandy shore of the cove thus discovered to my eyes, a row boat, far out on the bosom of the creek, here as wide as a river, was heading. It contained five negroes naked to the waist. Four had their backs to me and were rowing. The fifth, sitting in the stern, faced me and steered with a long oar. He it was whom we had heard humming, for as I looked he recommenced to a different tune, and I was able to distinguish the words of a song still current among our coast negroes. The song moved slowly and the boat fast:

> Gambler, Gambler, yo' dice am gwine deceibe you!
> Gambler, Gambler, yo' dice am gwine deceibe you!
> Gambler, Gambler, yo' dice am gwine deceibe you!
> Way down in the grabe!

By the time the song had progressed to that point, and it was rendered in a wonderful, sweet, sad voice, the boat had come so near that I could see the singer as plainly as I see Robert there. He was a very small man, thin to emaciation, and black as the pit. He had the head and face of a much larger man, and at first I thought that he was blind, for my vision in that first glance seemed to have embraced only the left side of his face which had a cavity instead of an eye. Indeed, when I first saw him his one eye must have been closed

or I could never have overlooked it. It opened now
and I saw what looked like the end of a disgusting yellow egg sticking from the man's skull. If that eye had
any iris it was of a yellow indistinguishable from its setting. I had a longing, hardly to be denied, to empty
my stomach of its contents and scream. I closed my
eyes and the nausea passed. While I lay with closed
eyes, Limb, for there remained no doubt under heaven
that it was he, began and concluded, with what cloying
sweetness of voice I cannot hope to describe, the second
stanza of his chantey:

> Mother, mother, yo' daughter gwine deceibe yo'!
> Mother, mother, yo' daughter gwine deceibe yo'!
> Mother, mother, yo' daughter gwine deceibe yo'!
> Way down in de grabe.

"I screwed my courage up to the looking point and
discovered that the oarsmen were in the act of giving
the boat the last impetus which should carry it to the
shore. The muscles on the great black backs and
shoulders rippled under the shining hides like deft fingers
playing indescribably complicated instruments. Limb
nodded his chuckle head as if he did not wish by speaking to interrupt himself in the train of thought inspired
by his own singing, the oars came inboard silently, and
the boat with diminishing speed drifted at once down
the creek and toward the shore. This would make the
landing further below me than my first conclusion had

dared allow, and the relief to my overstrained courage and imagination was so great that the saliva gathered head in my mouth and ran out between my lips. I saw now that amidships in the boat was a seaman's chest painted a sky blue and reinforced with heterogeneous pieces of sheet-iron nailed to the edges and corners. Limb sang a little louder, a little faster:

> Thunder, thunder, thunder, roll ober yonder!
> Thunder, thunder, thunder, roll ober yonder!
> Thunder, thunder, thunder, roll ober yonder!
> Way down in de grabe.

"And the boat ran on the beach. Before the rowers could move Limb hopped from his seat to the top of the chest, with a something in his movement that reminded you of a flea, set foot for the smallest fraction of time on the nearest black shoulder, and was ashore. The man who had been used as a stepping-stone turned his head slowly, all the while rubbing his shoulder, and gave Limb a grin, at once so sheepish, adoring, good-natured, and comical that my own mouth began to smile with his.

"My nurse had often regaled my youthful imagination with the magnificence of costume usually sported by pirates. What the poverty of raiment which covered the corpses of the pirates that I had been shown in the carriage-house had failed practically to establish (for all children struggle against fact to retain their grasp of the picturesque and romantic) was now certified. The men before me were clad only in dirty patched trowsers. They had neither hats, shoes nor weapons, unless Limb, whose diminutive waist was surrounded by a tawdry chequered sash, had one concealed therein. As events proved he had. But I saw none then, and began to pluck up my spirits, for I at least had a fowling-piece. Then it occurred to me to be dashed from that point of comfort by wondering if I had loaded it or not. Memory refused to be cajoled. Had I, if discovered, one shot between me and massacre was a speculation that I could not answer.

"Limb and the four rowers now drew the boat high and dry on the sands of the cove, and not without labor got the chest out of her. Limb then ordered one of the men to scratch his back for him and for several moments gave himself up to the process with the most evident signs of relish. After that they hove up the chest and staggered into the bushes with it.

"They did not go very far and presently the one who had scratched Limb's back returned to the boat and took out of it a pick and a shovel. He paused long enough to kneel in the sand and souse his head in the creek. Then he took up the tools and went back into the bushes.

"They were an unconscionable time burying the chest to their own satisfaction, owing, I suppose, to the tough and intricate network of roots, through which they must cut, and I was about concluding that the silence and suspense were to last forever when the most awful and sudden burst of screaming split my ears. There was a frenzied thrashing in the bushes, and out burst the negro who had grinned, running for his life. Behind him came, ran, hopped, flew—I know of no word that describes the kind or the speed of such unearthly locomotion—Limb. There was a blazing in my eyes like that of sun rays deflected and concentrated by a mirror. It passed and I saw Limb's black pipe-stem arm drive with a knife at the back of the runner's neck. I saw him wrench it out and, as the stricken man whirled and fell, drive it to the hilt in his convulsed face.

"Then, possessing himself of the knife which had been torn from his hand, he walked quietly back into the bushes from which he had just emerged with such demoniac speed. Presently I heard him speak in a quiet conversational tone that had the effect of a diabolic sneer:

"'Ain't you daid yet, Bluebell?'

"Then I heard the horrid sound with which I had become familiar, of a knife driven home—once—twice . . . and the drawling voice again:

"'Now you *is* sho daid, Bluebell.' And out of the bushes he strolled, singing, sweet and clear:

"'Sailor, sailor, yo' captain gwine deceibe you.'

"At the same instant a little voice began to say in my

head: 'You loaded that gun, I saw you. You put in buck-shot in case you saw deer or pig. Don't you remember. I saw you do it.' Whether I believed or not I do not know. Likely as not I did, for when Limb turned and bent to launch the boat I aimed very carefully at the little row of whitish knobs made by his spine just above his trowsers, and the gun went off. I saw no distinct picture in what followed, only a kaleidoscopic miracle of black pipe-stem arms and legs that whirled about a focus made by one awful yellow eye. I buried my face in my hands and screamed aloud. And I think, sir, that I must have passed into a state of unconsciousness. For when I once more saw the boat and one-eyed Limb there sat upon the gunwhale of the first three buzzards, and upon the chest of the second, one.

"And that, sir," concluded the old gentleman, "was the foundation of the Creighton fortune. And, sir," said he, glaring savagely, for the brandy was beginning to affect him, "I should like to see the man that would deny to my father the possession of the nicest sense of honor and integrity imaginable. He made no bones, sir, about accepting the treasure contained in the blue chest, and presented to him by an all-wise Providence and a dutiful son. . . .

"Creighton," said I, when the old gentleman, after a few indignant puffs, had given himself to the firm embrace of sleep, "it is not the part of a guest to impeach the veracity of a host's grandfather, but a little further down the coast, from the lips of August Lesage (dear old man!) I have heard a very similar story about a very similar pirate, according to which narrative, smacking with the first personal pronoun, was similarly founded a similar fortune. Did all your grandfathers eat pirates?"

"August Lesage's treasure chest was painted green, I think," said Creighton reflectively, "and *his* Limb lacked the right eye. My dear sir, all gentlemen are liars. My grandfather, with all due honor to his white hairs, has never been known to speak the truth or to tell an injurious lie. In the Northern States men lie for profit; we of the South lie only to entertain each other and our guests. It is to this fact more than to any other that my grandfather attributes the good fortune which has followed him for eighty years. Shall we go to bed? My grandfather will not be alarmed when he wakes and finds himself alone with what is left of the brandy. When that is gone, he will go to sleep, either here or in his bed, for, as he himself says, the power to sleep has not failed him for eighty years whenever he has found it necessary to put a snuffer on mental anguish."

"How *did* you Creightons make your money?" I asked.

A CAROLINA NIGHT'S DREAM

"One of us lied—for profit," said Creighton. "Rest his soul! He is the only one of all my ancestors for whom I have entire respect. Since for the benefit of his family he sacrificed those qualities which are most precious to a man—his integrity and his self-respect—he, no doubt, rests in peace."

"I believe you," said I, "while," said he, "our less provident ancestors—merely—*slumber*."

Fortunately I am not married and have no children, for ten minutes later I was merely slumbering.

The old gentleman came to my room late the next morning. He winked and said, "Let us visit the treasure chest."

We did. Among other precious things it contained ice.

VII

THE STOWING AWAY OF MR. BILL BALLAD

THE STOWING AWAY OF MR. BILL BALLAD

When Mr. Bill Ballad saw, through the wraith of white smoke which his pistol had made, the sudden and terrible contortion of Mr. Heigh's face, the staring eyes, the opening and shutting mouth, dreadfully grinning; when he saw Mr. Heigh's left leg buckle like an over-canvased spar in a squall; when he saw Mr. Heigh writhing on the turf, and when he heard the sheriff, panting from hard running, bellow, "Arrest that man!" then it was that Mr. Bill Ballad forgot the exquisite quixotism which had led him to make one of a duel with Mr. Heigh; then it was that he forgot the excellent nerve with which he had faced the detonation of his adversary's weapon, forgot his dignity, forgot his philosophy, forgot those debts and that unsuccess which, darkening the sun of his young days, had made him reckless; forgot the delicious face of Miss Gremley, with whom he was not acquainted, but in whose cause he had fought; forgot everything but his bump of locality, and incontinently took to his toes.

The sheriff and the sheriff's man ran over the graves

and in and out of the headstones with the celerity of staghounds, but Mr. Bill Ballad passed over the narrow houses of the dead like a swooping hawk, took the low wall of the burying ground in his stride, went down Eden Street like a gust of wind, turned into Turtle Lane and covered the length of it like a thrown stone, passed the place of business of his late adversary, was dimly conscious of the letters on the firm's shingle: *Flower & Heigh—seed merchants*, bolted down Ship Street toward the wharves, and finally took breathless refuge in the sail-loft of Messrs. Spar & Marlin, riggers of ships, and there, buried from view among ropes, rope ends, canvas, and old sacks, he lay and sobbed; for it is dreadful at twenty-two to be over ears in debt, a writer of philosophies to which the ears of the world are deaf, and liable at any moment to be laid by the ears for the killing of a man.

It was not until five in the afternoon that Mr. Bill Ballad looked up from his despair, ceased from his sobs, and remarked to the canvas ghosts in the sail loft: "When you are fallen as low as is possible, you can fall no lower; nothing is stable; all things move either up or down; wherefore, since I can no lower fall and since I may not remain stably fallen, I must in some measure rise. Food would boost me."

He now took measures to make his body more comfortable; a bunching of canvas here, a spreading of it there, a rolling over of himself, and a fine yawn.

"At least," said he, "I have done what I set out to do, for Mr. Heigh will not marry Miss Gremley in the morning—for the present I am safe, and blessings be showered on the head of the unfaithful servant who forgot to lock the door of this place on a holiday. As for the future, the darkness will provide. Come night— heavens be overcast—moon be hidden—stars be blanketed—and grant, O merciful Lord, that Jemmy be in his house when I do call."

Then he fell to thinking of that little book, "The Age of Folly," the gisty matter between the blue boards, and of the public—the great, blind, stuttering, strutting child which preferred the toys brain-y-factured by other men—and, tossing uneasily, he said: "I don't see why in hell it doesn't sell," and fell asleep.

Thick was the night, hidden the moon, blanketed the stars, and Jemmy was in his house at the time when Mr. Bill Ballad came to call. Jemmy had been in his house since noon. Jemmy, taking advantage of the holiday, had risen early and drank himself unconscious; unconscious he had lain on the floor of his library through the late afternoon, the evening, and part of the night. Unconscious he lay when Mr. Bill Ballad slipped through the open window, but when Mr. Bill Ballad shook him by the arm (as one testing the mechanism of a new pump) he began to awake.

"Wha' time is it?" he said.

"Midnight," said Mr. Ballad.

"Time turn in," said Jemmy, sighing.

"Wake up," said Mr. Ballad. "My life's in danger."

"What light's in danger?" inquired Jemmy. "Put it out."

"Wake up, you drunken swine."

"Swine yourself—swine herself—swine himself—all swine holiday this morning."

"Jemmy, does any ship sail from here in the morning?"

"Thish my library—ships don't sail from libraries. Library place to sleep in—nice to lie on snuggle rug an' sleep."

"Would a good kicking help you, Jemmy?"

It did. Jemmy sat up.

"What you kicking me for?"

"Beg your pardon," said Mr. Ballad, "but I thought you were dead. Will you try and pull yourself together, please? I'm in trouble."

"Wait till I wash my face, then." Jemmy arose and left the room somnolently. He returned much refreshed. "Now you may fire away," he said.

Mr. Bill Ballad shuddered. And then he told Jemmy his trouble. "Have you heard nothing of it?" he asked.

"No," said Jemmy, "I don't remember anything after noon. You may not have hurt him much."

"O Jemmy—I saw his face—I heard the breath whistle out of him—and, O God! I saw him fall."

Jemmy began to think hard.

"The *Mallow*," he said presently, "goes out in the morning tide, in hides, for Jamaica. If we can slip you aboard, and hide you, well provisioned——"

"Yes, yes," cried Mr. Ballad, "that's the thing—it's making up for a brute of a blow, and there'll be no one on deck. But where'll I hide?"

"I can't think of the name of the place," said Jemmy; "wait—no, I can't think—but I know the hatch that opens into it—it's below the fo'c's'le—where they keep spare stores—what in hell—no, I can't think."

"We must start at once."

"We must larder you first."

"What have you in the house?"

"We'll look. Then they began to rummage. They found a ham, two loaves of bread, one loaf of spice cake, and a fine hunk of cheese.

"You must have water," said Jemmy, and he filled a great stone jug. "Want any wine?"

"No—no," cried Mr. Bill Ballad, "I have had enough wine to last me till the Judgment Day, and to damn me then."

"I haven't," said Jemmy, "but I shall hope to have had. Come along, boy—take my blue cloak. . . .

Hold hard, you'll want flint and steel and a lantern
. . . have you your watch?"

"Herodotus, the Jew, hath it," said Mr. Bill Ballad
with a faint smile.

"You shall have mine. Now, then, I'll look abroad
a little; it may be that the coast is obscure."

The front door struggled in Jemmy's hands like a
live thing. "All the glims of heaven are doused," said
he, "and it's blowing like hell. Come along."

The streets were deserted, but lively with the rustling
of dead leaves, and the blowing about of all that was
unstable. Jemmy and Mr. Bill Ballad, each with a
sack of provisions over his shoulder, slunk through the
dark and blowy town like a pair of marauders laden
with plate. In Ship Street, a malicious inequality of the
paving caught Jemmy by one of his unsteady feet and
hurled him to the ground. "O Liberty!" he cried,
"what crimes are committed in thy name."

He gathered himself and his sack together, and they
went on. Jemmy owned a staunch skiff, out of which
the two friends had often shot at wild-fowls. They
found her riding snugly in the lee of Mr. Caruthers'
long wharf and embarked. Rounding the end of the
wharf, the wind and sea struck her in power.

"Can you keep her head to it, Jemmy?"

"Watch me." The oars tore at the water, the wind
tore at the skiff, the water slammed her on the bows,

but inch by inch she dropped the long wharf behind and made headway into the whistling dark.

"Where does the *Mallow* lie?" Mr. Bill Ballad was obliged to trumpet his hands and bellow the question.

Jemmy, his teeth gritted and his breath coming and going in great grunts, jerked his head backward for answer.

"Hope to—we can find her," bellowed Mr. Ballad. Twenty minutes later Jemmy rested on his oars and began to look about him, trying with sweat-filled eyes to pierce the black. At that moment, as a joker might suddenly snatch back the bedclothes from one sleeping, the storm fairly ripped a cloud from before the face of the Lady Moon. For an instant the backs of the charging waves glimmered; for an instant, as if revealed by pale lightning, the harbor became a shape and familiar landmarks flashed into view; for an instant the two friends beheld the great black bulk of a ship leaping back against the bite of her mooring chain; and then out went the moon, and Jemmy, heading the skiff in the ascertained direction, began to row like mad.

Ten minutes later, dripping and bruised, they had won over the side of the leaping ship and were creeping forward along her creaking deck.

Jemmy pulled the hatch to, and the roaring of the weather was cut off as clearly as a slice of bread is cut off by a sharp knife.

"Whew," said Jemmy.

"Thank God," said Mr. Bill Ballad.

They lit the lantern, and found that they were in a triangular place three parts full of undeterminate bulk, and wholly full of the nauseating odor of bilge water and unclean woodwork.

"You'll be very comfortable here," said Jemmy. "God bless you, my boy, and good luck. Will write you to Jamaica and give you the news." He held out his hand.

"Jemmy," said Mr. Bill Ballad, "you know Miss Gremley—a long time from now tell her my story; how I saw her but once, yet could not bear to think that so much loveliness should be sold to an old man; tell her that for the sake of all her excellence I fought and came to an unhappy end"—Mr. Bill Ballad was almost aburst with tears—"tell her this a long time from now, so that she may say in her heart: 'Ah, but one man loved me.' . . . God bless you, Jemmy . . . will you make back all right?"

"The wind will hand me ashore," said Jemmy, "just as after dancing with her a courteous gentleman hands a beautiful young lady back to the seat beside her mother. I hate to leave you with nothing to drink but water."

The trap opened—the howls of the wind sounded—the trap closed—and the howls ceased. Mr. Ballad found himself alone in the shifting, creaking, stinking asylum that he had chosen, and shed a few tears.

Nelson, eater of ships, sea-lion, scourge of Napoleon, etc., was often made dreadfully sick by the great billows of his chosen element, so that had there been no fighting to do, one might be tempted to exclaim: "Mon Dieu, qu'allait il fair dans cette galère?" But the business of fighting seems to have taken his mind off the dolorous motions of his flagship and toughened him inside to a whalish serenity. In short, cruising and ship's pork made the man sick; but when the battle was met, his constitution suffered a revulsion, and he not only ate ships, but kept them down, and, to use his own thought, "would not have been elsewhere for thousands."

The atmosphere in Mr. Bill Ballad's hiding-place, coupled with the fantastic and Gallic manner in which the hiding-place danced about, brought that young gentleman to inactive extremities, yet he was content to be where he was; and when, in the midst of a trance-like nap, an immense rat ran across his face, the excitement, as with Nelson at sight of the enemy, took away his qualms and rendered him once more fit to reflect and to endure.

"I suppose," he reflected, "that I must stick to this sty for at least two days, so that there may be no possibility of them putting me ashore. Then I shall throw open the hatch, discover myself to the captain, and be put at some disagreeable sea work, climbing masts perhaps," and he shivered.

His chief reflections, however, in that dark, bilgy and plunging place were upon the duration of time, the instability of human affairs, and the disregard of hard boards for the sensitive joints of the human frame. In the extremes of aching discomfort the events of the preceding day receded from his complaining mind. The terrible collapse of Mr. Heigh upon receiving the bullet, the breathless flight from the scene of the duel, and the lovely face of Miss Gremley, were pictures which came to visit him with less and less frequency. Eventually he thought about nothing but the disadvantages of bones to the human frame, and wished himself a jellyfish. But for all his uninuredness to hard surfaces, sleep visited him in dreamy snatches; once he awoke with a start and a half consciousness that for a moment the storm had howled down the hatchway and roared in his ears. Indeed, he fancied during those first startled, waking seconds that some one had opened the hatch, drawn it to, and descended into his hiding-place. But with complete wakefulness he attributed his impression to the machinations of a sea-rat. He never knew how many hours had passed of his incarceration when, being set upon by hunger and curiosity, he lighted his lantern, and discovered that the watch which Jemmy had loaned him had run down.

"Damn!" said Mr. Bill Ballad. But he began to eat of his provisions (in particular of the ham) with a great show of appetite. In the midst of a large and toothsome mouthful he had suddenly the horrible sensation of one who, fancying himself alone, becomes aware that he is being watched. His scalp seemed to bristle, and he stopped chewing the better to listen.

"I thought," thought he, "that I heard some one breathe." He listened hard. But the sound was not repeated. He heard only the thumping of his own heart, the faint and distant echoes of the gale, and the creaking of the ship. "I wonder," he thought, "if it is possible for a rat to breathe audibly. I fancy not. But possibly an old grandfather rat"—he became facetious, with fear going—"who was asthmatic or suffering from a cold in the head"—and, just as he was about to resume the business of untrammelled eating, there sounded from the deep dark that lurked upon the outskirts of the ring of light cast by his lantern a husky voice.

Mr. Bill Ballad never knew the precise words uttered by the husky voice. Fear petrified him, but not, unfortunately, in time to prevent his overturning the lantern, which rolled off, clashing into the sudden and absolute darkness caused by its own extinction.

Mr. Bill Ballad, trembling in every limb, gasped like a man coming to the surface after a long swim under

203

water. Sweat cold as ice ran down his sides . . . and then once more the silence was broken by the husky voice, which said tremblingly, "I beg your pardon, sir, but I forgot to bring any water, and I've eaten a lot of pickles, and I think I shall die of thirst."

Mr. Bill Ballad drew a long staccato sigh of relief. But he was angry at the voice for having frightened him so, and he said angrily:

"Why didn't you say so at first?"

"I told you not to be frightened the first time I spoke," said the voice.

"Frightened!" exclaimed Mr. Ballad, beginning to tremble again in spite of the gentle and plaintive quality of the husky voice. "I frightened; why, man, I'm *armed to the teeth.*"

"S—so—am—I," came back in a stuttering kind of a whine. "But why did you overturn the lantern?"

"As a precaution," said Mr. Ballad boldly, for he felt himself greatly heartened by the timidity now evident in the voice. "But come out of there—I won't hurt you, and you shall have a drink—if," he put in with courtesy, "you don't mind drinking out of the same jug."

Then was heard a bungling movement in the dark, followed by a sharp exclamation of pain.

"What's the matter now?" said Mr. Ballad, all patronage.

"My shin," said the voice, and exclaimed instantly again.

"Well?" said Mr. Ballad.

"My other shin," said the voice.

"Deuced clumsy, aren't you," said Mr. Ballad. "Oh, there you are." His outstretched hand came in contact with the top of a hatted head. "Here's the jug— for goodness' sake don't spill it."

The stranger drank greedily with a gluggling noise.

"Now," said Mr. Ballad, "you stay here—and keep saying where you are, so that I will know where I am, while I crawl about and look for that damned lantern. . . . I think I know where it rolled."

Mr. Ballad began to crawl cautiously in the direction in which he imagined the lantern to have rolled, while every now and then, to give him the location, the stranger said loudly, "Here I am." Between two of these pieces of data Mr. Ballad began to swear.

"What's the matter now?" said the stranger.

"My shin!" said Mr. Ballad furiously.

"Here I am!" said the stranger.

Presently Mr. Ballad swore again.

"Well?" said the stranger.

"My other shin," said Mr. Ballad, and, to do him credit, though he began testily, he finished laughing.

"Deuced clumsy, aren't you," said the stranger, rendered bold by Mr. Ballad's boyish laugh. . . . "Here I am." . . .

The next silence was terminated by an awful crash and a grunt of real pain.

"Here I am," said the stranger.

"Oh, you are, are you," said Mr. Ballad angrily, but with a ginger quality of voice. "Well, I've crawled off the edge of something, and here I am."

"Are you hurt?"

"I should think I was hurt. It's my knee . . . where are you? I'm coming back—damn the lantern —sing out, can't you."

"Here I am," said the stranger. . . .

"—— it," cried Mr. Ballad suddenly.

"What's the matter?"

"My other knee," said Mr. Ballad.

"Here I am," said the stranger.

"I should say you were," said Mr. Ballad furiously, "and heartily amused, I daresay. I've a good mind to punch your head—ouch—where are you?" No answer.

"Where are you?" No answer.

"I won't punch your head, you little fool."

The stranger raised his voice. "Here I am," said he.

"Have you a watch?" asked Mr. Bill Ballad.

"No," said the stranger.

"Then it doesn't matter about the lantern," said Mr. Ballad, "because my watch has run down, and I do not feel any particular curiosity to be gratified by a look at you. But you may as well tell me why you are here."

"Because I had to run away from home," said the stranger.

"You sound reasonably well bred," said Mr. Ballad. "So I daresay it is a question of bills which you are unable to pay. But I don't really care to know. What have you brought in the way of provisions?"

"Pickles, macaroons, jam, and a little candy," said the stranger.

"You never should have left your mother," said Mr. Bill Ballad. "You are the most ignorant youth with whom I have ever come in contact."

"You only came in contact with the top of my hat," said the stranger.

"I came in contact with every other damn thing in this ship," said Mr. Ballad, and he tried to caress all his bruises at once.

"I may be ignorant," said the stranger, "but I don't swear. I wonder where we are."

"I forget the name of the place," said Mr. Ballad, "but if you mean where the *Mallow* is, why, I suppose, she's well off shore. She must have sailed hours ago."

"It's pretty rough, isn't it?" said the stranger. "Are you a good sailor?"

"No," said Mr. Ballad, "in fact, some time ago I threatened to be very sick, but a rat ran over my face and startled me back into a pink glow of health. Then you appeared, and I must admit that your piquant conversation and absurd youthfulness have so shaken me with internal laughter that I feel as if I should never experience another qualm. What do you expect to have happen to you when we are discovered?"

"I don't know, I'm sure," said the stranger; "anything to get away. But why are you here?"

Mr. Bill Ballad reflected for a moment, but he loved talk for its own sake, had never suffered very acutely from discretion, and wished to play the man in the imagination of his young and callow acquaintance; therefore he said: "I will tell you."

"Do," said the stranger.

"Did you ever hear of a Miss Gremley," said Mr. Bill Ballad.

The stranger was silent for some moments. "A little pock-marked thing?" he said finally.

"Pock-marked yourself," exclaimed Mr. Bill Ballad. "She's the most exquisite girl that God ever made, and considering the practice He has had—well, never mind. Her parents are swine."

The stranger laughed. "In what way?" said he.

"In all ways," said Mr. Ballad. "They arranged, for instance, to marry this lovely child to an old, ugly, lean, underbred, rich, black-hearted ——, by the name of Heigh. It was simply a sale. The ewe lamb for the butcher—a fat commission for the parents."

"But if they were swine," said the stranger, "how could the child be a ewe lamb?"

Mr. Bill Ballad waved his hand in the dark and did not deign to reply.

"The wedding," he said, "was to have been to-day. That is, if to-day is to-day, and not already to-morrow, which is hard to establish in the dark. Well, a certain young gentleman of romantical nature who was not acquainted with Miss Gremley, but who worships innocence and beauty, was so incensed by the affair when it came to his ears that he sought out this Heigh and pulled his nose for him."

"Had the young gentleman been drinking?" asked the stranger.

"He had," said Mr. Bill Ballad.

"And what happened?"

"They fought back of the green church—and Heigh fell."

"Good God!" cried the stranger, "dead?"

"I don't know," said Mr. Bill Ballad with a shudder. "He fell horribly, and I ran away."

"Then it was you?"

"It was," said Mr. Ballad.

"You risked your life for the happiness of a young woman whom you only knew by sight?"

"I had been drinking," said Mr. Ballad.

"I do not believe it," said the stranger strongly; "you are trying to make light of a wonderful and beautiful piece of chivalry."

"Call it that if you like," said Mr. Bill Ballad.

"I would like to shake your hand," said the stranger. Mr. Bill Ballad (himself somewhat moved by the recollection of his own wonderful and beautiful, if spirituous, chivalry) thrust forth a hand in the dark, and as suddenly drew it back.

"What is that?" he said.

"My petticoat," said the stranger.

"Who are you?" said Mr. Ballad.

"I am Miss Gremley—where are you going?"

"After the lantern," exclaimed Mr. Ballad. It took him half an hour of painful crawling, during which he did not swear once, to find it. He crawled back in triumph, and lighted it. Then he held it aloft.

"Let me look at you," he said. He looked long into a pair of round, gray, glimmering eyes.

"Forgive me," he said in a faltering voice, "for what I said about your parents."

"I forgive you," said Miss Gremley.

"Forgive me for having sworn so abominably."

"I forgive you."

"Forgive me for boasting about the—the Heigh business."

"I forgive you—and I shall not forget."

During all this time he had continued to hold the lantern aloft the better to look into the gray eyes. His arm now began to tremble violently with the tension on it, and he put down the lantern.

"You are very beautiful," he said.

"You also are pleasant to look at," said Miss Gremley.

"My life has not been handsome," said Mr. Ballad with emotion.

"That," said Miss Gremley, "I shall never believe."

"Did you run away because of—of Heigh?"

"Yes."

"Poor child," said Mr. Ballad.

"I am rich in my defender," said Miss Gremley.

"Miss Gremley," said Mr. Ballad, "I am far from wishing to take an advantage of you, but the bulkhead against which you are leaning is, as I know by dolorous experience, harder than jasper. If you would care to regard my arm as a sort of buffer, and not as a part of the human male anatomy, I could contrive to make you a little more comfortable."

She leaned forward without hesitation and back against his encircling arm.

211

And then, having blown out the lantern to save the oil, they sat in the dark, until Mr. Bill Ballad's arm had lost all sensation, save that of bliss, and a great craving for food had settled in them both. Then they relit the lantern and ate heartily and with laughter.

"It seems warmer," said Miss Gremley; "we must have made considerable s—southing."

"It is smoother also," said Mr. Ballad.

"How long do you suppose we have been in here?"

"Not more than ten minutes," said Mr. Ballad politely.

"I don't know why it should," said Miss Gremley, "but my head aches and I feel faint."

"The air in here must be pretty well used up by now," said Mr. Bill Ballad. "But I think we would best stick things out a little longer. If we've been beating to windward all this—I mean the ten minutes we have been in here—why, we cannot have got far, and I for one don't wish to be put ashore."

"What shall you do when we get to Jamaica?"

"I shall try very hard to play the man and to look after you," said Mr. Ballad. A pressure of the hand, unexpected and delicious, rewarded him, and unconsciously his right arm, which Miss Gremley had been told to regard as an inanimate buffer against hard woodwork, tightened.

"Does your head ache very much?" said Mr. Ballad, tenderly.

"Very," said Miss Gremley.

He shifted his right arm a little, and drew her close to him. His free hand sought her right cheek, and, very gently, he drew the aching little head down on his shoulder. He tipped his own head to the right so that his cheek rested against hers.

"Jus' a few more buffers," he said in a breaking voice. "Are you more comf'able?" She did not answer. She hung upon him limply. He laid his hand over her heart, but could not discern a single beat. . . .

Mr. Bill Ballad never knew how he found the hatchway of their prison so easily and flung it open. It was a work of seconds only. Fresh air and the light of day rushed in, and Miss Gremley revived all at once, just as primroses open in the cool of evening.

"Come," said Mr. Ballad, and he gave her his two hands to help her rise, "and we will go on deck . . . and do not forget that I shall take care of you. . . . Kiss me, My Heart, and put heart into me. . . ."

He took her in his arms, and, just as he made sure that she was only going to let him kiss her cheek, she smiled and put up her mouth like a little child.

"My love—my darling—my heart—my treasure— my comfort—my sweetheart—my—" began Mr. Ballad in a choking voice, but with the manful intention of saying all the pretty names he knew.

"Better come up," came a loud laughing voice down the hatchway.

The grinning and rosy face of Jemmy was seen to be looking down upon the lovers. They went on deck.

Mr. Bill Ballad rubbed his eyes and looked about him. Then he rubbed them again.

During his incarceration the vessel had not moved, and he beheld, blinking, the familiar wharves of his natal town. The wind had subsided, and the afternoon, blue and sweet, shimmered exquisitely.

Jemmy leaned against the foremast and roared with laughter. "The game's up!" exclaimed Mr. Bill Ballad, and, in spite of him, his voice shook.

"We don't seem to have made as much southing as I had supposed," said Miss Gremley.

"Jemmy," said Mr. Ballad, "why is this ship here and where is her crew?"

"This ship," said Jemmy, "has been set aside by the authorities to be coated with tar and burned as a naval spectacle to celebrate the fifth anniversary of the founding of the Fire Hose Company. The *Mallow* sailed with the tide."

"Did you know that I was stowing away on the wrong ship?" asked Mr. Ballad sternly.

"Why, yes," said Jemmy, "for I knew that if you got to Jamaica I would never see my watch again. . . .

Miss Gremley, shall we go ashore? You have nothing to fear."

"How about me?" said Mr. Ballad.

Jemmy pulled as long a face as he could.

"Eater of men, manslayer, criminal, jail-bird," he said sternly, "the pistols were loaded only with powder. It has also transpired that one of the legs upon which your late adversary stood to face you was of Spanish cork, fastened to the heroic stump of its flesh-and-blood predecessor by an exquisite arrangement of straps, pads and buckles. On receiving your fire, the hero seems to have flinched to such an extent that one of the straps broke. Hence the dreadful *suddenness* with which he came to the ground——"

"But," cried Mr. Ballad, delightfully agitated, "why then did he open and shut his mouth as if dying, and make such dreadful noises?"

"It seems," said Jemmy, "that his false, fluting and perjured teeth were also dislodged, and by him swallowed. They stuck in his throat and his life was despaired of until early this morning, when Dr. Scalpel, aided by Dr. Setit and a buttonhook, succeeded in fishing them up. They are not injured in the least. . . . My dear boy, the whole town is laughing, Mr. Heigh has rushed from among us, his fingers in his ears, like Christian in 'Pilgrim's Progress,' and as for you, there is not a single copy of your book to be had for love or money. The printers are sweating out a new edition of five thousand copies."

"The Age of Folly," said Mr. Bill Ballad.

"As for you, Miss Gremley," said Jemmy, "I perceive that our young friend has told you those things which are best to hear, and as for me, I shall declare a holiday and get drunk." They helped Miss Gremley into the skiff, and Jemmy set himself leisurely to the rowing.

As the skiff neared the shore, it was seen that Mr. Caruthers' long wharf was densely packed with people. From among them cheers, laughter and hats began to rise. . . .

"Do you by any chance feel sheepish?" said Miss Gremley.

"Not in the least," said Mr. Bill Ballad; "it has always been my heartfelt ambition to be a great man."

VIII

THE EXPLORERS

THE EXPLORERS

I

In my early youth I had vacillated between so many trades and professions that I grew up jack of all. But, strictly speaking, I became a discontented graduate of the Physicians and Surgeons, and began to establish a practice in East Eighteenth Street. Materially I prospered from the first, but mentally I was in a turmoil of other ambitions and desires. It was my tragedy to believe that I was a born forester, landscape-gardener sailor or soldier, and had elected to live in a city, like a rat in a hole, and minister to the sick. The longer I practised, the more sharply did I feel myself caught between the horns of dilemma; I had neither the money to turn back and recast my lines nor the will to go ahead and land my fishes. Then, as is usual with dilemmas, fate stepped in, or, rather, dropped at my door William Dane, the Arctic navigator and explorer, overcome by the June heat.

Even before he had come to his senses, I took to the man, and was engulfed by his personality. He had a head and face and mane like the stone lion of Lucerne, imperturbable and vast; hard, smooth, colossal limbs; a chest like a bay-window, and hands at once the largest and most beautiful that I have ever seen; a man formidable in thought and action. "This," said I to Miss Ma, my assistant, "is somebody."

"This is who it is," she said, and showed me on the first page of the morning paper, which I had not had the inclination to read, two pictures—a ship and a man.

While I continued to apply restoratives, Miss Ma gave me brief extracts from the article below the pictures, which was captioned:

"Captain Dane morally certain to find the North Pole"

"Was going to sail to-day," she said; "put it off because doctor gave out—fifteenth Arctic voyage—sixty years old—doesn't look forty, does he?"

"Why did the doctor give out?" I asked.

"Panic," said Miss Ma, and she went on: "Many answers to advertisements for doctor—applicants unsuitable on various scores—Captain Dane says he will sail without a doctor rather than with a narrow-chested one—says that nine-tenths of good Arctic work has been done by blond men with gray eyes."

Here Captain Dane himself interrupted, his transition from insensibility to alert mental equipoise being nearly instantaneous.

"Damn the heat, anyway!"

"I can't agree with you," said I, "since it has brought me so distinguished a patient."

"I hope to be more so," said he; "will you call me a cab? I won't risk the sun again."

"Please call a cab, Miss Ma."

"What is your fee, sir?" asked Captain Dane.

"Five dollars," said I, "but I would like to contribute that much to your voyage. We have been reading you up in the paper, while you were coming to."

"I won't prevent your contributing," said he, "if you want to; but five dollars is a great deal of money. Money is a devilish hard thing to collect."

"By the way," I said, "the paper says that you have advertised for a doctor."

"I have," said he, "but the right one doesn't turn up."

A general restlessness and dissatisfaction with life, particularly at the advent of the hot months, impelled me to say: "Would I do?"

"You are built right," he said; "you have light hair and gray eyes, and I see by your diploma that you are a graduate of the P. and S.; but you aren't sure that you want to go."

"How did you know that?" I asked.

"Because you didn't answer the advertisement."

"I didn't see it."

"If you had been keen to go," said he, "you wouldn't have missed it."

"Well," said I, "I wasn't keen to go, that's the truth. But I am now."

"Why?" said he.

"You've made me," I said; "you make me more so every time you speak. I'd like to serve under you."

"Doctor's billet," said he, "is the hardest of all. Even I can lie up if I fall sick, but the doctor can't. I don't even allow my doctors to die when they want to. Up there," he said, thumbing northward, "men go down on their knees and ask to be allowed to die. Some of them I have to let die, but never the doctor. Do you still want to go?"

"Yes," I said, stoutly.

"Well," said he, "I'll drive around to headquarters, and if nobody better has showed up, I'll send for you."

"Hold on," I said, "I'm not so low-spirited as that. You can take me or leave me, but I don't dangle on any man's waiting-list."

"That's better," said he, and his voice, hitherto very matter-of-fact, became abundantly hearty. "You'll do."

Then he made me sit down and write a long list of things to get and where to get them.

"Take a cab," he said, "and hustle."

"When do we sail?" said I.

"The minute you're aboard."

"Where's the ship?"

"Off Thirty-third Street in the North River. I call her *The Needle* because she points toward the pole. Have you many good-bys, much to arrange?"

"No," said I, "I'll turn my practice over to the doctor across the hall, give Miss Ma a month's wages; and that's about all."

"Have you no relatives—no entanglements?"

"None of the first," said I, "that matter—and none of the last, not even a professional one."

"Blessed are the pure in heart," said Captain Dane, "for they have strong bodies and leave no trail."

Three hours later we were steaming down the North River through the blistering June heat. Every flag on the river was dipped to us, and all the whistles were blown.

II

From the first I was more interested in Captain Dane than in Arctic phenomena; just as, in my profession, I was ever more alive to the bearing of the sick than to their diseases. To which habit, more than to any skill in medicine, or determination to succeed, I attribute the ease which I had had in attracting patients to my practice. But, furthermore, the North is too overwhelming and magical to be interesting: the gorgeous blazing of the sun through the ice, the aurora flaming in the heavens at night, the very shape of the bergs, running to every grotesque of form and every shade of astonishing color, even the atmosphere putting to scorn the clarity of crystals and the sparkle of diamonds, are too astonishing and remote to excite in a man any but his dumber faculties, whose voices are exclamations. No man is truly interested except when his mental processes are engaged in analysis—processes which the Northscape in its mildest moments defies. A time soon came when I was sick to death of those wasted glories, obdurate against the most fascinating rainbow or the most emphatic green of the sea. But Captain Dane held my keenest interest from the start.

Prior to our acquaintance I had often asked myself— or a friend for the sake of discussion—"Why the devil does a man want to discover the North Pole? What's the use of discovering it?" and the like—questions which, properly answered, would, I thought, bring to bear a great light on many occult workings of the human mind. If Dane had any finite reason which bound him to that grail, he would not give them frankly, or else they shifted from day to day. "It's been such an endless sacrifice of lives," I said to him once, and he answered whimsically: "That's just it."

"Let us," said he, "for the sake of argument, call the pole hunt a nonsensical quest, to which are sacrificed many lives that might in other walks of life be valuable. Well, it's up to some one to stop the drain." Here he named a mighty list of explorers who had lost their lives in the Arctic. "Many of them," he said, "were strong and talented men, devoted thinkers, and brave beyond compare. Until the pole is found there will continue to be lost to civilization a constant trickling of the most elect citizens. Wouldn't it be service enough to put a stop to such a waste as that—a waste that humanity cannot afford and ought not to endure?"

"It would turn the course of the adventurous south," said I.

"It would," said he, "toward the other pole. When that, too, has been discovered there will be an end of the nonsense."

"You don't think it nonsense?" said I.

"As an act, yes," he said; "as an accomplishment, no. The man who sets his country's flag on the pole will save, or rather divert into more useful channels, many splendid lives that come after his."

But on other occasions his arguments were all at variance with this.

"Is it for the glory of finding it," I asked him, "or for the glory of being known to have found it?"

"I shall be content to find it," he said, "and to die then and there. You can carry out the proofs, and reap the honors."

"But," said I, "dead or not, your name would go down to the remotest posterity in big type. Doesn't that thought influence you?"

"I think not," he said, "but I will think it over."

The log-book of *The Needle* gives all the longitudes and latitudes, and scientific observations and data, of our voyage. These things are not important to my narrative. Suffice that we passed the winter, the coldest, bleakest, blackest winter, farther north than it had ever been passed before, and in the spring made our dash for the pole. The winter brought out great qualities in Dane—an overmastering humor and good-humor, a great gentleness to those who were impatient and sick, an almost god-like tenderness over those that died. He was like a great statue in the making, when each blow of the sculptor's hammer, instead of damaging the marble, brings out new strengths and beauties. Even at that time, before our hardships had fairly begun, we looked on our Captain as on one who had brought us out rather than on one who was leading us in. The day for starting came, and Dane spoke to those who were to go and those who were to stay.

"Men," he said, "it is as hard to stay as to go. Therefore I have divided you equally, as boys choose sides for a game. It is important that brave, patient men go with me, and it is important that brave, patient men remain. I wish I could take only those that want to go and leave only those that want to stay. But you all want to go. So I have had to pick and choose for myself. I shall think of those that stay as of a rock that will wait for me to come. That's the important thing, to find you waiting when we come back. You must not let yourselves get sick; and you must not let yourselves think too much about home; and you mustn't quarrel when you begin to think there is nothing else to do. When you have waited for us as long as you can, then wait a little longer, and then go. God bless you all."

No one of us that went ever again saw those that stayed. We parted forever, with laughter and shaking of hands.

As long as things went well, strength held, and food tasted sweet, our dash for the pole had in it something of a holiday lark. The dogs, strong, savage, and eager, strained at the sledges, the men lent their backs to the passage of rough places with deep-sea unison. Our supplies were calculated to a nicety, and we knew it. We believed that the plateau (it was neither ice nor snow, but a mixture of the two, at once firm and crumbling like sand) over which we were pressing held all the way to the pole. And at each resting-place, when progress would be calculated, we marvelled and rejoiced to know how far and how fast we had gone. Strung out over the white plains in marching order, we looked like some grotesque turn in a circus—a quantity of bears walking on their hind legs, behaving exactly like men, and driving the trains of dogs. It was Dane's scheme that each man should have his turn in leading the procession; thus one day bringing responsibility to one man, the next to another. Great rivalry rose among us as to who should have the credit of leading the longest march. As we neared the pole, excitement and jubilation rose among us. We had but fifty miles to go; there had not yet been any serious hitch. The far north had shown us whatever favors it had to show. We vied in health with our dogs. And then—whether it came from Billy Smith's furs, bought during the winter from an Eskimo, or where it came from I do not know—there leapt among us a germ of smallpox. I only know that the disease broke out with awful savageness, that we went into permanent camp at the very gates of the pole, and began to die. Billy Smith was the first to go. Captain Dane knelt beside him for seven hours, exhorting him to stay and do his duty. But the flesh was weak with the sickness, and weepingly suffered the spirit to depart. Captain Dane's face was furrowed with ice where the tears had run down.

III

Captain Dane looked me steadily in the eyes across a new-made grave.

"Where are my brave, patient men?" said he.

228

"They have gone," I said, bitterly, "all gone. But God knows I tried to save them."

"At work they were lions," said he, "in obedience, lambs. Not one of them cursed me. Think of that, all you who deride the splendor of the human soul. They came to the gates of the pole, like sheep to the slaughter. I brought them. They said I was their father, and they came with me—Americans, Englishmen, Germans—they all came with me; and they died without cursing—all the nations."

It was horrible to hear the man rave on, his eyes bright with fever, his face set like a stone.

"You must lie down, Captain, and rest," I said.

"Will the fever go out of me if I lie down and rest?" said he. "My God, no! Do you think that with my mortal sickness on me, and the pole just over there, that I'm going to lie down and rest? I watched them all die. When they were taken sick I made them lie down. But there wasn't one of them but would have marched and fought one day more if I'd told him to. When I lie down to rest, the pole shall be under me."

I pleaded with him to lie down, to husband his strength, to fight with the fever. I swore to him that I would bring him through. He laughed in my face. And what could I do? He was stronger than five of me, and mad, to boot.

"Go back to *The Needle*," he said, "and tell them

that I went forward alone, and discovered the pole. Will you go back, or won't you?"

I do not wish to make myself out a hero. If wishing could have taken me back to *The Needle*, or thousands of miles beyond, back I would have gone. But to make that long journey alone, to drive dogs, in which I had no skill, or even to find the way, I knew to be impossible. For me there was nothing but death—death to go back, death to stay. I preferred, not cheerfully, but still decidedly, and all things considered, to take my quietus in the immediate vicinity of the pole.

"I won't go back," I said. "Let's find this—— —— pole, and have done with it."

"Man talk that," said Captain Dane. "It's this way, Johnny, if we give in here, these men's lives will have been wantonly sacrificed. But if we can reach the pole, and die there, then *they* won't have died in vain."

"Who's to know?" said I.

"The cold," said he, "will preserve our bodies immaculately. Some day they will be found at the pole, with the record of our journey, and our names, and the names of those who died for us. Let's along, boy."

Then began a horrible nightmare that lasted seven days. Captain Dane, all broken out with the smallpox, and delirious with fever, trudged over the plain, laughing, shouting, moaning. Wild words poured from his deluded brain, and yet the idea that he must and would go forward, and his senses for direction and finding the line, by observations or calculating and the deviation of the needle from the true pole to the magnetic, never once forsook him. I think that all that was mortal of him died before we reached the end of our journey, and was dragged forward by his immortal soul.

We struck at length into a region that bore marks of terrific winds. For in many places the black bed-rock was naked and bare of ice or snow. As we progressed, the expanses of smooth, naked rock prevailed more and more in the scape, until, on the morning of the eighth day, all traces of ice and snow vanished. Here I first began to be sensible of difficulty, not altogether the result of fatigued muscles, in lifting my feet, which increased from hour to hour. Each of us carried a compass, and I noticed that the needle in mine was beginning to act in a queer, uncertain manner—like a hound that finds a trail, steadies to it a moment, and then loses it. Obviously, we were about to arrive. If I took any mental interest in the fact, it was a feeling of disappointment.

Some point ahead of that black rocky plain over which we were plodding, with feet that seemed to stick like plasters to the rock, was the great goal of explorers. There was nothing to mark it. It might be on a rise or in a depression. Measurements alone could mark it for us. There would be nothing to give one single moment of ante-mortem excitement to the eye. I was wrong.

We climbed painfully up a little ridge of rock, perhaps a dozen feet high. On the further slope lay seven corpses wrapped in fur.

"Here we are, Johnny," said Captain Dane suddenly. There was a complete sanity in his voice. And he fell to examining the corpses. As for me, I simply sat down and watched him. I was terribly tired, and did not want to die.

"My God!" cried the captain, "here's an old-timer. He drew a slip of sheepskin from the dead man's glove. "I don't make out the name," he went on; "but there's a date—August 9, 1798. This man discovered the pole, Johnny; take off your hat. And the others came after. Where's the last—here's the last—'98—1898. That was the year Jamie graduated. I belong next to him. Here goes."

Captain Dane laid himself down by the side of that last comer with a sigh, like that of a tired little child gathered into its mother's arms, and when I got to him he was dead.

I had, I think, no feeling of sorrow, or loneliness; I felt neither thirst nor hunger. I sat soddenly among the discoverers, and nodded my head. I sat for hours nodding my head. It nodded of its own accord, like the heads of those Chinese toys you buy on Twenty-

third Street. Then a shadow covered me, and it stopped
nodding. I sprang to my feet, wildly alert, and looked
upward.

Twenty feet above and slowly descending was a balloon; over the edge of the car peered a face, a tiny,
brown, man-monkey sort of face. A little fur paw
shot up to the face, salute fashion, and a shrill voice
called:

"*Salut!*"

The balloon came to earth, and a little Frenchman
hopped out (for all his great bundle of furs he actually
hopped).

"Is your party all asleep?" said he (this time in
French-English).

"No," said I, "all these are dead. They are men
who have discovered the pole at different times, and
died, and with each the news of his discovery. I was
this man's doctor—Captain Dane. He died of—"

A horrible fear seized me that if I said smallpox the
Frenchman would desert me. But he uncovered the
Captain's face and saw for himself.

"Smallpox," said he. "That is ghastly—what?"

He hopped into the car of his balloon and hopped out
with a kodak between his fur paws. He focussed the
thing on the dead man, made ready to press the button,
and suddenly desisted.

"Not nice," he said, "to kodak those brave, dead

fellows. Well, it is all very disappointing. Let us be off."

"You will take me?" I said.

"My God! of course," said he.

The little man bowed gravely and stood aside with many polite gestures while I climbed painfully into the car. He followed me with a single hop—like a flea.

"All my ingenuity go for nothing," said he; "all the cold and wind I have swallowed go for nothing. We come too late, the little balloon and I. . . ."

He threw out some blocks of ice that he had for ballast, the balloon began to tug at its braces, and presently to rise.

"Higher up," said the little Frenchman, "is more wind. Once up there we shall leave in a great hurry. . . . Farewell the dead heroes. . . ."

I heard no more. When I came to, we had left the pole a thousand miles behind and were scudding southward.

IX

THE LITTLE HEIRESS; OR, THE HUNTED LOOK

THE LITTLE HEIRESS; OR, THE HUNTED LOOK

I

The little heiress had a hunted look. And it was not the hunted look of the girl who is hunted for herself alone. Nor the hunted look that the hunted wears in full flight when the chance of capture is balanced by the chance of escape. Under fair conditions (had she been worth but one million, or even two), she might, like the nimble jack-rabbit of her native plains, have furnished rare sport. From two hounds, or even half a dozen, she might then have run like a ghost, foreseeing the strategy of their pursuit, doubling and dodging to confuse it, and vanishing finally, with a burst of speed and a joyous laugh. But she was weighted in the race by many more millions than two. On the day of her birth the first million had come to her in the form of a cheque, the signature in her grandfather's trembling and honored hand. On the envelope enclosing it he had written in the same trembling hand: "A Nest Egg, for Baby."

But after that the millions came to her in sad ways
and with sad words. First the heart that most loved
her ceased to beat, and the busy fingers that had vied
with Paris and Flanders in sewing for the baby were
still. And they gave the baby more millions, but for a
long time could not dry her eyes. When she was ten
the old grandfather died, and though they gave her
banks, and ranches, and oil wells and mines, she cried
for him. And after that she became the one flower in
the heart of a stern gray man who owned many gardens.
Him she loved with all her strength, and called *My*
father with immeasurable pride. Even governesses and
music masters faded before his iron will. She would
be snatched from her French lesson to flash across the
continent in a "special." In the midst of spelling,
likely as not at that very awkward word *phthisis*, would
come one in buttons and pride to say "would Miss
please be ready to ride with her father in twenty minutes." Then she would so hurry to be ready in time
that her cheeks would flush scarlet, and breeched and
booted she would clatter down the marble stair, and
appear before her father, gasping and speechless.
Sometimes, but after more preparation, they would ride
for days into the mountains, and always at evening
come suddenly in some wild place upon white tents, a
chef in his cap and apron, hot water to bathe in, brass
and linen beds to sleep in, a bearded demigod in a broad

felt hat to lift the weary little heiress from her horse, the smell of cooking to make her hungry, the mountain air to make her sleepy, and the exertion and admiration of all the world to make her glad. When the little heiress rode with her father into the mountains she carried a rifle, and on the stock she had burnt with a red-hot hat-pin A (for antelope) B (for bear) D (for deer) and L (for lion), but there were no notches after these letters, and sometimes when the Little Heiress came to be hunted herself she thought of this, and was glad. Though there were never any little girls for her to play with, she was not very different from the general run of them. When she ran furiously she got red in the face, when she fell down and bumped her nose it bled, when her garters broke her stockings came down; when she was thwarted she flew into a passion, and when her stomach ached she howled. The heavy millions had not yet begun to weigh her down. It may be that there were not enough. But many more were on the way, and, as before, to pay her for the death of somebody she loved. She waited up one Christmas Eve till very late for her father to come home. He had telegraphed that he would come. He would come, the secretary told her, over his pet railroad in his pet car with his pet engineer at the throttle, and he would make such time that the country would gasp. But the great man came home more slowly than had been expected, and in a conveyance in which he had never ridden before. He came feet first into the big house, carried by soft moving men in high silk hats, and he rode in a plain black coffin with silver handles. But they would not let the Little Heiress look at his face, and she learned somehow—from one of the servants, I think—that "fire had added to the horror of the accident."

But to comfort her there came the old man who was her father's lawyer, and he made her a present of the railroad that had killed her father, and other railroads, and other things, too many and too valuable to mention. He gave her this million and that—may be a hundred of them and more—but she could not be comforted. Nor did it comfort her, during the ten minutes in which the Bishop consigned the dust which was her father unto the dust of which he had been made, to know that all the locomotives of all the trains of all the railroads of all the United States stood still upon their rails during those ten minutes, and that all the travellers and engineers and conductors and brakemen and train boys in all the trains spoke of her father in low voices, and honored his memory, and said how great he had been.

Thus all those who really loved the Little Heiress passed out of her life, and she was taken to live with her father's sister, Aunt Katharine, who learned to love her after a while. Aunt Katharine and her husband lived when their household was stationary in one of several

houses. They had two white ones, made of marble—
one that stood on a corner and looked over Central
Park, in New York City, and one that was in Newport
and looked over the ocean. There was a red brick
house with white trimmings in London, and an old
house made of wood in Westchester, which Aunt Katharine's husband called "Home" and which they visited
for a week every year in the spring time; and they had
another wooden house, very new and comfortable, in a
little southern town called Aiken. And they had a
brown stone house with battlements in the city where
the Little Heiress had been born, but they only lived in
that when they had to "on business." But although
Aunt Katharine had so many pleasant homes to go to,
she was happiest when she was travelling. And some
people thought that she was not very happy then; and
everybody knew that she never went to Paris. And
even the Little Heiress knew why. Aunt Katharine's
little boy had died in Paris. That was why. He had
taken the scarlet fever, in London probably, and on the
way to Paris he had come down with it. And Aunt
Katharine had driven all over Paris with him, looking
for a bed to put him in. But that cold rainy day there
were no beds to be had in Paris; no, not for the million
francs that Aunt Katharine could have drawn her
cheque for. She tried the hotels, and they would not
have the sick boy; she tried to hire a house, but the

landlords feared the sick boy like grim death. And Aunt Katharine became desperate, and lied, and said that her little boy had a bad cold, nothing more; but nobody believed her, and all the doors were closed in her face. Finally the hack driver understood how matters lay and turned them out of his hack. And after that Aunt Katharine carried her little boy from house to house in her arms. And when her strength gave out she sat with him in a doorway, and called on the passers-by for mercy, just as if she had been a woman of the streets. There she sat in her sables, with pearls as big as cherries round her neck inside of her dress, and others in her ears, and wonderful rings on her fingers, and many bank-notes in her purse; but she was the poorest woman in Paris because she could not buy a bed for the little boy who lay drenched and burning in her lap.

Aunt Katharine had rung the bell of the door before which she sat, but it was a long time before the bell was answered; and when the door did open, and a woman's voice said, "What is the matter?" Aunt Katharine had lost all hope and could not answer. Then the woman who belonged to the voice took the little boy out of Aunt Katharine's lap and carried him into the house. The Little Heiress could never find out just what kind of a woman she was, or what kind of a house she lived in. She gathered only that she had never been a very good woman until she took the little boy into her house and laid him in her own bed to die, and nursed him and prayed over him. But that had made a very good woman of her—almost a saint. And she lived with Aunt Katharine now, and was her maid Thérèse; only she was never allowed to do any hard work, and Aunt Katharine loved her like a sister. She had refused Aunt Katharine's money and her pearls (that was after the little boy died), but she had gone on her knees to Aunt Katharine and begged her for honest employment and a chance to be good.

So it was the death of the little boy that prevented Aunt Katharine from being absolutely happy, and it was the coming of the Little Heiress to live with her that kept her from being absolutely sad. Indeed, as the Little Heiress grew older and wiser, Aunt Katharine grew younger and happier. And, of course, when they met in the middle they were the same age—seventeen—and loved each other dearly.

II

The Little Heiress had a hunted look. All the afternoon she had been hunted with cards and cut flowers. And now she was being hunted by the phalanx of shirt-fronts. Turn where she would a shirt-front blocked her path, and the slow-moving phalanx drove her into it from behind. But she, preferring to fall to the lot of the pack, would turn back and be surrounded by it. To matrons and girls less fortunate than the Little Heiress there would appear moving from one part of the ball-room to another a phalanx of black backs. Then it would stop and open to let forth the Little Heiress and the shirt-front with which she had agreed to dance; and the black backs, pivoting, would show white fronts and above them pairs of eyes that followed the progress of the Little Heiress in the dance. As a rule she looked very little and like a child against the man with whom she was dancing, and when it was time to tell him that she could not sit out the next dance with him in the conservatory, she had to turn up her face to him to do so. And then she looked so little, and so sweet and enticing, just the way a pansy looks, that, as one man, the phalanx ground its teeth. And the eyes belonging to the shirt-fronts tried to catch her eyes as she drifted past, and brains belonging to the shirt-fronts tried to calculate in just what part of the room she would be when the music stopped. And the phalanx, having calculated, would scatter and reform about the Little Heiress when she stopped dancing.

"If I were poor," she thought to herself, "there might be a man or two waiting for me (she had just seen her face, that was so like a pansy, in a long mirror), but now it has to be just shirt-fronts." And the Little Heiress sighed as the phalanx closed about her. She did not even look at the ring of faces above the ring of shirt-fronts; for she knew very well what faces were there; and more, she knew what face was not. The face that the Little Heiress liked to look at was rather a proud young face, that kept itself apart from the phalanx. When the man who owned the face thought that it was his duty to dance with the Little Heiress he would cut through the phalanx as a yacht cuts through water, and ask her. And she would be ready for him with her gladdest smile; just such a smile as the beautiful lady wore when the hero rescued her from the horrible sea monster. But gladdest smiles, and the little hand on his arm, made very little impression on Proud Face. When, for hospitality received, or any reason as good, it was his duty to ask her to dance, he asked her; when it was not his duty, he didn't. And there the matter rested. But when the Little Heiress did get a chance to dance with Proud Face she lost her hunted look. Twice, three times round the great room; the back of her neck ached a little with looking up at Proud Face, and her lips trembled a little, perhaps because they smiled at him so much. But she felt that she could go on dancing with him, and turning up her face to look at him—forever. "He won't ask me again to-night," sighed the Little Heiress to herself, "so don't stop, music—don't stop."

But the music stopped, and Proud Face, conducting

the Little Heiress to Aunt Katharine (and the advance guard of the approaching phalanx), bowed and said it had been a pleasure, and left her. Then the hunted look came back to her, and before she could smile upon her tormentors she had to deal with a restless tear.

"My dear," said Aunt Katharine, "somebody has put his foot through your gown."

"It was that clumsy man," said the Little Heiress, in her clear voice of a little child, and she pointed to one of the shirt-fronts. The face above the shirt-front reddened and began to mumble. But the Little Heiress broke into her clear laugh of a little child, for, though she could not escape from the hounds, she dearly loved to tease and to annoy them.

"You had better go to Thérèse," said Aunt Katharine, "and get her to put in a stitch."

The Little Heiress had seen Proud Face leave the room, and she thought that if she hurried she might overtake him on his way to the smoking-room, and—just overtake him and pass him, and that would be all. But she had not noticed that one of the shirt-fronts had detached himself from the phalanx and left the room by the same door.

"I'll go at once," said the Little Heiress. In her eagerness she forgot that she was no longer a little child and, the long, torn flounce of her dress streaming behind, she danced across the polished floor, a flash of pink, a twinkle of pink slippers, and vanished.

But she was not in time to catch up with Proud Face. And, beyond a shirt-front that suddenly blocked her way, she saw him lift the portière of the smoking-room and pass in.

"How you frightened me," said the Little Heiress swallowing her disappointment.

"I'm sorry," said the shirt-front.

"Forgiven then," said the Little Heiress, and she made to pass.

"Give me a minute. I *must* speak to you."

"To me?" said the Little Heiress, and she looked straight up into the eyes of shirt-front, and saw that he was one of those who had proposed to her before.

"Can't you change your mind," he said, "*dear?*"

"Often—often," said the Little Heiress. "But not my heart—but not my heart."

"Give me a chance," said shirt-front. "Give me a little hope. You know I love you. I love you with my whole heart and soul." But there was no more passion or conviction in shirt-front's voice than in a parrot's. There was neither hunger nor longing.

"A chance!" said the Little Heiress. "I give you the whole wide world in which to make a name for yourself. I give you a will to keep you straight——"

"Then you do care for me," said shirt-front, though

the remarks of the Little Heiress were not meant to be so construed.

"I!" cried the Little Heiress. And she meant to say no more. But shirt-front's words had carried to her clear nostrils a smell of drink, and she lost her temper. "I—when I love," said the Little Heiress, "will love a man."

"And what am I but a man?"

"You," she cried, "you are a shirt-front."

His face flushed and throbbed with fury.

"You will live to repent your words," he said.

"I shall more likely live to repeat them," said the Little Heiress. She escaped and ran up the stairs.

"Why are you out of breath?" said Thérèse.

"Because I ran," said the Little Heiress. "Look—" Thérèse knelt at the Little Heiress's feet and began to sew the torn flounce to its place. "First I ran after a man," panted the Little Heiress, "and then I ran away from a shirt-front."

"Why?" asked Thérèse.

"The first," said the Little Heiress, "because *I* was covetous, the second because *he* was."

"Is covetous, coveted?" asked Thérèse.

"No," said the Little Heiress. "But which do you mean——"

"*Miss* Covetous, I mean," said Thérèse, "who else?"

248

"No," said the Little Heiress, "she is not coveted."
And she sighed. . . .

"It is finished," said Thérèse.

"Thank you," said the Little Heiress. "Tell me
that I look like new."

"You look like a flower," said Thérèse.

"Like a pansy?" said the Little Heiress in a coaxing
voice.

"Like a pansy," said Thérèse.

The Little Heiress laughed her clear laugh of a little
child. But she went slowly down the stair, and had a
hunted look.

Just as she reached the foot of the stair, however,
Proud Face came out of the smoking-room.

"You!" said the Little Heiress.

"I," said Proud Face.

"I've been to be mended," said the Little Heiress.
"What have you been doing?"

"I have been smoking," said Proud Face, "and
losing money at cards; and now I am going to thank
your aunt for a delightful evening."

"But it's so very early," said the Little Heiress.

"Not for me," said Proud Face. "You see, I belong to a great banker, and if I oversleep he will get
somebody else to stand in my shoes."

"Let him," said the Little Heiress, defiantly.

"And if I did," said Proud Face, "who would pay

249

brother's expenses through college, and who would keep the wolf from mother's door?" Proud Face smiled at the Little Heiress.

"I should think if you need money so badly," said the Little Heiress, and, although she was only perpetrating a joke, she blushed at certain thoughts which it roused in her, "I should think that you would rather stay up town and try to marry me. Lots of men do."

"*Men?*" queried Proud Face.

"Shirt-fronts," corrected the Little Heiress.

Proud Face laughed.

"I've no doubt it would be very pleasant," he said.

The Little Heiress turned a fiery, a defiant red.

"Try it," she said.

"Princess," said Proud Face gravely—sometimes he called her Princess in a mocking voice—"turn your face to the light and let me look at you."

She turned her face obediently to the light and her lips quivered.

"I see," he said very gently, "I see." And he stood a while in thought.

The Little Heiress turned her face away from the light.

"You do see?" she said in a voice that was barely audible, "you do?"

"Is it bad," he said, "very bad?"

250

THE LITTLE HEIRESS

The Little Heiress took his hand and placed it over her heart. He could feel the heart beating and fluttering against it like a distracted bird.

"What does my heart say?" she whispered. "What does my heart say?"

"But if I don't love you?" said Proud Face.

"I will make you," said the Little Heiress. She reached up her little hands to his big shoulders.

"I love you with all my heart and soul," she said. Her slim body rocked and she held fast by his shoulders. "I'll give you the truest heart that ever beat for a man," she said.

But it was in Proud Face's mind to shock her love to the death.

"And how many millions will you give me?" he asked.

"All that I have," she said.

"And how many have you?"

"How many shot are there in a load?" asked the Little Heiress. "How many roses in a rose house? How do I know."

Proud Face stood in thought.

"I tried to offend you," he said.

"But how could you succeed?" said the Little Heiress. "I love you."

Visions of ease and plenty assailed Proud Face.

"I don't love you," he said after a time, "but I will be good to you."

"You will *love* me," said the Little Heiress, "I will make you."

She stood upon the tips of her little pink slippers.

"Take that to your mother," she said, "and say I sent it."

.   .   .   .

"Mother—mother!" It was not Proud Face, but Shame Face, that knocked upon his mother's door.

"Come in."

His mother lay in her bed reading.

"Mother," he said, and again, "mother!"

"What has happened, my dear?"

"I am going to marry the Little Heiress, mother."

She looked him in the face for a long time.

"Do you love her, my dear?"

Shame Face buried his face in the bedclothes and sobbed aloud.

.   .   .   .

But there was nothing shamefaced about the Little Heiress. And she returned to the ball-room almost blazing with beauty. And as the shirt-fronts of the phalanx closed about her, her eyes shone with a wonderful proud light and she cried in her clear voice of a little child:

"I am all mended, now—gentlemen!"

252

III

The Little Heiress had a hunted look. Never since congratulations were invented were any so cold as those which she received. The very night of the ball, after she found that sleep would not close her eyes, she got up and, regardless of anybody that might see her, ran down the hall in her night gown and knocked at Aunt Katharine's door. Aunt Katharine was sound asleep, but she waked up and made room at her side for the shivering Little Heiress. When the Little Heiress had stopped shivering she hid her face in the pillows (because there was a night light in the room), and told Aunt Katharine that she was going to be married.

"To whom?" asked Aunt Katharine, with fear and suspicion in her voice, for she had been terribly afraid all along that some undeserving, fortune-hunting shirt-front would capture the Little Heiress. The Little Heiress said to whom; and at first Aunt Katharine gave a little sigh of relief, for he was a great favorite with her, but then she began to feel suspicious even of him, and after sliding her arm about the Little Heiress and giving her a hug, she said:

"Are you sure he loves you?"

The Little Heiress had been preparing herself for that question; but her preparation went for nothing because when it came to the point she could not lie.

"I love *him*," she said, "with all my heart and soul, and I got him alone in the hall and told him so, and asked him to marry me. I told him that I would make him love me, if he would marry me, and finally he said he would."

"Does he love *you?*"

"No, but he's going to; I'm going to make him. Didn't any man ever tell you that if you would only marry him he would *make* you love him?"

Aunt Katharine was made very miserable by what she had heard, but she laughed.

"Dozens of men have said that to me," said the Little Heiress, "dozens."

"But, dearie," said Aunt Katharine, "your uncle and I won't hear of your engaging yourself to a man who doesn't love you."

"Why?" said the Little Heiress. "He's poor and loveless, and I give him love and millions. If *I* were a man, and he were a girl, everybody would say 'how beautiful!'"

"Not if the girl didn't love the man," said Aunt Katharine. "The man would be buying her."

"I want him," said the Little Heiress, "why shouldn't I buy him?"

"Because you wouldn't want a man that could be bought."

"But I do," said the Little Heiress. "And besides, he's going to love me."

"Until that happens," said Aunt Katharine, "there mustn't be any talk of engagements. I won't hear of it."

"Nonsense!" said the Little Heiress. Neither of them spoke for some time. The Little Heiress began to get very sleepy.

"Are *you* sleepy?" she asked.

"I don't feel as if I should ever sleep again."

"I am," said the Little Heiress. She drew her knees up and made herself very comfortable.

"It's beginning to be daylight," said the Little Heiress. "When I get up I'll have breakfast, and then I'll go see his mother, and ask for his hand in marriage."

"You'll do no such thing," said Aunt Katharine.

"I will," said the Little Heiress.

Then there was another silence.

"Aunt Katharine—" The Little Heiress's voice was very sleepy.

"What?"

"I shall always be very good to him."

Aunt Katharine set her mouth firmly and did not deign to answer.

"I shall find out when his birthday is and give him a railroad."

255

"You'll be sent to a lunatic asylum if you're not careful."

"Nonsense!"

Another long silence.

"Aunt Katharine——"

"What?"

"Nothing." . . .

When she had had her breakfast, for she was up by eleven o'clock that morning, the Little Heiress wrote notes to all the men who had ever proposed to her, and told them that she was going to be married. The notes were all exactly alike, and she wrote them as fast as she could. Except for the different names at the beginning of each note, they were like this—spelling included:

—— Because you often say you have my happiness at heart, I tell you as fast as I can that I am happy for allways now, and going to be married to the best man God ever made, and live with him allways and be happy. I hope that you will allways be happy. And that everybody will——

Then she went to see his mother.

"Please say," she burst out with, "that you don't mind my marrying your son. I love him so, and I will be a good daughter to you, and a good wife to him always. Did he give you the kiss I sent you? And may I give you another, please? I want to kiss everybody and everything that belongs to him."

His mother's eyes were full of tears.

"Dear child," she said, and she folded the Little Heiress to her heart, "you mustn't think of marrying him."

"Just what my aunt says," said the Little Heiress. "But why—but why?"

"He doesn't love you," said his mother.

"But he will," said the Little Heiress, "I will make him."

"He is going to you this afternoon to say that he cannot marry you."

"Nonsense!" said the Little Heiress, but she turned white at the thought. "There are law courts, and suits for breach of promise," She laughed. But his mother didn't laugh.

"I don't know why he doesn't love you," she said. "I wish to heaven he did. I do."

"Do you?" cried the Little Heiress. "Oh! I love you for loving me. And by and by he will love me for loving him. He must; mustn't he must?"

It was Saturday, which the Little Heiress had forgotten, and just as she had spoken the door opened and in *he* came.

"Oh," he said.

"Oh," said the Little Heiress. And his mother left them. He was no longer Shame Face, but Proud Face again.

"I have told our engagement to everybody I could," said the Little Heiress.

"You haven't," said he.

"I have," she said.

"Don't tell me," he said, "that you meant what you said last night."

"Mean it!" cried the Little Heiress. "Why am I here but to tell your mother that I love you, and ask her permission to marry you, and say that I will be a good daughter to her?"

"Is that why you are here?"

"Yes."

"What did she say?"

"She threw me down—she threw me down," said the Little Heiress. "But it's a poor love that shies at opposition."

"She was right."

"She was wrong. And you haven't seen me for hours, and you have promised to marry me, and you ought to come forward and kiss me."

He came forward smiling, but a little distressed.

"Wait," said the Little Heiress. "Is it to be all for my pleasure and none for yours? Do you want to kiss me?"

"I think," said Proud Face, "that I can go so far as to say that I do." He came still further forward.

258

"Wait," she said. "Last night—did you want to kiss me?"

He thought carefully.

"Not exactly, I think," he said.

"But *now* you want to," cried the Little Heiress triumphantly. "That's something—that's something. Oh! my dear love."

In spite of himself the kiss thrilled Proud Face to the heart.

"And what," said the Little Heiress, "is all this talk of me giving you up? I won't."

"How old are you?" said Proud Face.

"I am seventeen," said the Little Heiress. "But I look younger, and I know my own mind, if that's what you mean."

"It's like robbing a cradle," said Proud Face.

But the Little Heiress turned up her face, which was so like a pansy, to him, and there was an immense seriousness in her eyes.

"My God!" began Proud Face with a kind of sob in his voice, but he could not go on, and he said, "My God!" again.

"How are you going to help loving me," cried the Little Heiress, "when I love you so. Tell me. Are you *trying* to help it?"

Proud Face thought for a moment, and then he smiled.

"Perhaps I *am* trying," he said.

"But you mustn't try *not*," said the Little Heiress. "You must try *to*. Think how happy you will be when you do."

"I am not worthy," said Proud Face, "to kiss the dust on your little shoes. May I?"

"If you do," said the Little Heiress, "I will kiss the dust on yours."

IV

"If I come to see you," wrote Proud Face to the Little Heiress, "you will hypnotize me and I won't be able to say what I mean. Can I tell you to your face that I do not love you, and, not loving you, cannot, will not marry you? No. Not to your lovely face. Do you think it is easy to write it? And to confess that I am a fool? Sure anybody but a fool would love you, and most of the fools, too, as I think. But this fool doesn't. Hate me—hate me! Hate me!"

And the Little Heiress wrote back:

"I draw the line at any further humiliation. I give you up. Give my love to your stubborn heart. Think of me kindly if you can. We shall not see each other any more, except by accident. I can't think of any more to say. Good-by." . . .

Though this answer was what Proud Face told himself he had hoped for, it came to him as something of a shock. There were not, after all, so many flowers in the garden of his life that he cared to have the Little Heiress lifted from it, roots and all, and set in some other garden beyond the wall, where he could not even see her any more. All that day, and for many days, he would have in the midst of his work a sudden sinking feeling, and would realize after a moment or two that he was thinking of the Little Heiress and how that she was gone out of his life forever. He was not the least little bit angry with her for having first announced the engagement, and then the disengagement. He met the looks of his friends with an unabashed look, and nobody dared ask him questions. But in his heart he was ashamed, humiliated and troubled; and he did not do his work properly, and he felt his ambitions slipping away from him. He felt obliged, too, not to go any more into society for fear that he would meet the Little Heiress, and make her uncomfortable.

Meanwhile the shirt-fronts gathered once more about the Little Heiress and beset her goings and her comings with attentions. But she seemed an easier and more willing prey than formerly. When this shirt-front or that talked to her of love she listened as if she enjoyed listening, and she was always willing to sit out a dance, and was always "at home" when the shirt-fronts called, and she adorned herself with selections from the flowers that they sent her, and she gave this shirt-front her gloves to hold and did not ask them back, and her fan to that shirt-front, and her most inviting smiles to them all. And all the shirt-fronts believed that it could not be long before she would engage herself to one of them. And each shirt-front thought in his heart of hearts that it might be to him. For, very wickedly, she encouraged each one whenever she had the chance.

"I will make you love me," one would say.

"If you only can," the Little Heiress would answer earnestly.

"If you'll only give me the chance."

"Now is the chance."

But the suddenness of the opportunity always found the shirt-front unprepared and left him stuttering before the sweet gravity and readiness-to-be-made-to-love of the Little Heiress. Something of the Little Heiress's flirtations—heaven alone knows how—came to the knowledge of Proud Face. It may be that where she was concerned his mind was superhumanly alert. It may be that his mother heard things and hinted at them. Anyway, it was constantly in his thoughts that she was playing fast and loose with her chances of happiness, and, for none knew her impulsiveness and rashness better than Proud Face, might readily, because of pique and disappointment and general head-strongness, turn deliberately down some path that would lead to nothing but misery. "Ah," thought he, "if I only loved her." And, though he did not love her, yet whenever he thought of the two kisses she had given him (which was often), he wished that he did, and whenever he stopped thinking of them (which was seldom), he felt sad and disjointed.

Very late one night, as he was walking home from an usher's dinner, full of discontent, he passed by Aunt Katharine's house, and, looking up the shimmering marble face of it, saw that in the windows of one of the corner rooms there were still lights. "The Little Heiress is still up," he thought, and he stood in the shadow of a lamp-post and watched the lights. It seemed to him that not for a long time had he been in any employment that was so pleasant. He hoped that the lights would not soon be put out. The night was sweet and fresh and warm. The city was silent. Peace was upon it, and, above, the stars. Proud Face stood on and on, in the shadow of the lamp-post and still the lights burned in the corner windows.

The voices of the bronze-throated bells began suddenly to sound in the church steeples. But the silence returned. . . . Again the bells rang; and back came the silence, and the lights in the corner windows still shone.

"But they must go soon," thought Proud Face, "soon."

And with that, just as if they had been waiting for a signal, out went the lights.

Then Proud Face realized that he was tired and cold. But for a moment or two longer he kept his sad eyes upon the windows.

"They want me to take the California branch," he thought." Everybody wants me to, Mamma wants me to—and I think that I must—now that the lights are out—out. Oh," he thought bitterly, "there is nothing for me—nothing."

His shadow separated from the shadow of the lamp-post, and his steps rang in the street.

The next morning he accepted the California branch, and began his preparations for the long journey.

V

Whether or not a little bird told the Little Heiress that Proud Face was going to shake the dust of New York from his feet is unknown. It may be that any news concerning him was just a part of the air that she breathed. It doesn't matter. She learned that he was to go, and after that managed very quickly to learn when and how. Then she wrote him a note.

"Don't go without saying good-by. If you could come Satur-day at three. You start Saturday at five, don't you? Could you come then? I'd like to wish you good luck to your face."

THE LITTLE HEIRESS

When Proud Face came (Saturday at exactly three), he found the Little Heiress expecting him. She was hatted and gloved to go out, and she had a hunted look.

"So it's good-by," said Proud Face, "and good luck."

"Yes," said the Little Heiress. "But why did you stand so long and look up at my window—the other night?"

"Oh," said Proud Face, and he blushed.

"I watched you watch," said the Little Heiress, "until I thought it couldn't be good for you to stand so long in the night, and then I put out the lights, and you went away."

"Yes," said Proud Face, "and then I went away."

"And now you go on a journey. And I," said the Little Heiress, "go to walk in the Park."

"Alone?" said Proud Face, and he tried to smile.

"Alone," said the Little Heiress. "For you—all good things—all good luck. You'll not be coming back soon?"

"Not soon," said Proud Face. And he felt as if he were ringing the bells at his own funeral.

"Are you going alone?" asked the Little Heiress.

"Alone?" Proud Face did not understand.

"Are you going with gladness, I mean."

"Oh!" said Proud Face, "alone—so far as gladness goes."

"Shall we say good-by?" said the Little Heiress.

"Yes," said Proud Face. His voice was very gentle and tired. "Good-by."

"Do you feel a little wretched, too?" said the Little Heiress.

"Oh, yes," said Proud Face simply. "And," he faltered, "will you write to me when—you find happiness? There's an old absurd word, 'rejoice,'" he went on, "I would *rejoice* to hear that you were happy."

"Me? Happy?" said the Little Heiress, and she sighed.

"Don't," said Proud Face, "I can't bear it."

"Between us," said the Little Heiress, "there must always be good wishes."

She held up her face that was so like a pansy, a sad pansy, to Proud Face, and they kissed. The Little Heiress trembled a little; for she knew that she had shot her last bolt.

Presently, very shyly, she looked at Proud Face, and she found that he was beaming on her like the sun. His face was like a boy's; like the face of a prisoner that has been freed; like a demi-god's.

"Oh!" said the Little Heiress, "oh!" And then, very timidly, she said, "shall you go now?"

"Now!" said Proud Face, in a voice that rang like a bell. "I shall not go."

"When?" said the Little Heiress.

THE LITTLE HEIRESS

"Never," said Proud Face.

"Oh," said the Little Heiress. "They will say I have bought you."

"Not with millions," said Proud Face; "with loveliness."

"Oh," said the Little Heiress, "say it was the kisses—the three kisses. It was on those that I staked my all."

"I don't believe," said Proud Face, "that the kisses had anything to do with it. I think it was just you—just you. But I'm going to find out."

"Are you?" cried the Little Heiress, and she dodged him.

Aunt Katharine was surprised to find them on opposite sides of a big table. The Little Heiress still had a hunted look, but it was an entirely new kind.

X

THE BEST MAN

THE BEST MAN

I

Stanislas Odeskalki, the best man, and O'Gosh, the interpreter, helped, as did old man Openta. But Orloff Openta and Olenka were really married by the mayor. He made Orloff kiss Olenka; shook hands with them; said that he hoped they would be a loving couple; made the remark that everybody's name began with O, and wished them good-day. Then he turned to a document which demanded his signature, and puffed at his cigar, which had almost gone out.

Orloff, Olenka, Stanislas Odeskalki and old man Openta went up town by the Elevated, and hurried to the rooms in East One Hundred and Twenty-third Street, near the river, which Orloff had hired for himself and his bride and his father to live in. It was a bitter afternoon in January. Dark clouds hung low over the city, and occasionally flurries of snow were torn from them. In many windows lights already glowed. Old man Openta walked ahead, giving his arm to Olenka, who was so rosy and fresh-looking that

271

men turned their heads to look after her. The best man and the groom brought up the rear. The bridegroom's face was bright and smiling, and he kept his eyes steadily on the bride; but the best man scowled continually and complained of the cold. Only once did he speak of anything else.

"But you should have told me," he said, "what a pretty girl she is. You must look out or some fellow will take her from you."

He cheered up when the four flights of stairs leading to the Opentas' new rooms had been surmounted.

"Now we are going to feed," he said.

Old man Openta unlocked the door, and, motioning to the others to wait, crossed the threshold, turned and held out his hands.

"Welgub," he said. He affected the English language with ostentation, but the others clung to Polish. Olenka hesitated and looked at her husband, blushing.

"But go in," he said, and he pushed her gently toward the opening. "This is no time to hang back."

Old man Openta embraced her when she had crossed the threshold.

"Welgub do your hobe," he said.

Openta pushed Odeskalki into the room, followed and closed the door.

"Well, here we are," he said. "What do you think of it?"

Odeskalki began to look about critically. "It is easy to see that a woman has not lived here," he said. "You ought to have curtains. Mrs. Openta will be lonely without curtains. But how many rooms are there?"

"There is this one," said Openta, "for the cooking-stove and father, and there is that one"—he pointed to a second door, closed—"for us."

Odeskalki moved toward the closed door and laid his hand on the knob.

"Do not go in there," said Openta, a little sharply.

"Why not?" said Odeskalki.

"Because it would not be proper," said Openta.

"If I don't know what's proper," said Odeskalki angrily, "I don't know who does. But the rooms are yours—such as they are." He shrugged his shoulders. "You will say next that it will not be proper to light a fire in the stove. It is terribly cold."

"No," said Openta, "I will not say that"; and he began to busy himself with an old newspaper and some kindlings. Soon thick smoke was oozing through the cracks of the stove, but presently, as the pipe warmed, the smoke was drawn into it, and a fine crackling sound filled the room.

"That is better," said Odeskalki. "But the smoke has made me cough."

Olenka went close to the stove and spread out her

hands to catch the warmth. "I think a fire is so home-like," she said.

"But the room is warming up," said Openta. "Don't stand on ceremony. Let us all take our coats off." He started forward to help Olenka, but Odeskalki intervened.

"No, let me do it," he said.

"All right," said Openta, "and I will help father off with his."

In helping Olenka, Odeskalki pressed her shoulders with his hands, but very slightly, so as not to give offence.

"Openta," he said, "you will not need the stove with such a wife."

Openta and Olenka blushed and became greatly confused.

"Bud," said old man Openta, "be goodn't goog bidoud a stobe."

"And now," said Openta, "it is time for Olenka to enter upon her first duties as a wife." He pointed to a large, broad cupboard in one corner of the room.

"Obed id," said the old man.

Olenka approached the cupboard bashfully and hesitatingly, as if she expected that something of a comic nature would spring out of it.

"But open it," said her husband encouragingly.

"Id bill dod bide," said his father.

Olenka smiled over her shoulder at the three men. At times she fairly astonished by her prettiness. She was as out of place in that shabby room as an orchid would have been. You would not have been surprised to learn that she was a princess—even a fairy princess—in disguise. Her voice was tender and haunting, like the middle register of a fine old 'cello when a master is playing. Her feet moved in and out under the hem of her skirt, timidly and gently, like two mice. If you had been in the hall and had heard her laugh, you would have said, "Somebody is making a child happy in that room."

Presently, with a great show of courage, she flung open the cupboard door and at once began to emit exclamations of surprise and pleasure. For, aside from china and glass of permanent utility, the shelves of the cupboard displayed enough cold meats, salad, oranges, nuts, raisins, celery, jelly-cake and wine to give delight to the moment.

Soon the good things were transferred to the table, and a real feast began. Olenka presided; but so intent was she on seeing that the men's plates were always filled that she did not find time to eat more than a few mouthfuls herself. Old man Openta became loquacious. Openta himself beamed on the party and kept jumping from his seat to heap fuel into the stove. It began to get red-hot. Odeskalki scowled continually, but it was noticed that he ate and drank as much as he could get.

"But you mustn't mind his dark looks," said Openta to Olenka. "At heart he is not an ill-natured fellow."

Odeskalki only scowled the more, and, filling his glass, toasted Olenka. His voice was sulky and funereal, like that of a bishop consigning a dead person to the earth.

"May you be happy," he said, and shook his head gloomily.

"It is always so with him when he drinks," said Openta. "You would think him a dragon, not a man, but at heart he is not an ill-natured fellow."

"I gad ead do bore," said old man Openta suddenly, and probably for the first time in his life. He rose, carrying his glass of wine, and placed himself with his back to the stove. From this coign of vantage he beamed optimistically on the party.

Odeskalki drew out a fat silver watch and scowled at it.

"Time for us to be off," he said to Openta.

"It is really too bad," said Openta to the bride, "but I could not seem to make them understand. And if I were to stay with you I should lose my place. But next week I shall be put on the day shift. It was all I could do to get off this afternoon to be married."

"When do you think you will come back?" said Olenka.

"Perhaps not before one or two o'clock," said Openta.

"To-night," said Odeskalki sulkily, "there is to be a large dinner for men given by a young man who is going to be married. There will be a real lake in the middle of the table, with banks of ferns and red roses, and live ducks swimming in it. It is impossible to say when the affair will break up, for there will be a great deal of hard drinking—and not ordinary white wine like this, I can tell you. Those young fellows will not have anything but the best imported champagne, costing you, perhaps, six dollars the bottle. That's the kind of a feast to have."

"You see," said Openta gently, "this envious fellow and I will be kept busy serving courses and drawing corks until the last guest goes. There will be eight of us waiters, one for every four guests. But I will come home as soon as may be, and I will wake you up."

"But I shall not go to sleep until you come," said Olenka.

The young couple could not meet each other's eyes, but flushed hotly and looked down.

"Ahem!" said Odeskalki.

Old man Openta, from his position in front of the stove, began suddenly to speak in a loud, sing-song

voice. "Barriage," he said, "is dod all peer ad skid-
dles. Barriage is——"

An expression of acute pain suddenly covered his
face. He dropped his glass, clutched the seat of his
trousers with both hands, and sprang forward. Then
tears came into his eyes and he began to tremble.

"What has happened to you, father?" cried Openta,
rushing toward his parent.

"Don'd dudge be," said the old man.

"But what is it? Are you suffering?"

"Id is dotig," said the old man presently, in a choking
voice. "I haf purned by pridges pehind be."

Odeskalki scowled at the old man. "You ought to
have known better than to stand so close to the stove,"
he said. "Come, Openta, or we shall be late, and,
furthermore, God alone knows what may happen
next."

The old man scowled at Odeskalki.

The young men put on their overcoats. Openta
hesitated, looked for a moment sheepishly at Odeskalki,
and then, turning to the little bride, opened his arms
with complete frankness. She ran into them. And
for a few moments, so eager was the embrace, they
swayed to and fro.

Odeskalki fixed his handsome, scowling eyes upon
them. "I hope you will be happy," he said, "but I
do not think much ever comes of hoping."

THE BEST MAN

II

For about two hours Odeskalki, Openta, and six other waiters, representing nearly as many different nationalities, worked swiftly and in silence to promote the ease and comfort of thirty-two young gentlemen who had come to sit on the outer edges of a hollow square and make beasts of themselves. The hollow in the white damask square was occupied by four descending banks of maidenhair fern and Jaqueminot roses which terminated in physical reality at the edges of a square mirror-bottomed tank, and continued into it in lovely illusion. In the tank a pair of gorgeous mallard ducks swam and occasionally dove, seeking vainly to seize the reflected roses and ferns in their gritty bills. Occasionally food more substantial than shadows was tossed to them in the shape of bread pellets, celery ends and even olives, which they ate with avidity. But the supply became at length greater than the demand, and the water in the tank began to look less like good Croton than bad soup. Whenever their duties brought them close together Odeskalki whispered sour comments to Openta.

"Let them look to us for good manners. That fellow with red hair has no more breeding than a hog. Give me wealth and champagne, and I would not talk like a sewer. The little fat son of a dog is beckoning

279

to me and pointing to his empty plate. Let some one else fill it."

He became more and more displeased with his own lot and was inclined to visit his wrath on the meek and inoffensive Openta.

"Such a husband," he said. "You should have stayed with your wife to-night, even if you lost your position by doing so. Instead, you are skipping about like a monkey and currying favor with the rich. For God's sake, have some spirit; imitate me when you fill a glass. Do not look as if the act were a pleasure, but a condescension."

Odeskalki, for all his scorn and scowling, kept a clear and ready eye on opportunity and had already drunk enough champagne out of partially emptied bottles to make his blood boil. But alcohol did not cheer him. Ever since early in the afternoon, when he had seen Olenka for the first time, he had been bitter with fate. Her girlishness, innocence, and beauty had exerted a powerful physical attraction on the man, and as the champagne mounted to his head he began to imagine scenes in which he figured as her lover. "Only let this silly Openta have a care," he thought, "or he will wake up some morning with a pair of horns to add to his absurd appearance." At times the thought that Openta would possess Olenka made him furious. Unconsciously, the thought that Openta was absenting himself from her rather than lose his position in the restaurant made him more furious. Then self-pity would make his heart gentle and swell into pity for Openta and pity for Olenka. "It is simply terrible," he thought, "to think that I shall come between them."

A large screen of Spanish leather in one corner of the room shielded from view a table covered with removes and a great tub containing ice and champagne. Several times during the course of the dinner Odeskalki and Openta found themselves alone behind this screen. On one such occasion Odeskalki hastily filled two glasses with champagne, and said:

"Quick, man—to Olenka!"

Openta hesitated.

"Curse you," said Odeskalki in a fierce whisper. "I will not be friends with a man who will not drink to his own wife."

Openta had a weak head, and that one glass stimulated him wonderfully. It was not difficult, a little later, for Odeskalki to persuade him to take another.

"May you be fruitful and multiply," he said.

The third glass which Openta drank was at his own instigation.

"Come behind the screen," he said; "it is only right that we should drink your health now."

Odeskalki went willingly enough. "But don't take too much, Openta," he said, and experienced a virtuous sense of having done his duty. A few minutes later Openta dropped an armful of plates, and the other waiters cursed him.

Some of the young gentlemen had begun preparing for the dinner early in the afternoon by drinking cocktails. Others had been making up for lost time by drinking whole glasses of champagne at a swallow. Champagne had made its appearance with the oysters. By each plate were two glasses, one for champagne and one for water. But the water, for the most part, had been thrown into the duck pond so that each young gentleman might utilize the empty vessel for more champagne. Signs of drunkenness were beginning to be evident. The waiters were receiving considerable presents of money and secret directions to keep particular glasses filled.

Men left their places and carried their chairs to more alluring neighborhoods. Little groups surrounded the humorists and roared with laughter whenever these spoke. Men whom the champagne affected to seriousness drew aside in pairs, and with heads nodding close together, emptied their hearts of matters which for the moment seemed of paramount importance. Sometimes they sniffled and shed tears.

One or two, on mischief bent, left the dinner, went upstairs and for a few disgraceful minutes attended a small dance to which they had not been invited.

THE BEST MAN

John Tombs upset his coffee-cup; nothing came out but ashes. "Fat" Randall, sitting solemnly between two empty chairs, suddenly smiled a silly smile and poured upon his own head a whole cellar of salt. Jack Blackwell rose unsteadily and pounded upon the table with a gilt-edged plate until the plate broke. Having thus secured a sufficiency of attention, he raised his glass, so charged with wine that it slopped over the top and ran over his hand, and proposed the health of the bride. The young gentlemen surged to their feet, shouting and drinking. Jack Blackwell hurled his empty glass into the duck pond. Some followed this lead; others threw their glasses backward against the panelled walls of the room; others upward against the frescoed ceiling. Some threw plates. One man threw his glass by mistake straight into "Fat" Randall's face. It broke into a thousand pieces, but Randall was not even scratched. One man, a cigar nine inches long between his teeth, was hit on the back of the head by a plate. The cigar fairly flew from his mouth into the duck pond, and the man looked foolishly after it without the least idea as to why it had flown. Another man, dragging suddenly at a tablecloth, stripped one whole table of everything on it. The red shade of an overturned candle caught fire. John Tombs snatched a coffee-pot from a waiter and poured its contents on the conflagration. Openta, from whose hands the coffee-pot had been snatched, giggled. He was also drunk.

It was noticed by some that one of the ducks floated belly up among the flotsam on the surface of the pond. A sliver of glass had pierced its brain. The other every now and then reared itself, and, flapping desperately, tried to escape on clipped wings.

The dinner began to break up. The young gentlemen left the room by twos and threes. Downstairs in the main hall of the restaurant there was a great putting on of hats and coats; many of the latter were lined with expensive fur. Presents of money were freely taken by the boys in charge of the hats and coats. Electric hansoms received drunken cargoes on more pleasure bent. And, like the geese in the song,

> One flew east and one flew west,
> And one flew over the cuckoo's nest.

It was a great night for roulette wheels; a great night for young women who had plenty of time but no money.

But the future groom came back to the dining-room. He was a big man and, with his immense fur-lined coat and high silk hat, looked positively mountainous. His face was red and shiny with hard drinking, but he was not drunk.

"Where's the other waiter?" he said, in a loud, assured voice. "I've got something for all of you."

A swinging door was pushed open, and voices began to call for Openta to come back.

Openta, very unsteady on his feet and sure of only one thing—that he wanted to go home—had just reached the top of a flight of stairs leading to a lower corridor, at the end of which was a room in which the waiters deposited their coats and hats. Hearing his name called he turned, slipped and fell to the bottom of the stairs.

Those in the dining-room heard the sounds of the fall, mingled with a sudden burst of foolish laughter, and then a deep groan. Afterward there was silence.

The groom hurried, with the others, to the bottom of the stairs.

Openta had already picked himself up. His face was white and drawn with pain, but he did not seem to have received any serious injury. He kept feeling the small of his back with one hand, and taking quick, sniffling breaths.

"He's all right," said the groom, and he began to distribute greenbacks among the waiters. They bowed and scraped and gave thanks—even the gloomy Odes-kalki. The groom looked up the flight of stairs by which he had just descended.

"Can I get out of here without going back up those stairs?" he said.

"This way, sir," said one of the waiters, and he

walked off, followed by the groom, who muttered a careless good-night as he left.

The others, all but Odeskalki and Openta, hurried back to the dining-room for the remnants of the feast.

"What a stupid fellow you are," said Odeskalki, "to get drunk and fall downstairs. You might have broken your neck. Come, let us go."

"I have hurt my back," said Openta.

"Where?" said Odeskalki brutally. He prodded Openta's spine with his thumb. Tears of anguish ran out of Openta's eyes and he staggered.

"Curse you!" he cried.

Odeskalki was taken aback for a moment. "Don't be a fool, little man," he said presently. "Don't rail at those who are trying to help you. A nice figure you'll cut at your bride's bedside, drunk and snivelling. Pull yourself together, and don't curse your betters."

"I am sorry for what I said, Odeskalki," said Openta meekly; "I didn't mean it. But you shouldn't have punched me so hard."

"Punched you," said Odeskalki scornfully. "*I* punch you! Man, if I punched you you'd know it. My fist would come out the other side." He doubled up his fist and fell to admiring its bony outline.

Openta went up town by the Third Avenue Elevated and got out at One Hundred and Twenty-fifth Street;

but his back hurt him so that he could hardly walk, and very often he had to stop and rest. The pain made him cold and sober.

Olenka was sound asleep. Openta stood looking at her until the match which he had lighted burned his fingers. Then, walking on tiptoe, he went into the other room, and, having taken off his coat and trousers and folded them carefully, he crept into bed with his father. All night the old man slept and snored. All night the young man lay awake and moaned.

III

The next morning Odeskalki called to find out what had become of Orloff Openta. The invalid was asleep. Old man Openta and Olenka took Odeskalki to the furthest corner of the room and conversed with him in low tones.

"I woge ub ad he bas id by bed," said the old man.

"He fell down a flight of stairs," said Odeskalki, "and injured his spine. I hope that it is nothing, but injuries to the spine are not to be laughed at. He had just reached the head of the stairs when we called him to come back and receive a present of money. He must have slipped in turning. We heard him fall, and found him at the bottom of the stairs. He was on his feet, but evidently suffering. Just think, if he hadn't been called back to get the present this would not have happened."

"We have drawn the bed close to the stove," said Olenka, "because he complains that his legs are cold."

"Id is doo bad," said the old man.

"Have you consulted a physician?" asked Odeskalki.

"Yes," said Olenka, "and he said that Orloff must lie still for a long time."

"Has he any appetite?"

"Doe," said the old man.

Orloff Openta stirred in his bed and awoke. "Are you there, Olenka?" he said.

Olenka flew to the bedside. "Yes," she said, "and here is Mr. Odeskalki to ask after you."

"That is very friendly of him," said Openta. "I hope you are well, Odeskalki."

Odeskalki approached the bed in a slow and dignified manner. "I am well," he said, "but it seems that you are not well, my friend. Do you feel any pain?"

"No," said Openta, "I do not think that I feel any pain, but my legs do not seem to get warm."

Olenka, blushing a little, slipped her hand under the bedclothes and felt of his feet.

"They are like ice," she said. "Would you care to feel for yourself?"

Odeskalki felt a certain repugnance in accepting this

invitation; nevertheless he felt of Openta's feet and satisfied himself that they were very cold.

"Can you move your legs?" he asked.

"Yes," said Openta. "But if I do it hurts my back."

"Hum," said Odeskalki, and looked very wise.

"What worries me," said Openta, "is that all our savings will be spent, and that perhaps I shall not be well enough to work even then."

"But I shall find something to do," said Olenka; "and, besides, we agreed not to speak of that. Could you drink a cup of soup?"

"I am not hungry," said Openta. "I think I feel a draught."

"No," said Odeskalki, "there is no draught in the room. Both windows and both doors are shut."

"Perhaps," said Openta, "one of the windows in Olenka's room is open, and the door does not fit tightly enough to keep the cold air out."

"I will see," said Odeskalki.

Openta raised himself in protest, and sank back with a little gasp. Odeskalki returned in a moment.

"No," he said, "the windows are closed. Your room is more cheerful than this, Mrs. Openta. There is an outlook."

"Bud doe stobe," said the old man.

"Haf you purned your pridges to-day?" said Odeskalki, giving an execrable imitation of the old man's

English. And he added in Polish: "Some day you will be setting the house on fire."

When Odeskalki's back was turned the old man made a series of faces at him, indicative of scorn and sarcasm.

Odeskalki laid his hand on Openta's pillow and patted it lightly.

"It is your duty to get well," he said. "I must go now, but I will come every day, if possible, to inquire about you. Mrs. Openta, will you speak with me a moment?"

She went with him to the head of the stairs, closing the door behind her.

"Do you think he is seriously ill?" she asked.

"I do not know," said Odeskalki, "but I am afraid so. What I want to say is this. Do not hesitate to call on me if you run short of money. I have had a good position for a long time and I have saved nearly a thousand dollars. There is no one dependent on me. Furthermore, it would be a pleasure for me to do you a good turn. I am, it is true, a taciturn fellow, but not altogether bad. It may be that I can be of help in other ways. I will come again to-morrow. But you must not confine yourself entirely to the house. Perhaps I will make you go for a walk with me. Is it permitted?"

He had taken her hand and raised it to his lips. If

he kissed it with more ardor than mere friendship permits, Olenka did not know. She was very grateful to him for his offers of help and for the kind tone which he had adopted.

"How I have misjudged this man!" she thought.

Openta was waiting her return with that greedy eagerness for attention so habitual to novices in suffering.

"But what did he say to you?" he asked almost querulously.

"He spoke altogether kindly," said Olenka, "offering help, and even a loan if necessary. I tell you he does away with that scowling habit of his when people are in trouble."

"Didn't I always tell you he was a good fellow at bottom?" said Openta.

"I doe'd lige hib," said the old man, who had been dozing.

There was a knock on the door, and almost immediately it was opened and Odeskalki reappeared.

"Mrs. Openta," he said, "you are not to hesitate to send for me in case of need. The best way would be to send me a telegram direct to Sherry's. I will always leave word with the head waiter where I am to be found. Good-bye again. I shall be late; but I do not mind that."

"Really a sterling fellow," said Openta. "Didn't I always tell you so?"

THE BEST MAN

"I doe'd lige hib," said the old man.

Odeskalki came nearly every day. For the most part he wore a smiling mask. Sometimes he insisted on taking Olenka for a walk. Sometimes he read the papers to Openta and the old man. Once he brought a friend who played upon the violin with real genius. Openta was delighted, but the friend made eyes at Olenka and Odeskalki would not permit the visit to be repeated. Meanwhile Openta got a little better, but he could not use his legs without suffering torment, and his savings were nearly all gone. As a matter of fact, the doctor whom they had called in did nothing for him. He came often, felt of Openta's legs and back, nodded his head, pocketed his fee and went away.

The weather was bitterly cold; provisions were high, and more wood went up the stove chimney in the form of smoke than Olenka cared to think about. But through it all she preserved her charm, her childishness, her cheerfulness and her red cheeks. Often she was possessed of a real gayety, such as might be expected in one whose troubles had suddenly been brought to an end. At such times her laughter sounded in the sickroom like sleigh bells and she would not make serious answers to questions. Sometimes she would mimic old man Openta and talk as if she had a dreadful cold in the head. But Odeskalki, if he had wished, could have told of moments, carefully screened from the

Opentas, when the anxiety which was torturing her came to the surface—sometimes as a fleeting expression of woe, sometimes in the form of tears. Once, as they were mounting the last flight of stairs, having returned from a short walk, she caught hold of the banister and began to sob. On that occasion Odeskalki caught her in his arms and held her to his breast until she panted for breath. When she had stopped sobbing she freed herself from him, but gently and not as one who has taken offence. She seemed rather preoccupied and not concerned with what had happened.

On another occasion Olenka complained that she felt ill and dizzy. She let Odeskalki put his arm around her for support and half carry her up the stairs. At the second landing she seemed to lose consciousness for a moment, causing Odeskalki untold alarm.

"It is nothing," she said, "it is often so. I have a little something the matter with my heart. Sometimes it seems as if it were too big, and then I become dizzy and am ready to faint."

"But you should see a doctor and take a prescription."

"Oh, no," said Olenka, "it is nothing; it does not trouble me."

That same day Odeskalki informed the Opentas that in the future he would have to work on the day shift and that it would not be possible for him always

293

to come up early enough in the evening to find them awake.

"It is a pity," said Openta, "that your lodging is not in the neighborhood somewhere."

"I don't see," said Odeskalki, "why I do not live with you and bear a portion of the expenses. We could put another bed in this room. Furthermore, it is very lonely living by myself. But do not invite me unless you wish."

Two nights later Stanislas Odeskalki came for the first time to pass the night under the same roof which covered Olenka, and old man Openta whispered to his son:

"The roob bill be warber. Bud I doe'd lige hib."

IV

On a certain evening, when old man Openta was sleeping heavily, being on the outside of his son's bed, Odeskalki spoke to the young Opentas of matters which were troubling him.

"Will either of you deny," he said, "that you reached the end of your resources two days ago and that I am bearing all the expenses?"

Neither Orloff nor his wife was able to deny this.

"It is nothing," continued Odeskalki. "I ask nothing in return. Let things be as they are until Orloff is well. But there is one thing which I cannot endure much longer. And that is the constant hostility which is shown me by Orloff's father. He who, after all, is nothing but a burden, constantly shows his teeth at me and passes sarcasms. Let him only show a proper gratitude, and I will not complain. But he does nothing but sleep, or air his English, or demand that more wood be put in the stove. He is a trial not easily borne."

Orloff and Olenka knew that there was much truth in what their benefactor had said. Old man Openta hated Odeskalki and showed his teeth at him whenever there was opportunity.

"I am sorry that you have noticed," said Openta. "But I will speak to him myself. He does not realize, perhaps, that he is living at your expense. Furthermore, father is old and not very strong in his head. It is better to laugh at his sarcasms. But I will speak to him, and after this everything will be better."

Consternation seized even Odeskalki when at this point it was noticed that the old man had opened his eyes. He scowled malignantly at Odeskalki, and said shrilly:

"Id bill dod be pedder. I was dod sleebig."

He rose, muttering to himself, took his overcoat from the peg where it was hanging and began to put it on.

"I bill dod gub bag," he said; "I bill dod gub bag. I ab dod wanded."

Olenka tried to hold him, but he shook her off angrily and made for the door. She threw her arms about him a second time, but he turned and struck her in the face and on the breast with his fists. Odeskalki rushed between them and hurled the old man aside.

"But for God's sake let him go," he cried. "He will come back soon enough. We are not going to lose him so easily. It is cold out, and he will soon be hankering for the stove."

"I bill dod gub bag," shouted the old man.

He tore open the door and began to shuffle down the stairs. Openta and Odeskalki heard him burst into a storm of weeping, but Olenka did not hear him, for she was weeping on her own account. Odeskalki closed the door.

"Go into your room," he said to Olenka, "and put cold water on your face—" He hesitated and turned to Openta. "I will just go and see if she is hurt," he said.

Olenka poured water into the basin on her washstand, but for the moment she was using it only as a receptacle for her tears.

"Don't cry," said Odeskalki gently. He took her by the shoulders and turned her so that she faced him. "Your cheek is bruised," he said. "But that is a trifle. Did he hurt you when he hit you here?" He touched her breast lightly with his hand. She did not answer. And Odeskalki began to finger the third button of her dress. But there must have been some spark of good in the man, for he suddenly drew back from her.

Olenka's tears ceased.

"I was frightened only," she said.

"If he had not been an old man," said Odeskalki, "I would have struck him dead. You do not feel any pain?"

"No, but everything is going round."

Odeskalki caught her as she fell and carried her to the bed. He laid her on it and kissed her unresisting mouth hungrily. Then he brought cold water and began to bathe her temples.

Meanwhile Openta had turned his head so that he could see the door leading into his wife's room.

"He ought not to have closed the door," he said querulously. "He ought to come back and tell me if she is hurt."

In a few moments anxiety for Olenka began to torment him.

"Maybe father really hurt her," he said.

Then he began to call for Odeskalki, at first in a low tone, then more loudly.

Suddenly the door opened and Odeskalki, looking like a man on fire with anger, appeared in the frame.

"For God's sake, don't scream so," he cried angrily. "Mrs. Openta has fainted. I am doing what I can."

He disappeared, slamming the door.

Half an hour passed. Orloff Openta began to cry. Another half-hour passed. He got out of bed and crept to the door, for he could not stand. He reached the knob, turned it and pushed. The door did not open. Strength came to him. He stood and beat upon the door with his fists and hurled his light body against it again and again. In his frenzy it did not occur to him that in order to open the door he should have pulled and not pushed.

He desisted after a while and leaned wearily against the door. It was then that his father, slinking shame-facedly back, found him.

"We must go," said Openta quietly. "They are in there. They have been in there for a long time. We are not wanted here. Help me put on my clothes."

"Bud you gad walg."

"Oh, yes, I can walk."

Old man Openta helped his son down one flight of stairs. Then he said:

"Waid for be. I hab begodden subthig."

He was gone quite a long time. And when he returned he carried the key of the outer door in his hand.

When they reached the street he was still carrying it.
Coming to a drain opening he dropped the key into it.

"I hab logged theb id," he said, "ad embdied the
stobe. Loog!"

The windows of the room which they had quitted
glowed in the night like coals. Openta fell face downward in the gutter.

V

"Her heart must have been weak," thought Odeskalki, after he had labored vainly for nearly an hour
and a half to bring Olenka to. "She is certainly dead.
I must tell Openta."

He pushed open the door and sprang back from a
storm of flames. The door closed of itself with a bang.
Odeskalki ran to the window, threw it open and looked
out, right, left, down and up. There was nothing for
it, if the worst came to the worst, but to jump, unless
he could make a rope out of Olenka's bedding. He
rolled her body unceremoniously to the floor, and began
to tear the bedding into broad strips. He worked with
frantic haste, but not so fast as the fire in the next room.
The intervening door sprang inward from its hinges
as if it had been hit by a locomotive. Flame and
smoke poured through the opening. Cries began to
rise from the street below and the reverberations of
fire-gongs. Odeskalki thrust himself half out of the

window and screamed for help. In that moment of
agony and fear he saw, among the upturned faces in
the street, the face of old man Openta convulsed with
ghastly merriment. And the old man's shrill voice was
borne up to him, clarion and horrible like the yell of a
ghoul.

"I haf purned your pridges behind you, Odeskalki!"

Odeskalki sprang from the window. The cries and
the reverberations of the fire-bells seemed to combine
in one awful rushing shudder. The crowd fought
cruelly to get back from the place where Odeskalki
would land. Old man Openta did not move. He did
not seem to realize his danger. He stood as if rooted,
with upturned, malevolently smiling face.

It seemed to those who saw the catastrophe that the
old man was literally driven into the street to the head,
as a carpenter drives a nail into a shingle with one blow
of his hammer.

It happened that the train for which Orloff Openta
was waiting at the New York Central's One Hundred
and Twenty-fifth Street station was carrying two young
people to Greenwich on the first stage of their honeymoon. It was curious that the bridegroom was the
very man whose generosity had been the cause of
Openta's fall and of all his subsequent disasters. If
the bridegroom had known this he might have been

moved to tears, for he was big and gentle and kind. But he did not know it, and Openta did not give it a thought. He was waiting on the very edge of the platform for the train. He did not know where he had passed the night or the morning nor how he had come to the edge of the platform. He considered to have gotten there as the only piece of good luck that he had ever had. That was all. . . .

"Heavens!" cried the bride. "What's happened?"

"You wait here, dear, and I'll go and find out."

The bridegroom hurried to the end of the car and looked out. He saw the body of a man, almost torn in two, being dragged from under the train. The sight made him feel sick all over. But he turned and went back to the bride, forcing a smile to his face.

"Was some one hurt?" said the bride, her face full of concern.

"No, dear—a man got knocked down—that's all. They—he picked himself up and walked away with a silly smile, and everybody is l-l-laughing at him."

XI

THE CROCODILE

THE CROCODILE

I

The first locality of which I have any recollection was my father's library—a tall, melancholy room devoted to books and illusions. Three sides were of books, sombrely bound, reaching from the floor to within three feet of the ceiling. Along the shelf, which was erroneously supposed to protect the tops of the top row of books from the dust with which our house abounded, were stationed, at precise intervals, busts done in plaster after the antique and death-masks. Beginning on the left was the fury-haunted face of Orestes; next him the lachrymose features of Niobe; followed her Medusa, crowned with serpents. The rest were death-masks— Napoleon, Washington, Voltaire, and my father's father. The prevailing dust, settled thick upon the heads of these grim images, lent them the venerable illusion of gray hair. The three walls of books were each pierced by a long, narrow window, for the room was an extension from the main block of the house, but over two of these the shutters were opaquely closed in winter and

305

summer. The third window, however, was allowed to extend whatever beneficence of light it could to the dismal and musty interior. A person of sharp sight, sitting at the black oak table in the middle of the room, might, on a fine day, have seen clearly enough to write on very white paper with very black ink, or to read out of a large-typed book. Through the fourth wall a door, nearly always closed, led into the main hall, which, like the library itself, was a tall and melancholy place of twilight and illusions. When my poor mother died, in giving me birth, she was laid out in the library and buried from the hall. Consequently, according to old-fashioned custom, these apartments were held sacred to her memory rather than other portions of the house in which she had enjoyed the more fortunate phases of life and happiness. The room in which my mother had actually died was never entered by any one save my father. Its door was double locked, like that of our family vault in the damp hollow among the syca- mores.

The first thing that I remember was that I had had a mother who had died and been buried. The second, that I had a father with a white face and black clothes and noiseless feet, whose duty in life was to shut doors, pull down window shades, and mourn for my mother. The third was a carved wooden box, situated in the exact centre of the oak table in the library, which contained a scroll of stained paper covered with curious characters, and a small but miraculously preserved crocodile. I was never allowed to touch the scroll or the crocodile, but in his lenient moods, which were few and touched with heartrending melancholy, my father would set the box open upon a convenient chair and allow me to peer my heart out at its mysterious contents. The crocodile, my father sometimes told me, was an Egyptian charm which was supposed to bring misfortune upon its possessor. "But I let it stay on my table," he would say, "because in the first place I am without superstition, and in the second because I am far distant from the longest and wildest reach of misfortune. When I lost your mother I lost all. Ay! but she was bonny, my boy—bonny!" It was very sad to hear him run on about the bonniness of my mother, and old Ann, my quondam nurse, has told me how at the funeral he stood for a long time by the casket, saying over and over, "Wasn't she bonny? Wasn't she bonny?" and followed her to the vault among the sycamores with the same iteration upon his lips.

It was not until I was near eight years old that my father could bear the sight of me, so much had we been divided by the innocent share which I had had in my mother's death. But I was not allowed to pass those eight years in ignorance of the results of my being, or of the constant mourning to which my father had devoted the balance of his days. I was brought up, so to speak, on my mother's death and burial. Another child might have been nurtured thus into a vivid contrast, but I ran fluidly into the mould sober, and came very near to solidifying. Death and its ancientry have a horrible fascination for children. And for me, wherever I turned, there was a plenitude of morbid suggestion. Indeed, our plantation—held by the family from the earliest colonization of Georgia, spread along the low shore of a turbid river tributary to the Savannah, and dwindled, partly by mismanagement and partly by the non-success of the rebellion, into a sad fulfilment of its bright colonial promise—was itself moribund. In the swamps, still showing traces of the dikes, which had once divided it into quadrilaterals, the rice which had been our chief source of income no longer flourished. The slave quarters, a long double row of diminutive brick cubes, each with one chimney, one door, and one window at the side of the door—such dwellings as children draw painfully on slates—still standing, for the most part, damp and silent, showed that the labor which had made the rice profitable was also a thing of other days. The house itself, a vastly tall block of burned bricks, laid side by side instead of end to end, as in modern building, stood on a slight rise of ground with its back to the river, among lofty and rugged red oaks, rotten throughout their tops with mistletoe. An avenue, roughened by disuse into a going worse than that of a lumber road, nearly a mile long, straight as justice, shaded by a double row of enormous live oaks, choked and strangled with plumes and beards of gray moss, led from the county road through the scant cotton fields and strawberry fields to the circle in front of the house. I used to fancy, and I think Bluebeard's closet lent me the notion, that the moss in the live oaks was the hair of unfortunate princesses turned gray by suffering and hung among the trees in wanton and cruel ostentation by their enemies.

Nothing but a happy and cheerful woman, a good housewife, ready-tongued and loving, could have lent a touch of home to our melancholy disestablishment. Women we had in the house, two black and ancient negresses, rheumatic and complaining, one to cook and one to make the beds, and old Ann, my mother's Scotch nurse, a hard, rickety female, whose mind, voice, and memory were pitched in the minor key. We had a horse, no mean animal, for my father had known and loved horses before his misfortune, but ugly and unkempt, and it was the duty of an old negro named Ecclesiastes, the one lively influence about the place, to look after the interests of this little-used creature. My father and myself completed the disquieting group of living things. Concerning things inanimate, we had enough to eat, enough to wear, and enough to read.

And the clothes of all of us were black. Until I was twelve years old I believed fervently that to mourn all his life long for dead wives and mothers was the whole end and destiny of man. In my twelfth year, however, my uncle Richard, a florid, affectionate, and testy sportsman, paid us a visit on matters connected with the mismanagement of the estate. He stayed three days. On the first he shot duck, on the second quail; on the morning of the third he talked with my father in the library; in the afternoon he took me for a walk. In the evening he went away and I never saw him again.

"Richard," he had said, for I had been given his name, "I want to see the vault before I go. I haven't seen it since your mother was buried."

It was a warm, bright, still December day, the day before Christmas, and my uncle seated himself nonchalantly on the low wall which surrounded the vault, his knees crossed, his mouth closed on a big cigar, and his eyes fixed on the "legended door."

"People who go into that place in boxes," he said, "never come out. Has that ever occurred to you, Richard?"

I said that it had.

"You never saw your mother, my boy," he went on, "but you wear mourning for her."

"It seems to me almost as if I had known her," I said, "because——"

THE CROCODILE

"Yes," cut in my uncle, "your father has kept her memory alive. He has neglected everything else in order to do that. Now tell—what was your mother like?"

I hesitated, and said finally, "She was very tall and beautiful."

My uncle smiled grimly.

"You would know her then," he said, "if you saw her? Answer me truthfully, and remember that other women are sometimes tall and beautiful."

I admitted a little ruefully, that I should not know my mother if I saw her.

"No, you wouldn't," said my uncle, "and for this reason, too; your mother had an amusing little face, but she was neither beautiful nor tall."

"But—" I began.

"Your father," my uncle interrupted, "has come to believe that his wife was tall and beautiful because he thinks that the idea of lifelong devotion to a memory is tall and beautiful. He is a little hipped about himself, my boy, and it makes me rather sick. I will tell you an anecdote. Once there was a man. He met a girl. For three weeks they talked foolishly about foolish things. Then they were married. Nine months later a son was born to them, and the girl died. The man mourned for her. At first he mourned because he missed her. Then because he respected her mem-

ory. Then because he liked to pose as one ever-
lastingly unhappy and faithful till death. He made
everybody about him mourn, including the little child,
his son, and finally he died and was put in the vault
with the girl, and no one in the world was the better by
one jot for any act of the man's life. . . . Let me hear
you laugh. . . ."

I looked up at him, much puzzled.

"Not at the anecdote," he said, "which isn't funny—
but just laugh."

I delivered myself of a soulless and conventional ha-
ha. My uncle put back his head and roared. At first I
thought he must be sick, for until that moment I had
never heard any one laugh. I had read of it in books.
And as a dog must have a first lesson in digging, so a
child must have a first lesson in laughing. My uncle
never stopped. He roared harder and louder. Tears
ran down his cheeks. Something shook me, I did not
know what. I heard a sound like that which my uncle
was making, but nearer me and more shrill. I felt
pain in my sides. My eyes became blurred and sting-
ing wet. With these new sounds and symptoms came
strange mental changes—a sudden knowledge that blue
was the best color for the sky, heat the best attribute of
the sun, and the act of living delightful. We roared
with laughter, my uncle and I, and the legended door
of the tomb gave us back hearty echoes. In the desert

of my childhood I look back upon that oasis of laughter as the only spot in which I really lived. When my uncle went away he said: "For God's sake, Dickie, try to be cheerful from now on. I wish I could take you with me. But your father says, no. Remember that the business of living is with Life. And let Death mind his own business."

The door closed behind that ruddy, cheerful man, and left us mourners facing each other across the supper table.

"Papa," said I presently, "haven't we a picture of mamma?"

"I had them all destroyed," said my father. "They were not like her. The last picture of her—" here he tapped his forehead—"will perish when I am gone. Ay, but laddie," he said, "she is vivid to me."

"Tell me about her, please, papa," I said.

"She was a tall, stately woman, laddie," he said, "and bonny—ay, bonny. Life without her has neither breadth nor thickness—only length."

"What color was her hair?" I asked.

"Boy," he said, "you will choke me with your questions. Her hair was black like the wing of a raven. Her eyes were black. She moved in beauty like the night."

Here my father buried his white face in his white hands, and remained so, his supper untasted, for a

313

long time. Presently he looked up and said with pitiful effort:

"And what did you with your uncle Richard?"

"We sat on the wall of the vault," I answered, "and laughed."

It was a part of my father's melancholy pose to renounce anger together with all the other passions, but at the close of my thoughtless words he sprang to his feet, livid.

"For that word," he cried, "ye shall suffer hellish."

And he dragged me, more dead than alive, to the library. But what form of punishment he would have inflicted me with I do not know. For a circumstance met with in the library—a circumstance trivial in itself and, to my mind, sufficiently explicable—shook my father into a new mood. The circumstance was this: that one of the servants (doubtless) had opened the carved box in the centre of the table, taken out the crocodile, probably to gratify curiosity by a close inspection, and forgotten to put it back. But I must admit that at first sight it looked as if the inanimate and horrible little creature had of its own locomotion thrust open the box and crawled to the edge of the table. To instant and searching inquiry the servants denied all knowledge of the matter, and it remained a mystery. My father dismissed the servants from the library, returned the crocodile to its box, and remained for some moments in thought. Then he said, very gravely and earnestly:

"The possession of this dead reptile is supposed to bring misfortune upon a man. For me that is impossible, for I am beyond its longest and wildest reach. But with you it is different. Life has in store for you the possibility of many misfortunes. Take care that you do not bring them upon yourself. Pray that you have not already done so by giving vent to ghoulish laughter in the presence of your dead mother. Now take yourself off—and leave me with my memories."

That night there was an avenue of moss-shrouded live oaks in dreamland, down which I fled before the onrush of a mighty and ominous crocodile.

The next day was Christmas, and we resumed the monotony of our stolid and gloomy lives.

II

At eighteen I was a very serious and colorless youth. It may be that I contained the seeds of a rational outlook upon life, but so far they had not sprouted. My father's pervading melancholy was more strong in me than red blood and ambition. With him I looked forward to an indefinite extension of the past, enlivened, if I may use the paradox, by two demises, his and my own. I had much sober literature at my tongue tips, a condescending fondness for the great poets, a normal appetite, two suits of black, and a mouth stiff from never having learned to smile. I stood in stark ignorance of life, and had but the vaguest notion as to how babies are made. My father, preserved in melancholy as a bitter pickle in vinegar, had not aged or changed an iota from my earliest memory of him—a very white man dressed in very black cloth.

One morning my father sent from the library for me, and when I had presented myself said shortly:

"Your Uncle Richard is dead. He has left nothing. He was guardian, as you may know, of Virginia Richmond, the daughter of his intimate friend. She is coming to live with us. Let us hope that she is sedate and reasonable. You have never seen anything of women. It may be that you will fall in love with her. You may consult with me if you do, though I am no longer in touch with youth. She is to have the south spare room. You may tell Ann. She will be here this evening (my father always spoke of the afternoon as the evening). You may tell her our ways, and our hatred of noise and frivolity. If she is a lady that will be sufficient. I think that is all."

My father sighed and turned away his face.

"To a large extent," he said, "she has been educated abroad. I hope that she will not bore you. But even if she should, try to be kind to her. I know you will be civil."

"Shall you be here to welcome her?" I asked.

"I shall hope to be," said my father. "But I have proposed to myself to gather some of the early jasmine to— If I am urgently needed for anything I shall be in the immediate vicinity of the vault."

Virginia Richmond arrived in an express wagon, together with her three trunks and two portmanteaus. She sat by the driver, a young negro, with whom she had evidently established the most talkative terms, and did not wait for me to help her deferentially to the ground, but put a slender a foot on the wheel, and jumped.

"It's good to get here," she said. "Are you Richard?"

"Yes, Virginia," I said, and felt that I was smiling.

"Where's Uncle John?" she said. "I call him Uncle John because his brother was my adopted uncle Richard always. And you're my cousin Richard. And I'm your cousin Virginia, going on seventeen, very talkative, affectionate and hungry. How old are you?"

"I shall be nineteen in April," I said, "and my father is somewhere about the grounds"—I did not like to say *vault*—"and I will try to find you something edible. Are you tired?"

"Do I look tired?"

"No," I said.

"How do I look?"

"Why," I said, "I think you look very well. I—I like your look."

A better judge than I might have liked it. She had a rosy face of curves and dimples, unruly hair of many browns, eyes that were deep wonders of blue, a mouth of pearl and pomegranate.

"You," she said, "look very grave—and—yes, hungry. But you have nice eyes and a good skin, though it ought to be browner in this climate, and if you don't smile this minute I shall scream."

So I smiled, and we went into the house.

"My God! cousin," she cried, to my mind most irreverently, "can't you open something and let in the light?"

"My father," I said, "prefers the house dark."

"Then let it be dark when he's in it," she cried, "and bright when he's out of it." And she ran to a window and struggled with the shutter. When she had flung that open she braced herself for an attack upon the next; but I bowed to the inevitable, and saved her from the trouble of consummating it. The floods of light let thus into the hall and dining-room seemed to my mind, sophisticated only in dark things, a kind of orgy. But Virginia was the more cheered.

"Now a body can eat," she said. "Ham—hoe-cake —Sally Lunn—is that Sally Lunn? Oh, Richard, I have heard of these things—and now—" wherewith she assaulted the viands.

"Don't you have ham in Europe, Virginia?" I asked.

"Ham!" she cried. "No, Richard, we have quarters of pig cut in thick slices—but meat like this was never grown on a pig. This," and she rapped the ham with her fork, and laughed to hear the solid thump, "was once part of an angel—a very fat angel."

"And you are a cannibal," I said. It was my first gallantry.

She gave me a grateful look.

"I had not hoped for it," she said. And for twenty minutes she ate like a hungry man and talked like a running brook.

"And now," she said, "for the house. First the library. Uncle Richard told me about all the death heads with dusty brows."

"Did he tell you about the crocodile?" I asked.

"Which crocodile?" said Virginia gravely.

"We have one only," I answered. "And I'm afraid it won't interest you very much. . . . This is the library."

She was for having the shutters open.

"My father wouldn't like it," I said.

"This once," said she, and I served the whim.

"Yes," she said, after examination, "it *is* dreadful. Show me the crocodile, and then let's go."

But she was more interested in the scroll.

"It's Arabic," she said; "I can read it."

THE CROCODILE

"You can read Arabic?"

"Indeed, yes. When papa's lungs went bad we lived in Cairo. He died in Egypt, you know. . . . Listen. . . . It says: 'That man who holds me (it's the crocodile talking) in both hands, and cries thrice the name of Allah, shall see the face of his beloved though she were dead.'"

"That's not our version," I said. "We believe that the possession of that beast invites misfortune."

"But you don't read Arabic," said Virginia. "Quick, Richard, take this thing in your two hands and call 'Allah' three times—loud, because it's a long way to Egypt—why, the man doesn't want to play—"

I had taken the crocodile in my hands, but balked, and I believe blushed, at the idea of raising my voice above the conversational pitch to further so absurd an experiment.

"Don't you want to see the face of your beloved?"

"I have none," said I.

"Then I'd cry 'Allah' till I had," said she. "Please—only three times."

So I held the crocodile, looking very foolish, and called three times upon the prophet. Then I turned to Virginia and met her eyes. The same thought occurred to us both, for we looked away. It was then that my father entered.

"Richard," he said, "the shutters——"

320

I made haste to close them, for I was blushing.

"This is Virginia!" said my father. "Welcome to our sad and lonely house. I thought just now that I heard some one calling aloud."

"It was Richard," said Virginia. "This scroll—" and she translated to my father.

"Oh, for faith to believe," said he. He took the crocodile in his hands and examined it with sad interest. "I have just come from her tomb, Virginia," he said. "I have been laying jasmine about it."

"Oh, the dear jasmine!" cried Virginia. "It's splendidly out, and to-morrow I shall fill the house with it.

"The house—" said my father hazily.

"Don't you like flowers, Uncle John?"

"I neither like nor dislike them," said my father.

"Then why, for heaven's sake—" but she stopped herself. "And you, Richard, don't *you* like them?"

"I have grown to think of them," said I, "if at all, as something odorous and sad, vaguely connected with funerals."

"Oh, no!" cried Virginia. "They are beautiful and gay, and they are connected with weddings—"

"Don't," said my father quickly. He was still holding the crocodile. "But I do not blame you, child. You will soon learn our ways. Since our great loss we have kept very quiet. . . . Ay, my dear, but you should have seen Richard's mother—was she not bonny, Richard?"

I bowed.

"I could fain look upon her again," he said. "And the scroll—does it not say '*even though she were dead?*' . . . Who was it called 'Allah'? . . . You, Richard? . . . And what face did you see? . . ."

"Tell him," said Virginia.

"Ay, tell me," said my father.

"I saw Virginia's face," said I.

Then we left him. But in the hall Virginia laid her hand on my shoulder.

"Haven't you noticed?" said she.

"What?" said I.

"Your father," said she.

"No," said I; "what ails him?"

Virginia tapped her forehead.

"Mildewed here," said she.

"I don't understand," said I.

"Never mind then, Richard," said she; "I'll take care of you."

That night I dreamed that I heard my father calling the name of Allah. But in the morning I rose early, and, going to the woods, gathered an armful of jasmine for Virginia.

She received it cheerfully.

"Is this—er—in *memory* of any one?" she asked.

"Yes," I said boldly, "it's in memory of me."

"Then I will keep it, Richard," she said. "Flowers are for the living."

"Yes," I said.

"And crocodiles," said she, "are for the dead."

III

For a long time I looked upon the innocent gayness and frivolity of Virginia with blinking eyes, as a person blinks at the sudden match lighted in the middle of the night. I had been pledged to darkness from my earliest years, and now, while my character, still happily plastic, was receiving its definite stamps, I blinked hankeringly at the light that I might have loved, and at the same time steeled myself to go through with the prearranged marriage. As in the Yankee States children are brought up to believe that it is wicked to be joyous on Sunday so I had been taught to believe of every twenty-four hours in the week.

I cannot think peacefully of that unhappy period in Virginia's life forced on her by us two moribunds. She was the sun, soaring in bright, beneficent career, brought suddenly to impotence by a London fog. And I take it that to be bright and happy, and to fail in making others so, is the most grievous chapter in life. But Virginia's glowing nature had its effect on mine, and in

323

the end she set my spirits dancing. With my father, however, the effect of a madcap sunbeam in the house was altogether different. For it served only to plunge him deeper into gloom and regret. If we came to dinner with him fresh from the joyous morning and in love with laughter, the misery into which he was too palpably thrown reacted so that for all three of us the afternoon became clouded. Sometimes his sorrow would take the form of mocking at all things peaceful and pleasant. In particular the institution of marriage aroused in him hostility.

"Ay, marry," he would say, "Richard, and beget death. It may be hereditary in our family. Exchange your wife, who is your soul, for a red and puling inconsequence, that shall serve down the tiresome years to remind you day and night of the sunshine which has been extinguished for you."

And I remember once retorting on him sharply to the effect that if he threw me so constantly in my own face I would leave his roof, and in the intemperance of the moment I fully purposed to do so. "I will do no worse among strangers," I said, "or in hell, for that matter."

My father fairly shrivelled before the unfilial words, and retreated so pathetically from his foolish position that my attack melted clean away.

"But why," I said afterward to Virginia, "wouldn't

he let me go? Why did he say that he could not live without me? And why, in God's name, when it was all over, did he cry?"

And Virginia thought for a few moments, which was unusual with her, and said presently: "Richard, either your father is the greatest lover that ever lived, or else he is a tiresome egomaniac. Frankly, I believe the latter. You are an accessory, a dismal carving on the mouldy frame in which he pictures himself. When I first came I used to tell him how terribly sorry I was that he had lost his wife. But I've given that up. Between you and me, it made him a little peevish. Now I say to him, 'Uncle Richard, you're the unhappiest man I ever saw,' and that comforts him tremendously. Sometimes he asks me if I really think so, and when I say that I do he almost smiles. And I have caught him, immediately after a scene like that, looking at himself in the mirror and pulling his face even longer than usual. . . . There, I've shocked you."

"No, Virginia," I said, "but I should hate to believe of any man what you believe of my father. His grief must be sincere."

"It may be," said Virginia, "or it may have been once. I believe it isn't now. I believe that if your mother came to life your father would——"

Virginia did not finish. We were seated in the cool hall, for the porch was piping hot, and our conversation was interrupted by a loud cry emanating from the library.

"Allah—Allah—Allah!"

"If I weren't charitable, which I am," said Virginia, "I would say that that was done for effect. He knows we're here. Bet you, he's looking at himself in the glass."

"Virginia," I began angrily, and I was for telling her that she was ill-natured, when the library door opened and my father came out.

"Oh!" said he, with a fine start, "I did not know you were there. . . ."

Virginia gave me one look, at once hurt and amused. Then she turned to my father and said gravely: "Did anything happen, Uncle Richard, when you called? Did you see the—the face—of——"

"No, child," said my father sadly. "I was so foolish, I may say undignified, as to try a childish and foolish experiment. It is unnecessary to say that the tall and stately form and classic face of Richard's dear mother did not appear to me. But I caught a glimpse of another face, Virginia—a face white and broken by sorrow and regret, a face that it was not pleasant to see. . . . How it all comes back to me," he went on. "Here I stood by her casket, ignorant of time and place—ignorant of all earthly things but loss—and for the last time looked upon her beauty. No, not for the last time,

326

THE CROCODILE

"'For all my daily trances
And all my nightly dreams
Are where thy bright eye glances
And where thy footstep gleams.'

"Ay, child, but she was bonny! Was she not bonny, Richard?"

I do not know what prompted Virginia to ask the sudden question which turned my father's face for a moment into a painful blank, and placed him in a position from which he extricated himself, I am forced to believe, only by a real and searching act of memory.

"What was her name?" said Virginia quickly.

It was a full half minute before my father managed to stammer my mother's name. But during the ensuing days it was constantly on his lips, as if he wished to make up to it for the oblivion into which it had been allowed to drop.

.   .   .   .

That afternoon it rained violently, and Virginia persuaded me to explore with her the mysteries of the ancient and cobwebby attic which occupied the whole upper floor of our house. It was a place in whose slatted window-blinds sparrows built their nests, and in which a period, that of my mother's brief mistress-ship, had been perfectly preserved. It was the most cheerful part of the house.

327

THE CROCODILE

Among other things we found in a trunk of old fashion my mother's wedding regalia. A dress of apple-green silk embroidered about the neck and wrists with tiny forget-me-nots, faded to the palest shade of lilac; a pair of tiny shoes of the same apple-green silk, with square toes and dark jade buttons; a veil of Venetian point, from which a large square had been cut, and the brittle remnants of a wreath—my mother's wedding wreath, which old Ann had often told me was combined of apple and orange flowers. When Virginia stood up and held the neck of my mother's dress level with the neck of her own it did not reach to her ankles, and she smiled at me.

"Richard," she said, "I could not get into this dress. Your tall and stately mother was no bigger than I."

"And no sweeter, I fancy," said I. For the being together with Virginia over my mother's things had suddenly opened my heart to her.

"Oh, Virginia," I went on, "it makes me sick to think of your living on in this dead house. I want you to be happy. I want to make you happy. You are the only good thing that was ever in my life. I know it now. And I—I want to be happy, too. . . ."

We explored the attic no more that day, and after supper we told my father.

THE CROCODILE

IV

From the very announcement to him of our engagement a marked change came over my father. Hitherto his influence had been for darkness, but of a silent and quiet character, like that which clouds spread through a wood at noon; but now he had become baleful and pointed in his efforts to make us unhappy.

To set in motion any machinery of escape was too impracticable and tedious to be thought of. Had I been for myself alone, I would have left him at this period and endeavored to support myself. But with Virginia to care for—and I could not leave her while I made my own way—the impulse was empty. He made attacks on our happiness with tongue and contrivance. He descended to raillery and sneers, even to coarseness. Yet when the confines of endurance had been approached too closely, and I threatened to cross them, he clung to me with such a seeming of feeling and patheticalness that I was forced to hold back. Through these harsh times Virginia was all sweetness and patience, but her cheeks lost their color and her body the delicious fulness of its lines.

My father was at times so eccentric in his behavior that I had it often in mind to ask the investigations of a physician. But as often the horror of a son prying after madness in his father withheld me. As always, his actions centred around the observance of his private grief. And to that great mental structure which he had made of my mother's beauties and virtues, he added incessantly wings and superstructures, until we had portrayed for us a woman in no way human or possible. To draw odious comparisons between Virginia and my mother, between his capacity for loving and my own, were his constant and indelicate exercises.

"Do you think you love, Richard?" he would say. "If she were to die this night, where would your love be at the end of the year? Is she bonny enough to hold a man's heart till death shall seek him out too? She's well enough in her way, your Virginia, I'll not deny that. But does a man remember what was only well enough? Does a man remember the first peach he ate? Nay, he will not remember that. But will he forget the first time that he heard Beethoven? Your mother, she was that—rich, strong music, she was— the bonny one—the unforgetable. Ah, the majesty of her, Richard, that was only for me to approach!"

And such like, till the heart sickened in you. Often he made us go with him to the vault and listen to his speeches, and kneel with him in the wet. Finally he played on us a trick that had in it something of the truly devilish, and was the beginning of the end. He began by insisting that we should be married and appointing a day. There was to be a minister, ourselves, and the servants. We were glad enough to be married, even on such scanty terms, and I well remember with what eagerness I arose on the glad morning, and slipped into my better suit of black, for I had no gayer clothes. Virginia did not come down to breakfast, but toward the close of that meal, at which my father was the nearest he ever came to being cheerful I heard her calling to me from the upper story. When I knocked at her door she opened it a little and showed me a teary face. "Richard," she said, "they've taken away my clothes and left only a black dress. I *won't* be married in black."

"Does it matter, dear?" I said. "Put it on and we will ransack the attic for something gayer."

But we found the attic locked. My father had provided against resistance.

"Does it matter, dear?" I said. "It's not your clothes I'm marrying—it's my darling herself."

So she smiled bravely and we went downstairs. The ceremony was appointed for eleven in the morning. But at that hour neither the minister, nor my father, nor the servants were to be found. We waited until twelve. Then I went out to look for my father. I went first to the vault and there found him. He was kneeling in the wet, facing the door, and holding in his hands the stuffed crocodile. He had, I suppose, been ealling the name of Allah in the wild hope of seeing my mother's face.

"Have you forgotten that we are to be married to-day?" I said.

He rose, hiding the crocodile beneath his coat.

"No," he said, "I had not forgotten that. Why should I be forgetting that? But the minister, he could not come—at the last minute he could not come."

"Then you should have told us," I said sternly.

"Would you be angry with me, Richard, my son?" he answered gently.

"Why couldn't the minister come?" I said, giving no heed to his question.

The gentleness, which must have been play-acting, went out of my father's voice.

"The minister," he said sneeringly: "faith, the minister, he had a more important funeral to attend."

My gorge rose and fell.

"What have you done with Virginia's trunk?" I said.

"It will be back in her room by now," said my father.

"Thank you," said I, "and good-day to you."

"Good-day, Richard? Good-day?"

"Yes," said I. "I am going to take her away."

"You'll not go far without money," said he.

"With heart," said I, "we shall go to the ends of the earth."

332

My father turned to the vault and addressed the shade of my mother. "Hear him," cried he, "hear him that took you from me. He's going to the ends of the earth. He turns his back upon your hallowed bones. . . ." His words became unintelligible.

. . . .

During the packing of my trunk I left off again and again to go to Virginia's door to ask if all were well with her. For there had been a look in my father's face which haunted me like a hint of coming evil. And although nothing but good came of that afternoon, still its events were so strange as to make me believe that men are often forewarned of the unusual. It was about three o'clock that suddenly I heard my father shrieking aloud in his library. Thinking that sickness must have seized him, I bounded down the stairs to offer assistance or search for it if necessary. But except for a pallor unusual even with him, he was not apparently sick. The crocodile lay belly up on the table, as if it had been hastily laid down.

"What's the matter?" I asked.

"Richard," said my father, in great excitement, "the door of the vault is open. But now I heard it creaking upon its hinges——"

Virginia, who had heard the shrieks, now joined us, her face white with alarm.

"What is it?" she cried.

"The resurrection of the dead!" cried my father, and, thrusting my detaining arm suddenly aside, he literally burst out of the house. I followed at my best speed, and Virginia brought up the rear. In this order we raced through the woods, brightly mottled with sunshine and shadows, in the direction of the vault. Run as I would, I could not gain on my father, who seemed to possess the speed of a pestilence. As he ran he kept crying: "God is merciful! I shall see the face of my beloved."

I cannot account for what happened. A little lady, dressed in apple-green silk, with a wreath of flowers upon her head, appeared suddenly in the path, ahead of and facing my father. She held out her arms as if to detain him. But he bore down upon her at full speed, and I cried out to warn her. Then they met. But there was no visible or audible sign of collision. My father literally seemed to pass through her. He ran on, always at top speed, and the little lady in the apple-green silk was no longer to be seen in any direction. Yet she seemed to have left an influence in the bright forest, gentle and serene, and I could swear that there lingered in the air a faint smell of apple blossoms and orange blossoms. And it may be the echo of a cry of pain—the ghost of a cry.

When I came to the vault its door was wide open, and I found my father within, breaking with his thin hands the lid from my mother's coffin. I was not in time to prevent him from completing his mad outrage. The lid came clean away with a ripping noise, and my father gazed eagerly at the face thus rudely revealed to the light of day. But what horrible alchemy of the grave had brought into shape the face upon which my father looked so eagerly is not for mortal man to know. For the face was not my mother's, but his own.

Gently he laid his hand on the forehead, and gently he said: "Was she not bonny, Richard? . . . Was she not bonny?"

V

Our honeymoon was nearly a week old, when one morning Virginia and I were taking breakfast in the glass dining-room of the old Hygeia Hotel. The waiters, the other guests, the cups, saucers, knives, and spoons all made eyes at us, but we were wonderfully happy. An old gentleman approached our table with a kind of a sad tiptoe gait. Tears were in his eyes.

"My dear boy," he said, "I have not the heart to congratulate you on your happiness, for I cannot help remembering what a good father you have so recently lost. I was present at his wedding, and I have not seen him since. But as you see—" and the old gentleman drew attention to the tears in his eyes.

"Aren't you mistaken, sir?" said I. "Aren't you thinking of somebody else's father?"

"Why, no," said he, "your father was —— ——. Don't tell me that he wasn't."

"I shall have to," I said, "for he wasn't. My father was a crocodile."